Heart Words

The Sweetbriar Mountain Series

Nora Everly

Heart Words

Editing: Rebecca Kimmel

Cover: Yummy Book Covers

Heart Words

The last person I wanted to see was the hot jerk who broke my heart.

Unfortunately, his daughter is the newest and most adorable kindergartner in my class, and he is the newest, hottest, and most annoyingly determined cop in town.

Falling for Trevor again was not part of my plan. Burying my feelings, avoiding him at all costs, and keeping him out of my heart. That was the plan.

But this flame flickering between us refuses to die and he still seems to be everything I've ever wanted. Protective, sexy, and kind, and that doesn't even get into how I feel when I see him with his kids.

He asked me for a second chance. But how can I take it when it feels like we never really took the first one?

Chapter 1
Rose

I sipped my hazelnut latte and smiled gratefully at my older sister. Violet always gave good coffee. Sometimes she also provided unwanted advice and nosy observations, but I decided to ignore those and focus on the positive aspects of having her as a volunteer in my classroom. If the first day of school was hectic, then the first day of kindergarten was utter insanity. Nervous children barely out of toddlerhood combined with teary-eyed, emotional parents made for an intense morning. Volunteers were necessary. Volunteers who provided coffee were invaluable.

"Are you ready, Violet?" I asked after taking another sip.

"Yep. But the real question is, are you ready?" She peered at me over the top of her coffee cup, eyebrows standing at attention and hazel eyes twinkling. She expected the scoop, but I wasn't ready to give it up. "Madison is going to be in your class this year, which means Trevor will be here any minute to drop her off." Madison was the adorable daughter of my—well, he wasn't even my ex. Trevor was my almost. He'd never fully owned my heart, yet he'd broken it all the same.

Trevor Hale was the delicious new detective on my police chief-father's force. I wanted him from the second I saw him over a year ago, standing in my sister's living room looking gorgeous and irresistible. For a while, he wanted me too. But it didn't last. Nothing ever lasts for me, because something about me was forgettable. Easily-replaceable Rose. Well, no more of that. I had made a sacred vow to myself to find a man who wanted me as much as I wanted him. No more complicated, messy relationships and no more settling for second place.

"Earth to Rose . . ." Violet teased.

I took another sip of my latte and smiled at her. "I'm ready. You know, the first day of school is always my favorite." She looked at me skeptically as I smoothed down my navy blue, red apple-printed shirtwaist dress. I tapped my red T-strap flats on the floor, and flashed my matching red manicure at her, making her laugh. I could go over the top with my school attire. My goal in life ever since I was a child was to be just like Ms. Frizzle from *The Magic School Bus*. She always wore dresses inspired by her lessons and made learning fun. Seeing a child become inspired in my classroom meant everything to me. I refused to allow the thought of seeing Trevor this morning throw me for a loop. This was my world, and I had important work to do.

"We have about ten minutes 'til game time. Just enough time for you to spill about what went on between you and Trevor," she said as she sipped her coffee and walked the room, making sure everything was in its place. Every year, Violet helped me set up my classroom. This year we decorated with a black chalkboard and neon rainbow theme. Violet owned a hugely successful coffee shop in town called *Violet's*. But before becoming the coffee guru of Sweetbriar, Oregon, she was an educational assistant. She kept herself on the volunteer list and usually spent the first week or two of school with me. Kindergarteners were like kittens for the first few weeks; all hyper and easily distracted. Herding cats was a multi-person job.

"Nothing happened," I lied as I checked my makeup in the mirror hanging behind my desk. After fluffing my long, curly red hair, I applied more lip gloss. I wasn't usually a primper, but I was nervous as all heck. The closer it got to start time, the more fidgety I became. I didn't usually get nervous on the first day of school. In fact, my classroom was the only place that I felt confident. Every other aspect of my life was kind of a disaster. And now, because of Trevor and our almost-thing together, I was pretty much a nervous wreck in the one place that made me feel good about myself.

Damn it, Sexy Trevor. Get out of my brain.

"Oh, come on. You met him at Lily's, right? And then you had a secret affair with him. Is that it? Did he move here to be with you? Come on, I won't tell anyone!" She waggled her eyebrows at me. Lily was our sister, and my identical twin. Trevor was her late husband's partner on the police force. I did meet him at her old house; Violet was half right.

"I don't want to talk about this Violet. Now is not the time," I insisted as I continued with my excessive primping.

Violet's voice greeting a student snapped me out of my vain reverie. Whipping around, I hastily stashed my lip gloss in my desk and hurried to join her at the door to say hello to the little early bird. I'd met most of the students at back to school night last week, but not this little cutie.

"Good morning. My name is Miss Barrett. What's your name?"

"I'm Anna," she answered distractedly as she stared at me. "Your hair is just like Merida's. From *Brave.* She's my favorite princess." I tried my best to tame my curls, but they had a mind of their own. I kept my hair long because the longer it was, the easier it was to take care of. The weight of it hanging down my back kept me from looking like a frizzy red Q-tip.

"Well, thank you. I like that movie too." I looked up from cute little Anna and shook Anna's mother's hand. "Would you like to go to your table and write your name on the paper, then match it to your name on the wall and put it in the slot?" Anna looked intrigued. All the tables had a label with each student's name, blank slips of paper, and baskets full of crayons. Violet called them over to Anna's table.

The second she turned from me to go to her table, Trevor popped right back into my brain just like a freaking whack-a-mole. I'd like to whack him out of my mind, but ever since I'd seen him at my mom's Sunday dinner with Lily and the kids, I couldn't get him out of my thoughts. That day, I'd taken one look at him, turned around and rushed out of the house. I have been actively avoiding him ever since. He hadn't attended back-to-school night with his kids; his mother had brought them, which was a relief at the time. But now, I wished I'd seen him and gotten it over with. The anticipation was killing me.

My younger brother Jude came through the door next, which distracted me enough to allow me to whack Trevor back into his hole in my brain. Jude was with Bella, the daughter of one of his good friends. Poor Harper had to work this morning and couldn't bring Bella herself. Little Bella was crying and Jude was doing his best to console her, but it wasn't working. "I'm trying, Rose, but she just wants Harper."

I bent down to talk to her. "Hi, Bella. You remember me

and Violet, right?" She nodded through her tears. "Yay! Do you remember that we're both super nice, and extra awesome?" I teased with a big smile. She looked up at me and returned a tiny smile. "You'll be fine today. I know that your mom is going to pick you up right after school, and you can tell her all about how much fun you had on your first day of kindergarten." She took a deep breath and nodded. Violet waved her over to her table. Jude mouthed 'thank you' to me, then followed them.

It went on from there. Kids arrived, Violet and I gave greetings and introductions, the little tables filled up—but there was no sign of Trevor. I was a jumble of nerves. I just wanted to get the part where I had to see him over with, so I could go on with my day.

I heard him before I saw him. His voice was a trigger, popping him back up to fill my thoughts. Only this time, all the memories popped up too. Trevor and I had been long distance. We'd built most of our relationship over the phone —as in every night before bed, plus here and there throughout our days—for a little over three months. We'd never even kissed, and sadly, it was the best relationship I'd ever had. What did that say about me? *Pathetic, that's what it said.*

Violet bustled around the room, talking to parents and helping kids write their names. I had to suck it up. Tamping down my feelings, I headed to the door to greet Madison and Trevor. "Hi, Madison. Are you excited for your first day of kindergarten?" I asked with a big, partially-fake smile.

I briefly glanced up at Trevor and he smiled at me. Damn, he looked edible—tall with strong, lean muscles on glorious display in the black polo shirt that stretched over his broad chest. His brown eyes twinkled at me and that gorgeous smile weakened my resolve to never speak to him again.

I shook my head slightly. *Quit it, Rose, you're at work, look away.*

I refocused on Madison, who clung to Trevor's hand with fear on her face and a trembling chin. As her big blue eyes filled with tears, I forgot all about Trevor and lost my nervous jitters.

I knelt in front of her. "We're going to have a great day, Madison. We'll sing songs and color pictures. We'll play outside and go for a walk around the school so you will know where everything is. I promise to teach you everything you need to know about being a kindergartner. Then you can go home and tell your dad all about it. Deal?" I held my hand out to her, and she shook it with a shy smile. *Yes!*

I stood up, slipping a bit on the carpet. Trevor held my elbow to steady me.

"Thank you," I whispered, as the electricity from his touch zoomed through my body. *Damn it, no sexy electricity allowed!* Trevor was like catnip, and I was the stupid cat.

"You're welcome, Rosalie." he said, not letting me go. He studied my face while I squirmed under his observation. I guess I hadn't tamped my feelings down far enough. Who was I kidding? I had so many unresolved feelings for Trevor that I'd have to turn my heart into a landfill to bury them all.

Violet called to Madison and waved to her from her table. She looked up at Trevor, who nodded encouragingly. Madison headed over to Violet and sat down.

"You haven't been taking my calls," he said softly, once she was out of earshot. No way I was taking his calls. Trevor was irresistible over the phone. His deep, smoky voice did things to me—things that were too inappropriate to be thinking about here.

I sighed, frustrated and confused by my lingering feelings for him. "I've been busy. Getting ready for the school year to start. I'm sorry," I murmured.

"If I call you tonight, will you answer?" I shook my head as his deep voice washed over me and I shivered. Damn him and his hotness. "I know I hurt you. It hurt me too, Rose. But we could have another chance together. Please? Can we try again?" he whispered intently. Gorgeous eyes burned into mine, drawing me in. I had to look away from that eyeball tractor beam, lest I end up headfirst in the garbage again.

"I can't do this right now." He looked like he wanted to argue. "You can call me tomorrow night," I said, simply to placate him and get him to go away so I could attempt to have a normal day.

"Okay, tomorrow then. I'm going to say goodbye to Madison." Violet had switched name tags and moved her to sit by an also-crying Bella. Over the years, I had found that when you put two crying little girls together, they always ended up as friends. I shot Violet a thumbs up.

I pulled myself together. I had until tomorrow night to come up with something to say to him. Trying to avoid him wasn't going to work anymore. It was clear he would not be giving up any time soon. Madison beamed up at him as he tugged one of her pigtails, straightening the corkscrew curl. And he just got hotter.

Chapter 2
Trevor

The walls of my tiny office closed in on me as I sat at my desk, tapping a pencil on the blotter and thinking about Rose. My ex-wife, Tara, also flitted through my mind, along with the regret over how I had let her fuck up my life. I probably shouldn't have married her, but it was hard to regret it too much because Madison wouldn't have been born if I'd made another choice. We got married after she got pregnant with Mikey, my soon-to-be seven-year-old son. We were never in love, and I think she resented me for trying to settle down with her. When I found out she had been cheating on me, I filed for divorce immediately; it was the last straw. Our divorce was almost final when I met Rose.

The whispers at my door jolted me out of my thoughts. "How was school?" I asked as my kids burst through the door. My mother followed quickly behind. I stepped around my desk, knelt, and opened my arms. Madison ran to me and crashed into my chest. I picked her up and kissed her cheek with a laugh. She was just like the nursery rhyme: sugar and spice and everything nice. She looked exactly like her mother—golden blonde curls and big blue eyes.

She leaned back in my arms with a big smile on her face. "I love Miss Barrett," she answered with a big toothy smile. "She sings all the time! She took us to the big kid playground. If we're good, our class gets to play on it every Friday! And look!" She pulled a pink heart cut out of construction paper and tied onto a red string from under her shirt and stuck it in my face. "I wrote this all by myself! It says "love." It's my first heart word because I know it by heart. L-O-V-E spells love. I love you, Daddy, and I love Miss Barrett!" She wiggled, so I put her down. She ran around my desk and started doodling on the blotter.

"I love you too, sweetheart," I said to her, and she smiled huge at me.

"Oh, Daddy, call me Maddie. My friends all have nick-names and I wanted one too."

"Okay . . . Maddie." Wow. What a difference from the scared, quiet tears from this morning. Rose was a miracle worker. I felt a curious pride in her.

"How about you, Mikey?" Mikey, on the other hand, was all me. He had my nose and my build and the same dark brown hair that he insisted be cut just like mine—short on the sides, and a bit longer on top. Every time I looked in his eyes, I saw my own brown looking back at me. Except his eyes held a spark of mischief that mine never had; I had to watch him constantly.

"Dylan and Mark are in my class and they're my best bros, so that's awesome." I watched him wander around my office and stop to flop into the chair in the corner. "This office is way smaller than your old one. But I'm glad we live in this town now, even if we're all squishy in here. Plus, Grandma picks us up from school. No more daycare. I can sit around in my underwear at Grandma's. They wouldn't let me do that at daycare."

I chuckled and met my mom's eyeroll with one of my own. I never knew what was going to come out of Mikey's mouth. "Do you like your teacher? She seemed nice," I prodded.

"Yeah, she's okay. I like her. Can we have pizza for dinner?" he asked.

"I'll get one before I pick you up. Sound good?" He held up his fist and I bumped it with my own. I'd take that as a yes.

"Thanks for picking them up, Mom."

She nodded and hugged me. "I'm so glad you're here, honey. Tacoma wasn't the place for you. It never was." She'd been against my marriage to Tara. I had been too, but I'd done it for my kids, and I'd do it again if I had to.

Moving here was the best decision I'd made in a long time. Sweetbriar was a small town, so the pace of my job would be slower here, my hours more flexible. In Tacoma I was one detective out of many. Here, I was the only one so far.

Sweetbriar is where I would start my life over. I'm closer to my parents, closer to Lily and her kids, but most of all closer to Rose. Letting her get away was one of the worst mistakes of my life. There was no room for more mistakes. Rose wouldn't get away from me this time; I was determined to make her see how good we could be for each other.

Chapter 3
Rose

I pulled into my garage with a scowl. No matter how loud I blared my radio I couldn't get Trevor out of my thoughts. His bedroom eyes and irresistible deep voice haunted me. The way he looked at me this morning had imprinted on my brain, while the memories of the months and months we had spent talking and planning and getting to know each other raced through my mind. It all left me breathless and frustrated in the front seat of my car. *Stop it, Rose.*

The sound of my frustrated grumbling filled the garage as I swung open the door to my powder blue VW Beetle. I had to get him off my mind. I mean, I still had work to do; I couldn't start moping yet. There were few phone calls to make. I had two shy little girls in my class who had spent most of the morning crying and Maddie was one of them. They commiserated with each other over missing their parents, a friendship was born, and just like that there were no more tears for the rest of the day. However, I felt that if a child spent a lot of time crying or upset in my class, I had to call their parents. It was one of my rules.

So, now I would be the one to call Trevor. With a huge sigh, I got out of my car, collected my stuff, and headed inside. I had bought this house about seven years ago, right after I'd started teaching. It's in the middle of town and just a street over from my grandmother's house. Gram moved into my parent's garage apartment and now rents out her house, so we're not neighbors anymore. Her new tenant is—wait for it—*Trevor*.

I could see where this whole thing was headed. Trevor was slowly becoming embedded in my life. He had ties with Lily. My nephews were his son's best friends, my dad was his boss, Gram was his landlord, and my brother Cade was a cop and therefore a coworker. He probably bought his freaking coffee in the morning from Violet's shop. And sweet little Maddie was in my class. They all liked Trevor and once they all found out we'd had an almost-thing together, the matchmaking would start. The one person I wanted to avoid the most was slowly becoming unavoidable.

I had refrained from putting up a for sale sign in my yard, despite the proximity to Trevor's place. I bought my house for a steal. To call it a fixer-upper would be an understatement. Luckily, my dad was a big time do-it-yourselfer and since remodeling was his favorite hobby, he'd helped me out. Now, instead of a big mess, my house was like a cute little box. I had a detached garage, which was a bummer when it rained—and this was Oregon, where it rained a lot—but I had a big covered front porch and huge backyard to make up for it. Dad and I and a revolving team of my brothers had repaired and remodeled everything in this place. Once we'd finished all the construction type stuff, Dad was finished too. This was okay with me, because I enjoyed the decorating part. I liked having my own space. Especially on days like this one, when I wanted to be alone to brood and mope around my backyard.

I had big afternoon plans to lie around, drink Diet Coke, eat a bag of Doritos, and pout. Luckily, pre-Trevor I was almost always . . . well, if not happy, at least content with my life, and not prone to sullen, broody bad moods. Thus, I had to stop at the store before I came home to pick up my Doritos. Rose and Doritos were always a bad idea. I didn't know how to *not* eat the entire bag. But I always had Diet Coke at home, so no worries there.

I slung my stuff on top of my big coffee table, kicked off my flats and flopped onto my huge, dark blue sectional couch. My living room was like a man cave—I decorated for comfort—and being able to lounge was important to my well-being. My television was massive and mounted to the wall. Dad helped me build shelving and cubbies to surround it. It held all my books, family photos, my Xbox One and other odds and ends. I also hid snacks in there, because my brothers always inhaled all my good snacks when they came over to play *Call of Duty* with me.

I took out my list and called the first parent of my shy little criers. I called, discussed, and said goodbye. Easy-peasy. Squeezing my eyes shut to brace myself, I called Trevor and tried not to have a panic attack as it rang—only to end up disappointed when it went to voicemail. Disappointed wasn't the right word; I almost burst into tears. I didn't *want* to talk to him, yet, I got sad when he didn't answer. Sorrow and shame burned through me. *Talk about a mixed message.* Even mixed messages to oneself are bad.

Grumbling all the way, I headed into my room to change clothes, tossing my dress at the hamper as I went. It flittered to the floor instead, somehow emphasizing what a mess my life was. I threw my bra on the floor to join it and slipped into my pajamas. Now fully settled into my relaxed, at-home zone, I was determined not to leave my house until tomorrow morning. My cell ringing from the couch sent me flying down the hall to answer it. Trevor's name flashed on the screen and I inhaled a huge breath to calm my sudden near-death heart attack. I answered. "Hello?"

"Rosalie, hello. You called?" His deep voice was like a massage through the phone. I swear I could feel it on my skin, and whenever he used my full name it made me feel all warm and squishy inside. Kind of near my heart, but also near my—gah! *Damn you, sexy Trevor!* Turning me on with just his voice was not allowed.

"Um, yes, I called. I wanted to talk about Maddie for a minute—"

"What's wrong? Is everything okay?" His voice had changed into what must be his dad-voice. Which was debatably hotter than his regular voice.

"Yes, she's fine," I soothed. "You remember how she was crying this morning? She started up again after you left, along with two other girls. I put them together at a table, because sometimes a peer can provide the most comfort. They sat together at lunch and played at recess, friendships blossomed, and I think she will be fine tomorrow. But I will let you know if I have to try another tactic. Don't worry Trevor."

"She's in good hands with you. I knew she would be. Thank you." He sounded proud of me, and that messed with my head. I wanted him to have *all* the feels for me, not just pride. But I also wanted him to go away. I wasn't making any sense, and it was exhausting.

"Well..." It was definitely time to get off the phone.

"Since we're on the phone, can we talk about—"

"I'm sorry, Trev, I actually have to go. I have other parents to call." *Liar, liar pants on fire.*

"Baby, please don't blow me off," he said softly in that irresistible velvet voice.

"I . . . um . . ." *Damn it.* "I will answer when you call tomorrow. Promise, Trev."

"Until tomorrow then, sweetheart," he said before ending the call.

He'd called me baby *and* sweetheart. I was so screwed. It was Dorito time, damn it.

I'd spent the last year or so trying not to think about Trevor. I should probably change that tactic and just deal with my crap. But it hurt too much, and I didn't know how to stop the pain. When I'd met Trevor, I'd felt like I had met my soulmate. Was that silly? Probably, but I couldn't help how I felt. When I'd lost my chance with him, it had hurt in a way I'd never experienced before.

I slipped on some flip-flops, crossed through my laundry room, and headed out the back door to go outside. My destination was the small patio in the rear corner of my backyard. I had a few Adirondack chairs, ottomans and little end tables set out to surround a small fire pit.

I didn't have rear neighbors because my yard backed up to Sweetbriar Park in the middle of town. Tall trees surrounded my property, but my favorite was the massive oak tree near my patio. Someday I would climb it, but today was not that day. I had a birdbath and bird and squirrel feeders distributed throughout my yard so I could sit out here like an old lady and watch the little critters do their thang. It was relaxing and peaceful back here, and I loved it.

I set my armful down on the glass cover of the firepit, popped open my Diet Coke, then plopped back into my chair, propping my feet up on the ottoman to fully commit to the experience.

I munched on Doritos and watched the birds at the feeder. But I still remembered all the things about Trevor that I was trying to forget about, like his beautiful brown eyes and charming sense of humor. The sound of his deep, sexy voice saying sweet and naughty things still echoed in my ears. I got up and walked around, pacing and pouting like a toddler. I could still picture his big biceps that I tried so hard not to stare at this morning, and his strong forearms with the lovely looking veins running up and down. And he was so tall. I couldn't stop thinking about what it would be like to kiss him, to touch him like he was mine.

Damn it Rose, just stop.

It had been about a year since I'd had a marathon brooding session in my backyard, a year since Trevor had called off his divorce and gone back to his wife.

I stood under my oak tree and looked up. A lone squirrel sat munching corn from the little picnic table feeder I had attached high up on the trunk of the tree. He watched me, though I really couldn't tell if it was a he or she. Since my mood was a bad one, I decided Mr. Squirrel was male. Plus, his eyes were beady and judgy, just like a man—a stupid, stupid man.

"Don't judge me!" I called up to him.

He tapped the tiny picnic table with his little feet—or were they paws? Whatever—and slid a corn kernel off the tiny table at me. It landed in my hair, and I clumsily tried to swipe it out. He chattered at me and pushed off another. I sat down on the grass as the tiny rodent bastard continued to flick—I swear he was aiming—corn at me.

"I can't even get a squirrel to like me," I mumbled into my soda. "Who do you think puts the corn in your feeder, you little butthole?" I shouted up at him, then collapsed backward onto the grass. I stretched out and stared up into the tree while that freaking squirrel chattered and knocked corn off the table.

Was this rock bottom? It couldn't be. I'd never, ever tried drugs. I'd only smoked that one time in high school, and I hardly ever drank alcohol. I did drink a lot of Diet Coke though. Was there a Diet Coke and Dorito rock bottom?

I set my empty glass in the grass. Covering my eyes against the corn assault, I tried to clear my mind and relax. At least I wasn't thinking about Trevor. *Damn it.*

"Rose! Are you out back?" Lily was my identical twin, except everything in her life was tied together like a neat little bow on a sneaker, and I was just a frayed end with no aglet.

I groaned in answer. The fence gate creaked as it opened to let her in the backyard, but since I had no energy left, I didn't move to greet her. All this thinking and pouting and remembering had worn me out. I did move when I felt hot breath and a wet doggy tongue on my cheek. I opened my eyes to see Rocky, Luke's boxer, staring at me. Luke—my sister's husband, and our non-official, non-incestuous triplet —was born on the same day as Lily and me. Our mothers had been best friends and had thought it would be fun to be pregnant at the same time. Luke had stolen my sister's heart from day one. They were close as could be until he joined the army, developed PTSD, and left her for seven years. Now they're back together, married, and she's expecting a baby. See? Neat little bow. Rocky grinned his doggy grin at me and barked up at the squirrel.

"That squirrel is being mean to me. Sic him, Rocky," I commanded. But he just laid down at my side and put his head on my chest. I hugged him; I needed a freaking hug. "I thought dogs chased squirrels, like they were tennis balls from God or something. Come on, Rocky, get him." Rocky just stared at me and licked my face again—typical male.

Lily sat down crisscross-applesauce next to me on the grass. "So, what are we pouting about?" she said with a laugh.

"Nothing. You're so cute," I deflected, and patted her tiny bump with the side of my hand. I was happy for her, I swear. One hundred percent.

"I brought tacos." She gestured to the bag beside her on the grass. "We were supposed to have Taco Tuesday tonight and talk about the first day of school. Obviously, you forgot, Miss Whiny McPoutFace. Dude, you have corn in your hair." She brushed some of it out. Crap, I'd forgotten about that. And damn that squirrel. Lily was the new librarian at Sweetbriar Grade School and I was thrilled that I'd get to see her every day.

I shook my fist up at the tree. "That squirrel is my nemesis."

She looked up. "What squirrel?"

I looked in the tree. The little corn-eating doody-head was gone. "Typical. I can't even get a squirrel to stick around. I even feed him corn! Does Trevor like corn? Why am I always second best?" I sat up and shook my head. Corn kernels fell out of my hair, and a tear almost fell out of my eye. Rocky sniffed at the corn, then ate it.

"You're not second best. Why did you say that?" she asked.

"It's just—I'm never *the one*. I'm expendable, replaceable. I wasn't even the maid of honor at your wedding and you're my identical twin. If I can't even get you to put me first, what chance do I have with the squirrels?"

She passed me a taco. Lily was fond of stress eating. Maybe I should try that instead wandering around my backyard with a bag of Doritos and a heart full of angst. I sighed and took a huge bite of taco. Tears formed in her eyes. *Crap.* This was why I always kept my feelings to myself.

"I didn't know you felt like that," she said. I looked at her and shrugged, because words had failed me. She was quiet for a minute before continuing her thought. "Remember when you were joking around, and you said that Violet could be maid of honor because you outranked her? You said that us being identical twins made it obvious that I loved you the most and you didn't need to be maid of honor. Do you remember that?"

I nodded. Yeah, I remembered. I usually hid my hurt feelings from everyone. I never told her how much it had hurt me.

"Rose, look at me please." I shoved the rest of the taco in my mouth and looked at her. "I thought you knew it was true," she said.

I chewed and swallowed quickly, so when my mouth dropped open it wouldn't be full of taco—because that would be gross. "What?" I breathed.

"I do love you the most. You know me better than anyone. You're always there when I need you. You're my identical twin—we were wombmates for crap's sake. How could you not know?" she asked.

I sat there blinking at her. I couldn't think right now. My brain was too full of self-doubt and hurt feelings and buried pain to think clearly. I didn't know what to say, and I was too sad right now to make up a lie to spare her feelings. "I'm sorry I didn't talk about it with you," I blurted. "I should have been honest. I guess it's easier to have hurt feelings quietly, than risk being disappointed."

She nodded and held my hand. "I get that. But you can talk to me. I know my life has been a mess for the last couple of years, and you've taken care of me a lot. But I promise I'll be there for you like you've always been there for me." Tears shone in her hazel eyes and threatened to spill over.

"Okay. I promise I'll talk to you," I answered.

"Good. Now tell me about Trev. What went on between you two?" she prodded with a gentle smile.

"Why does he have to be so hot?" I whined. "It's like a knight in shining armor mated with a sexy mermaid siren and spawned Trevor. It's too much for me to handle right now."

"Yeah, he's definitely a looker and a total sweetheart. He's a good dad, too. Tell me what happened."

"I met him after Will died. When you were on bedrest with Calla." Lily had moved back to town over the summer from Tacoma, about a three-hour drive north of Sweetbriar. Her first husband, Will, had been Trevor's partner on the police force. While on duty, a hit and run driver struck and killed him. Days later, Lily discovered she was pregnant. It was a hard pregnancy, and for the last few months of it she'd been on bedrest. I made the trip every weekend to help take care of her and Dylan, my adorable nephew. Trevor had also helped Lily out a lot. It was weird that I'd never met him before then. The three-hour distance and timing were the only explanation. Plus, Lily and Will had always come to Sweetbriar for holidays and such. I'd hardly ever driven up to Tacoma for visits. Trevor had been Will's partner and best friend for years and was super close to Lily too. But, nevertheless, that had been my first encounter with him.

"That's when you met Trev?"

I nodded sadly. She looked at me with sympathy and passed me the taco bag. Rocky got tired of looking for my squirrel nemesis and flopped over to lay on my feet with a groan. I patted his head. "He told me he was divorced. I didn't know it wasn't final."

She frowned and shook her head. "Really? That isn't like him."

It bothered me too. It was the chink in his armor that I couldn't get over. "Lily, we talked every night and he would text me every day. I would see him when I came to help you. It was months. It went on the entire time you were on bed rest."

"So, three and a half, almost four months? God, that sucks. The whole thing sucks. His wife was just a terrible, horrible person. They only got married because she was pregnant with Mikey. She cheated on him all the time. He filed for divorce years ago and she left right after Maddie was born. But she wouldn't sign the papers and he didn't have money to keep paying for an attorney. He only took her back because she was dying of cancer. She was on his health insurance and if he had divorced her, she would have lost coverage. She couldn't take care of herself anymore and if she had moved in with her dad, she would have had to switch doctors and hospitals. So, he took her in."

I already knew all of that. "But what he did for her made *me* into a mistress. I was 'the other woman' and that's not who I am. I don't do that kind of thing. I know why he took her back. I respected him for it—even admired him for it. I just couldn't be a part of it. And I'm upset that he didn't tell me he was still married, even if it was only on paper. I would have waited, and I wouldn't have—" I stumbled over my words at the end.

"You wouldn't have fallen for him so fast if you'd known. Is that it?" she deduced.

"Yeah. I thought I'd finally found the one for me. We

were making plans to be together, for me to meet his kids. He treated me like I was special. But I wasn't, and he ended it. I feel like a selfish ass for being resentful that he dumped me to take care of his dying wife. But I can't stop thinking about him. And I can't stop my jumble of messed-up, guilty, hurt feelings. He wants to talk to me. What do I do?"

"You already know what to do. Think about it." She looked at me expectantly. But I didn't answer.

"Oh, come on, Rose. I've never known you to be afraid of anything. This is a new experience—usually I'm the messed-up wuss in our relationship." I laughed as she teased me. "If you can't stop thinking of him, then you have to talk to him. Don't make yourself live with regrets." She clapped her hands together, like she had solved the problem.

"That's it?" I asked. I was incredulous. I had been super helpful while she'd rebuilt her relationship with Luke. He was the love of her entire life and now she was constantly smiling, full of bliss, and married. A large part of that was due to my matchmaking efforts. Damn it, she owed me. I expected more from her. I added a "*pffft*" sound effect to emphasize my disappointment.

My epic "*pffft*" didn't faze her in the slightest; she just laughed at me. "Yeah, that's it. Remember when I was scared to talk to Luke? You told me to stop being a pussy and go get my man. Concise, to the point, and correct. So, Rose, don't be a pussy. Trevor is a good man. Did he make mistakes? Yeah, but his heart was in the right place. I bet letting him make this up to you will be worth it."

That was a little bit better. "Good effort," I said with a nod.

"Thanks, glad you approve," she answered smartly.

"I'm supposed to talk to him tomorrow night. He's going to call me."

"Nope, you're going to *see* him tomorrow morning. He's the new police department volunteer for the school. He's going to be at morning assembly talking about stranger danger. And he also added himself to the parent volunteer list for his days off," she informed me.

My heart flipped, my stomach swirled, and my head spun. I would be seeing him no matter if I wanted to or not. It was out of my control. And I still hadn't figured out how I wanted to feel about him.

Chapter 4
Rose

I had to leave for school in ten minutes. I got up a half an hour earlier than normal so I could beautify, and I still wasn't finished. *Who am I?* I wasn't a beautifying kind of girl. Usually the mascara, lip gloss, bun/ponytail thing sufficed, and I called it done. Today I had tried winged eyeliner and I had regrets.

I had to pre-caffeinate with a home-made cup of coffee before I saw Violet and she was going to be so pissed. She always got huffy when we drank coffee other than hers. I tipped my head back and squirted more eye drops in. I was exhausted and my eyes were red. *Gah*, forget that squirrel—the lack of sleep from crying all night over Trevor like a lovesick fool was my real nemesis.

Examining myself in the full-length mirror in my bedroom, I turned side to side. Black fitted cropped pants, a red flowy camisole—that I'd finally gotten back from Lily—and a lightweight black blazer with white polka dots. I found my rainbow beaded lanyard on my dresser top and decided to be done with this crap. There is nothing wrong with doing yourself up, but I had gone next-level obsessive and it had to stop. I had been wasting too much of my time in the mirror lately. Tomorrow, I would take that half hour of sleep back. I could learn to do winged eyeliner faster, and who really needed highlighter anyway?

Even my favorite *NSYNC songs blasting through the speakers of my car couldn't quell my Trevor obsession. He was a permanent fixture in my brain. I couldn't say "Bye Bye Bye" to my fantasy filled Trevor daydreams—I failed so hard. This Trevor situation was worse than my *NSYNC crush back in junior high. I never chose a favorite member. As a practical pre-teen, I loved them all because it increased my odds of marrying one of them. As I drove through town, I found myself wishing my life could be that simple again. I was stupid over Trevor. My defenses were up, then down. I was angry at him, then over it, and back again. He was "Tearing Up My Heart," dammit. When would it ever be me?

Lily was getting out of her car as I pulled into the lot. "Where's Dylan?" I asked. He attended first grade here at Sweetbriar Grade School. He was in the same class as Mikey, Trevor's son. I was afraid to talk to Trevor, but not afraid to find out all the information I could.

"He wanted to be a bus rider this year. Luke is waiting with him at the bus stop," she answered. Her eyes bugged out after I stepped out my car and she saw me. "What are you wearing Rose?" she hissed. "I had that shirt at my place."

"I know. I saw it on your dresser, so I took it back. I love this camisole. It goes great with my blazer."

"I was going to buy you a new one," she said.

"Why? You didn't get anything on it. It's fine," I answered as I looked down at myself and smoothed it out.

"Oh no," she groaned. "Remember when I told you

about me and Luke in his office?" Her face was red, and she wouldn't meet my eyes.

"You mean, when you dry humped each other on his office couch?" I smirked, then realization hit me, and my mouth dropped open. "Oh my god, you were wearing this shirt, weren't you? This shirt is full of your horny sex juju. Ahh! I can't wear a sex shirt around Trevor!"

Lily darted forward and put her hand over my mouth. "*Shhh,*" she whispered loudly. "He'll be coming over here. He just parked his car."

I leaned closer to her. "Lily, you don't return sex clothes. Everyone knows that," I huffed.

"I didn't return it, stupid. You snooped and took it," she shot back.

"I didn't snoop. I was babysitting Dylan. We were watching *Moana* in your room. I saw it, so I took it back." Rose doesn't snoop. Stalk hot guys? Yes. Snoop? Nope.

"Okay." She shook her head. "Okay, never mind, that's not important now," she urgently insisted as her eyes darted behind where I stood. I started to argue some more, but she smacked my arm to stop me. "Hey, Trevor. How are you?" she called, voice high and bright with false cheer.

I jumped and spun around. Crap, I almost blew it and blabbermouthed all my stuff in front of him. Lily and I could become wrapped up in a good argument. It was very adolescent. Sometimes we regressed to our teen speak when we were together.

"Hi Lily. Rose," he called back. Did his voice get lower when he said my name? I knew I hadn't imagined it when Lily raised her eyebrows at me.

"I've gotta run inside." She pointed to Trevor. "I'll talk to you later Trev. Stop by the library when you're done."

She rushed past him. But then turned around long enough to stick her tongue out at me. *Hmph.* I'd deal with her later.

"You're here early today. Where are Mikey and Maddie?" I asked as he got closer to me. He was wearing dark denim that fit him perfectly. It took a lot of self-control to keep myself from trying to sneak a peek at his booty in those jeans. He had on another polo shirt today. This one was navy blue and had "Sweetbriar Police Dept." embroidered on it, right over his exceptionally well-developed pectoral muscle. It was tucked in at the front, behind his belt buckle. The badge clipped to his belt made him officially look like a badass. Between the badge in front of his abs, and his cop arms, I didn't know where to look. I bet he could easily punch out a bad guy, or rescue someone from . . . stuff, things, whatever. His arms were tanned and luscious and muscle-y and I wanted to feel one up so bad.

"My mother will be taking the kids to school and she'll pick them up when I have to work. I'm doing a presentation today. How are you this morning?"

I blinked myself out of my daze and snapped my eyes to his. I realized I was indeed staring at his arms and I felt myself turn red. "Oh, you're the stranger danger dude this year," I said lamely.

He grinned down at me. He was so tall—at least six-foot-three. I was five-two and wearing flats, I had to look way up to see his face. The way he leaned forward to look at me was mesmerizing; I had every bit of his attention and it intoxicated me. He had a fascinating hint of dark stubble on his jaw that I bet would feel good against my—I blinked again and looked up. His grin grew wicked. He knew he was getting me all flustered and he liked it, the big hot jerk. He chuckled at my bemused expression and I melted.

"You're adorable. You look beautiful today, Rosalie. That shade of red suits you."

I stammered out a thank you and my face turned even redder. It had to be as red as this stupid freaking sex shirt. Damn this shirt and its sexy juju powers.

"I'm going to call you tonight, remember? You promised we'd talk, and I've been looking forward to it since yesterday. We have a lot to say to each other, don't we?" I could only manage a nod as I stared up into his eyes. His voice had grown deeper, so seductive. If the devil had a voice, it would sound like Trevor: captivating, tempting, and so luscious. He was dangerous to my heart, and yet I felt myself swaying closer toward him instead of turning away.

Memories of the nights we'd spent talking on the phone ran through my mind. We'd spent so much time spent whispering our secrets, planning the future. The sound of his voice as he spoke to me and the way he always made me feel surged to the forefront of my thoughts and I couldn't make myself turn away from him. God, *the things he would say to me.* He could be so sweet, then turn on a dime and get so deliciously dirty I would blush. But most of all, he was always full of hopeful plans and promises. When none of them came true my heart was left empty and broken. I tilted my face back as he stepped even closer to me. My back was against my car as I stood there like a fool. I didn't move as he planted a hand on the roof to cage me in on one side. His eyes never left mine as his face slowly descended. The tender look that crossed his face sent an unwanted bolt of hope to my heart and I sighed. My eyes drifted shut as he got nearer. Parting my lips, I slowly inhaled. Wow, he smelled so good. His breath fluttered gently over my lips.

Is this it? Would this be our first kiss?

"Rose! Where are you? I've got my hands full of coffee and scones. Help me!" Violet called, loudly. The moment was ruined. Trevor jerked back and stood straight. I let out a huge breath and put my hand on my car to steady myself. I didn't know whether to be grateful or pissed at her. "There you are. Oh, hi, Trevor. I'm—did I interrupt you? I should have looked before I started yelling. I'm so sorry." Violet stammered as she handed me my coffee.

"It's okay. Thanks for the coffee," I said. I couldn't be mad at her when she brought me coffee from her shop. She handed me a bag—coffee *and* scones. Yum. Although, I suspected Trevor would have been yummier. *Damn.* That was a close one. I needed to get my head straight before I got my lips involved. I needed to know where he stood, where I stood. I needed clarity and assurances and other important things that I couldn't remember right at this moment. But later, I would remember them. Then I would be glad I hadn't kissed him. Really. So glad.

He escorted me to the front entrance. Then he and Violet left to go to the office. I was surprised when they *both* came back with volunteer stickers stuck to their chests. Violet made googly eyes at me when Trevor wasn't looking. Trevor came with us to pick the kids up from the cafeteria after their breakfast was over. Trevor stayed, and we started to get the class situated. I was off my game; he was a big distraction and I had to use all my mental powers—already diminished by my lack of sleep—to ignore him. Violet sent him to the hall to help the kids find their hooks to hang up their backpacks and put their folders and lunch boxes in the right spots. I mouthed "thank you" to her. She winked. Best big sister ever. And I promised myself no more sleepless nights. This was the worst.

By late morning, I was a mess. Luckily, we had finally made it to assembly time where I could have a break from the feels Trevor had been sparking throughout my body all morning. His stranger-danger presentation was going well, and the kids loved him. The fact that he handed out color changing pencils and lollipops had nothing to do with it, I was sure. He was charming and funny and kept the kids engaged and informed without freaking them out, which was awesome. My crush, my admiration—whatever it was I felt for him—grew as I watched his presentation. I glanced at Maddie, who was all adorable and proud of her dad as she watched. He winked at her when he caught her eye and I had to go sit down. It was too much; I couldn't take it. I plopped next to Lily on one of the benches that lined the gym and sighed dramatically. Violet sat with my class, after having waved me off. She could tell I needed a minute. Bless her.

"He's so hot," Lily whispered to me.

Wait, what?

She leaned closer to me. "I mean that in a way that conveys that I think he's very good looking, but I don't harbor any lustful feelings for him. I mean, I have Luke, and you've seen him," she whispered to me. Luke was hot, I guess. But I grew up with Luke. Thinking Luke was hot would be like thinking one of my brothers was hot. Yuck, ew, and barf. "Anyway, you'd better lock that down. He's hot, he's sweet, and he's a great dad. You can't find that very often."

I rolled my eyes. She kept forgetting about the fact that he told me he was divorced when he *was not*. I needed to get to the bottom of that, then decide how I felt about it. I stood up when Trevor was through with his presentation. It was lunch time for the kids, which meant lunch time for me.

Violet and I lined them up, walked them down the stairs and to the cafeteria, squirted hand sanitizer into their little palms, and sent them off to grab their lunch boxes or line up for hot lunch.

She grabbed my hand and held it as we walked down the hall back to my classroom. "I have to leave early today Rose, remember?" I had forgotten. I guess that's why she was carrying her purse with her. I shrugged. It would be okay. I was pretty sure I was going to have an easy class this year. After last year and the curse of the three rowdy Jadens, two bratty Olivias, and the disturbingly deviant Ethan—this year's trio of little criers and benign chatters were looking all right to me. Plus, I only had one set of kids with the same name this year: Mason M. and Mason F.

"No problem, Vi." I appreciated her taking time from her shop to help me out. I especially appreciated the fact that she'd brought me lunch and put it in the mini fridge in my classroom. I hugged her goodbye and she took off.

I finished the trip back to my classroom, sat in my chair, then spun around to retrieve my food. My desk faced out toward the room, with filing cabinets, shelves and the mini fridge behind it along the wall off to the side and under the windows that lined the main portion of the rear wall of my room. My classroom was huge. I had a small class library, areas set up for small groups, and a big storage closet in addition to my main teaching area. My room shared a bathroom full of tiny little toilets with the kindergarten class next door, which made it easier for the kids. No worries about getting lost or falling into a big toilet. However, I don't recommend trying to take an emergency pee in one of those tiny toilets. Peeing with your knees tucked up to your chest was seriously uncomfortable.

I was just about to take a bite of my chef's salad when

Trevor tapped on my door and walked in. He had a sexy half-grin aimed my way and he still looked gorgeous. I put my fork down and waved. *I waved at him. How lame.* He must like lame weirdos though, because his half-smile turned to a full one and lit up my room. Did he smile like that when we were on the phone together? I was never able to resist him on the phone. How would I survive in person?

"Are you hungry, Trevor? Violet left two salads here. I guess she forgot she was leaving early today," I offered.

"Are you inviting me to lunch? I accept," his grin broadened to a full, glorious beam of irresistableness as he crossed the room to my desk and I felt my heart stutter to a stop then crash to a booming crescendo in my chest.

I grabbed the second salad from the fridge and brought it to one of the small group tables. I sat down, but he just stood there for a minute before he laughed and joined me. I giggled at the sight of his tall body in the tiny chair, his knees bent to almost touch his chest. "I'm sorry, Trevor. I don't have any regular human sized chairs in here."

"I'll sit anywhere if it means I get to have lunch with you," he answered. I sucked in a huge breath. Wow, that was nice. Trevor had always been so sweet to me and interested in what I had to say. He was a good listener and remembered everything I'd ever told him. We'd had the best conversations together, lying in our separate beds sharing our lives over the phone. It was a major contrast to how I had spent my entire dating life. I was used to being disappointed, cheated on, or ghosted. All this attention from Trevor was irresistible. I couldn't figure out how to handle it. Other than blushing, stammering and acting like an idiot, of course. I was really good at that.

"Oh, that's sweet of you to say. Thank you." I smiled

and took a bite of salad. He smiled back at me and sipped his water.

We talked about Maddie and how well she did this morning. We chatted about our jobs and other small-talk kinds of things while we ate our salads. Then suddenly, his mood changed, and he was finished with small talk. Intensity burned in his eyes as he put his fork down and turned his chair fully toward mine. He was serious, and he looked determined. Neither of which I was ready for—at all. I gulped. "I wanted to apologize again for how I ended things with you," he said. "I wanted to make sure you understand why I had to do it."

"I do understand. I understood it then. It's not a big deal. I'm okay," I answered. The look on his face told me it was the wrong answer.

"I don't understand how you can say that. I'm not okay about any of it." Hurt flashed across his expression before he hid it.

I tried again to explain. "We spent time on the phone, chatting. We texted. We didn't have a relationship. We didn't have a commitment or anything." I was trying to make him feel better about hurting my feelings, but everything I said came out wrong.

He shook his head, clearly getting frustrated with me and my attempts to dodge the truth of our almost-relationship. "No, what we did was spend months getting to know each other and making plans to spend time together. I know your hopes. I know your dreams, and you know mine." His eyes grew intense as he gazed at me. "I know what you want from a man Rosalie, and I had intended to be the man to give it to you. It was a big deal to me then, and it still is. We have chemistry. Don't deny it now that we finally have a chance to be together. Don't brush it aside like it meant nothing." He leaned forward; our faces were less than a foot apart. I could see the sincerity in his eyes; it shined there, warming me up and making me want him.

I pushed back in my chair. I had to get away. "I'm not denying anything, Trevor. We did almost have a chance," I conceded.

"We have a chance now, Rose. There is no *almost* about it. Take that chance with me, please. We're in the same place now and there are no more complications. It's just you and me. Have dinner with me?" His eyes—had they looked like this when we were talking on the phone and I couldn't see them? So intense, so hopeful, so beautiful. Maybe it was a good thing we talked so much on the phone. The way he looked at me was overwhelming.

Yeah, we had chemistry, all right, lots of it.

"I . . . I, um. Trevor. I have to ask you something first." I really didn't want to do this now. But I had to know. I had to know before I said yes to him.

"Ask me anything," he said. His eyes were earnest as they held mine.

"You told me you were divorced, and you weren't. I think, I mean . . . I wouldn't have let myself get so wrapped up in you if I'd known that you were still married to her." I shut my eyes and waited for him to answer. But instead of an answer, the sound of the bell rang through the room. A nervous giggle escaped me as I stood up. My class would be waiting for me. "I guess we have bad timing again."

"We're not done," he declared as he stood up. *No, we weren't.* My gaze never left his as he moved closer. My head tipped back as his tipped forward. Something stopped me from doing what I should and stepping away. I froze in place as he inched closer to me. Something kept my face tilted up to his as his eyes dropped to half-mast. His full lips formed a devastating half smile, then parted slightly as he moved even closer. He was too sexy for me to resist. And I forgot why I was even trying to resist him in the first place.

Wife, wife, wife.

Shut up, brain.

He ran his nose down the side of mine. Then nuzzled his face into my neck. His slightly scratchy stubble gave me goosebumps and I shivered. My stomach dropped to my feet, came back up, and flipped over. Warmth flooded through me, all the way up to my face which I was sure had turned bright red. Goosebumps rose on my skin, right in that spot where my neck curved into my shoulder as he kissed it, then brushed his lips against me as he nibbled gently, tasting my skin. He smiled against my neck; his breath was warm, his lips were soft, and I was about to fall to the floor.

"*Gumph,*" I said. It was not a word, but it didn't stop me from saying it. I grabbed onto his arms to steady myself because I was going down. My knees shook, and my stomach wouldn't stay where it was supposed to

"Rosalie." His lips tickled my skin as he spoke.

"Hmmm?" I tried to answer. I should turn and walk away. But I felt my stupid eyelids drift closed and my traitorous lips part in anticipation instead.

He grinned softly as his face lowered to mine. But the butthead didn't kiss me. "I'll call you tonight, sweetheart," he whispered against my lips.

I could only manage a dreamy, dazed nod as an answer. I was in some kind of horny, loved-up haze and incapable of forming words.

"I promise to kiss you properly after we understand each other." My eyes got big while his smile broadened.

"Have a good rest of the day, baby." He kissed my forehead, cleaned up the trash, and left.

I sat back down for a second and gulped down some water. *Sweet mother of sexy . . .*

I was in trouble.

Chapter 5
Trevor

"Trevor, come here." Shit, it was Lily. I'd hoped I could get out of here before she saw me. I loved Lily like a sister, but I didn't want to talk to her. She knew something that I desperately wanted to forget about. And she wasn't letting it go.

A few months ago, Lily had a stalker and she ended up kidnapped and held for a day. Everything was fine now, but for a few weeks over the summer no one knew who was after her. When it was all over, we'd discovered my late wife's brother, Jeff, had been trying to scare Lily so she would move in with her parents or get protection from one of her brothers. He had gotten into trouble with a loan shark after borrowing money to pay off one of Tara's lovers who'd been blackmailing her with the information that I may not be Maddie's biological father. Jeff went to Will for help with the loan shark, and it ended up getting Will killed. His death was not a random hit-and-run like it had seemed. Lily had been pressuring me to get a paternity test done ever since.

If Madison looked like me, maybe I could worry less.

But she was a mini Tara. Every time I looked at my little girl my heart broke a little bit. I couldn't see myself in her, but no matter what a paternity test could possibly say, she would always be mine and I would never give her up. I was the parent who had always been there. I was the one to get up at night to feed and change her then rock her back to sleep. After Maddie was born, Tara left the hospital, then left us to move in with one of her boyfriends. She refused to sign the divorce papers and was a pain in my ass, but she tried to be a good mother.

"Hi, Lily," I said with a sigh and followed her into the library. Lily was just as beautiful as Rose. But something about Rose was irresistible to me. It was curious that I had never, not ever, had an attraction to Lily. But the second I'd seen Rose I'd wanted her. Not just physically, either; I had wanted to know everything about her.

"I talked to Jane." Jane was Lily's best friend and my late partner Will's sister. She was like family to me, but most importantly, she was a doctor. "I didn't tell her about Maddie, but I asked her about paternity tests. She said she can do it, if you'd like. You can't keep putting this off. The last thing you need is to be blindsided."

As much as I hated it, she was right. That guy was out there somewhere. He'd blackmailed Tara; who knows what else he was capable of. Unfortunately, I did not know his name and neither did Tara's family. When her brother got the money, he gave it to Tara and she handled the payment. What kind of man blackmails a woman dying of cancer? What kind of man wouldn't want to know if he had a child? "You're right. I need to handle this." I started pacing the library. Lily tried to keep up, but I paced fast when I was pissed off and stressed out. I felt bad for avoiding her. She was only trying to help me. I stopped pacing to apologize.

She crashed into my back, making both of us laugh and breaking the tension.

"I'm just trying to help, Trev. I love you guys," she said.

I met her eyes. "I love you too, and I'm sorry I've been avoiding you. I don't know what I would have done without you all these years. You taught me how to take care of a girl —how to fix her hair and potty train her. You helped me so much and you still do . . ." I looked away. I felt tears pricking at the back of my eyes. I couldn't stand the thought of losing my baby girl. I wanted to punch something or someone. I needed to go for a run and burn off some of this fearful energy burning through me. Instead, I sat down. At least the chairs in here were bigger than in Rose's classroom.

Lily took a seat in front of me and took my hands. "Trevor, we're going to figure this out. But the first step has got to be finding out the truth. We might not even need to do anything else—she might just be yours."

"Can you talk to Jane? Can you set it up? I can't—" Just thinking about it was killing me inside.

"I'll take care of everything," she promised. I nodded and deflated into the chair. She smiled at me and patted my knee. "There is something else I need to talk to you about," she said. I braced myself. The look on her face told me I wasn't going to like what she had to say.

"It's about Mikey. Technically, today is my first work day. I volunteered in the boy's class yesterday. Mikey was acting up." I raised my eyebrows at that. Mikey always acted up, that wasn't new. She shook her head and continued, "It went beyond his usual shenanigans. Trevor, it was bad. He wouldn't stay in his seat and he walked out of the classroom a few times. He was openly defiant and disrespectful. His class had library today, so he was here earlier. He was disrespectful toward me. He's never disrespected me before in his life. Something is going on with him."

He had never done anything like that before. In kindergarten, he was just talkative and high energy—nothing like what she just described. We had been talking a lot about Tara's death and how we all felt about it, both at home and with our family therapist. Was Mikey holding something back? It occurred to me that my life was a mess. I had just moved to a new town and started a new job. My kids' mother had died only months before, and we were still dealing with it. I was renting a house and I still needed to find one to buy. My daughter might not be *my daughter*. And now, something was up with my son, and I had to figure out how to help him. On top of all of that, I was trying to pursue Rose. Did I have any business getting into a relationship? Was it fair to Rose to pull her into the chaos that my life had become? I leaned back in the chair and brushed my hair back, leaving my palms on top of my head to dull the headache that began when I started adding up all I had to deal with.

"Hey, it will be okay. One thing at a time. Quit thinking about it all at once and I'll be here for you like always. Don't worry," Lily soothed. How did she always know? Lily had a preternatural way of reading me. I lifted my head and shook it at her, making her laugh. "Now, tell me about Rose. What is up with that? And don't say nothing." I opened my mouth to answer. Then I shut it. I didn't know what to say. Lily knew what to say though, "You like her. You more than like her, and she more than likes you too." She bounced in her seat like a kid. "I'll babysit for you, so you can go out," she offered, and I laughed bitterly.

"I have no business asking her out. She doesn't need

someone with this much baggage. I should have just left her alone"

"Rose is an adult. She can decide for herself. You're a good man Trevor. Rose deserves to have a good man in her life. And you deserve a good woman. Don't try to wait for a better time. You have a chance right now. She's been hurt enough. Don't pull back and hurt her again."

"She's been hurt?" I didn't like the thought of Rose being hurt. It made me want to punch something again. Or find whoever had hurt her and punch him. That would be satisfying.

"Not abuse type of hurt. Just the lying, cheating, can't-find-a-good-man, country-music-song type of hurt. I want her to be happy, I want her to have love. I want you to be happy, too. You obviously like each other, so you should explore it. And if it works out, you would be my brother-in-law. Oh my gosh! Our kids would be cousins. Well, step-cousins, or whatever! Yay!" she said with a huge smile.

"Don't get ahead of yourself. I do like her, a lot. I more than like her. She's beautiful and funny and great with kids —she wants kids, doesn't she?" I asked. Now *I* was the one getting ahead of myself.

"Yeah, she wants kids. Rose loves kids, and kids love her. You two would make beautiful babies, and Rose would make a great step-mother. I am so excited. Now I am getting out of control." She started bouncing in her seat again, it made me laugh. "Just ask her out, Trev."

"I will. Hopefully she isn't turned off by the mess that comes with me." I sighed. I still wondered if it was fair to go after her. She deserved so much more; she deserved the best.

"Trevor, I know what you're thinking. Just listen to me —a loyal, kind hearted man with good intentions is worth her time. It's worth everything. Do you have a lot going on? Yes, you do, but the fact that you want so badly to include Rose in your life says a lot."

I nodded at her, she made good points. "What am I going to do about Mikey? He was already a handful."

"Talk to him. He's a good boy at heart. I'll talk to him too."

"What would I do without you?" I asked. I couldn't imagine not having her as a friend. Moving here was the best decision I had made in a long time. And if I played my cards right, she may end up being my sister-in-law. I grinned at her.

"Let's not find out," she said. "You've been there for me so many times Trev, especially after Will died. It's my turn now." She leaned forward and hugged me. I kissed her cheek then stood up to go.

"I have to get to work. The last thing I need is for your dad to fire me for being late." I laughed.

"Okay, I'll talk to you later. Ask her out," she encouraged as I headed for the door.

I would ask her out as soon as I saw her. I had made up my mind. It had only wavered because I wanted what was best for her. Thoughts of Rose filled my head as I took off to head into work.

Chapter 6
Trevor

After my shift, I was home trying to clean up before my mother dropped the kids off. We'd been in this house for just over a month and it was already a mess. I rented it furnished from Rose's grandmother, so I had to take care of everything. Her furniture was very . . . grandmotherly. And floral. There were flowered fabric and lacy table covers everywhere. Lily had stayed here before I moved in, and I had her to thank for the kid's rooms and the removal of all the breakable stuff that had previously made up the décor. Now instead of breakable figurines and collectibles, toys were all over the place. We had been drowning in dirty laundry, but I was finally on the last load.

I grimaced and pulled some of Maddie's tiny socks from behind the couch. Seriously, was laundry ever really done? I would have to talk to the kids about their sloppy tendencies. My face scrunched up in disgust as I pulled used tissues from underneath the couch cushions, Mikey had just gotten over a cold. I also found a bunch of smashed goldfish crackers and the wrappers of the gummy fruit snacks that went missing last week. *Sneaky little turkeys.*

I didn't mind the housework. Tara sure never did any when we were married, so I got used to doing it all myself. It was mindless work. Well, I didn't care if it was half-assed, so it was mindless for me. I also wasn't a neat freak and would rather spend time playing with the kids instead of nagging them to pick up after themselves. But dirty tissues in the couch? No way. I pictured finding dirty tissues when Mikey was older and amended that to a "hell no." I knew what teenage boys used tissues for; I used to be one. Now I did it in the shower, like a responsible adult. Though when Rose and I used to talk on the phone, I'd used a baby wipe. And . . . now I'm hard.

I adjusted myself with a sigh and a glance at the clock above the fireplace. I had some time—if I hurried. Bolting upstairs, I dashed into the bathroom and started the shower. After I stripped and got in, I let images of Rose in that sexy red shirt drift through my mind. I pictured tugging the straps down and letting it fall around her waist. Would it catch on her nipples before it fell? I'd never seen her naked. My forehead thudded against the tiled shower wall as I stroked harder, imagining what she would look like: creamy, pale skin bared for me to touch, legs spread wide, ready for me to take her . . .

I was close already. She had me wound up tight.

I already knew what she would sound like. Her voice always got so soft and breathy right before she came, but I'd never heard it in person. With my eyes shut to reality, I could almost hear her voice in my ear, and I let it push me over the edge.

"Yoo hoo!" my mother called from downstairs. I almost slipped and fell on my ass at the sound. "Trevor, honey, we're here." The kid's footsteps bounded up the stairs and was glad I went for the shower instead of the baby wipe.

"I'm in the shower. Just give me a minute and I'll be right down." I shouted. Fuck me, that was a close one.

"Daddy! Hurry up Daddy!" Maddie shouted.

Mikey piped in, "Leave him alone. A man needs his privacy. He's probably eating Oreos in there. That's what I do in the bathroom when I need some alone time." That explained what happened to most of the Oreos anyway. "Or maybe he took a big dump." His laughter echoed in the hallway.

"Michael Austin Hale. Enough of that mouth," my mother scolded. I finished toweling off and threw on some sweatpants and a T-shirt. Back to reality.

I braced myself and unlocked the door. I smiled as Maddie raced down the hall and jumped into my arms. "Hi, sweetheart. Did you have a good day at school?" I asked before I put her down.

"Yes. I made something for you. It's in my backpack downstairs." She turned around and started running.

"No running on the stairs." I called. She slowed down. At least one of them listened to me.

"Hey, Ma." I greeted as I entered the kitchen. Mikey was at the table emptying his backpack, slumped down in his chair. He silently passed me a yellow slip of carbon paper, then put his head down.

"Mikey is having a time out. I've set the timer for seven minutes," my mother informed me. She turned to Mikey, her face softening. "Look at me, Mikey." He looked up, tears in his eyes. "I know you can do better. Just because I got mad at you, doesn't mean I don't love you. I adore you, sweet boy. Tomorrow I expect you to make better choices."

He nodded and put his head back down.

"Trevor. I've already talked to him about his mouth. I won't abide cursing in my house."

"He cursed at you?" *Cursing? Mikey?* I couldn't believe it.

"No. Not at me. He cursed when Maddie spilled her juice. Then he said she would get a spanking. I don't spank, and I know you don't either. Did Tara spank them?" I had told Tara my thoughts, and she'd agreed not do it when she had the kids. My heart sank in my chest as ice entered my veins.

"As far as I know, she didn't. I'll have a talk with Mikey tonight," I said through the thick fog my thoughts had drifted into.

"Okay, honey. And you can handle that too." She pointed to the yellow paper on the table.

"I'm sorry, Mom. Thanks."

"You're welcome, sweetie." She patted my cheek, and turned toward the table. She leaned down and kissed Mikey on top of his head, then whispered in his ear. He looked up and whispered that he loved her too.

After collapsing into a chair, I jumped as Maddie rushed in with a piece of red construction paper cut out in a lopsided heart. "I love you Daddy" was written clumsily in the middle. "I love you too, sweetheart."

"I learned more heart words today," she informed me. I watched while she unzipped her backpack and unearthed several sheets of pink paper. "These are heart word flash cards. We cut them out and then you have to practice with me. If I read them all at school, then I get the purple ones." I glanced at the papers, then pointed to "sit". "What does that one say?" I asked.

"Sit," she replied with a huge smile.

With a laugh, I pointed. "What about this one?"

"Down." She grinned.

"And this one?"

"Now." Her giggle lifted my spirits. Even Mikey smiled.

"Can I have Oreos?" she asked. I got up and collected the rest of the Oreos, some milk, and cups. I had a feeling we were going to need them. I got us set up right as the timer went off.

Mikey's head popped up, just like toast from a toaster. "I got a Yikes," he announced.

"And, what is a Yikes?" I asked.

"It means he got in big trouble." Maddie informed me through a mouthful of Oreo. She already had a milk moustache and had made a milky puddle on the table. That was quick.

"What happened, Mikey?" He looked away, not even touching the Oreos.

"I don't know. I got mad," he answered without looking at me. He was busy staring out the window with great concentration.

"What made you mad? Mikey, look at me."

"I saw it at recess," Maddie answered for him. Her entire hand was in the glass of milk. I reached around to the counter and grabbed a dishtowel. I should have kept her bibs.

"Mikey, start talking."

"It was all stupid Blake's fault," he finally answered.

"Blake from next door?" I asked, and Mikey nodded. Blake was in second grade and—I hated saying this about a kid—he was also a little asshole. His father was a prick too, and his step-mother . . . well, let's just say she hit on me last week when I was unloading groceries.

"He kept asking me where my mom was. Then he told

everyone I didn't have a mom. Dylan got in trouble too. He told Blake to shut up."

Maddie gasped. "I didn't hear Dylan say shut up. That's a bad word, Miss Barrett said so."

"Did Rose—I mean, Miss Barrett—see what happened?" Mikey shook his head. Maddie stuffed a milky Oreo in her mouth and shook her head too. I shook *my* head at the mess she was making. It was kind of unbelievable. I winked at her and she smiled a black and white cookie smile at me.

"It was at lunch recess. Classroom teachers don't go to lunch recess. The recess teachers do," he answered sullenly.

I picked up the Yikes and read it. It was a form describing misbehaviors. Boxes next to "disrespectful" and "refused to follow instructions" were checked, and "Mikey wouldn't line up and come in from recess when asked. He hid under the slide." was written at the bottom.

"Did you hide because you were upset?" I asked.

He raised his eyes to me, but not his head. "Yeah," he whispered.

"I'll make you a deal. You won't get into trouble for this Yikes if you tell me what is bothering you. Sound good?" I held out my hand, and he took it. Tears filled his eyes, and I lifted him onto my lap.

"Why is Mikey sad? Does he miss Mommy? I don't miss her anymore," Maddie announced through a mouthful of Oreo. Mikey clung to me as he cried.

"I don't know yet, sweetheart," I answered. "Take that dish towel and wipe your mouth, then go and wash your hands. You can turn on Netflix in the living room when you're done. There are new *My Little Pony* episodes."

"Okay, Daddy," she said, then ran out of the kitchen.

"Do you miss your mom, bud?" I whispered.

"No," he answered quickly and firmly.

"Oh, I thought you did. You seemed sad about it before. Can we talk about it, Mikey? Why don't you miss her?" I was winging it now.

"She was mean. She went away again and again and again. I didn't like her house and I didn't like her. She was a mean mom." He sobbed.

Why was I just now hearing about this? I'd always asked them how it went when they were with her and I never would have sent them to her if they didn't want to go. I'd had full custody and visitation was at my discretion. I had thought it would be good for them to know their mother. The more Mikey spoke, the more my stomach sank.

"Mikey, why didn't you tell me any of this?"

"At first, I didn't want you to be mad because I liked going there. She was nice most of the time, and fun too. Then she was just mean. She drank stinky red juice and made me take care of Maddie and help clean up and stuff. She said she needed your child sports and she wouldn't let Maddie come home if I told you."

My body coiled tight with rage. But I had to bury it, so I could get to the bottom of whatever the hell was going on. Tears filled my eyes, but I blinked them away. He was just a little boy. What had she been thinking? Mikey shouldn't know a thing about child support. It wasn't even official child support. I gave her money to help when she had the kids for the occasional weekend. How could I have been so stupid?

Breathe. One thing at a time.

"Mikey, did she spank you?"

"Not at first." He pulled back and looked at me, "And don't worry, Daddy, I didn't let her spank Maddie. I made Maddie play hide-and-seek." He leaned against me again and I couldn't stop it this time; the tears spilled over. Mikey had tucked himself into my chest and curled up like he did when he was a baby. I didn't want him to see me cry, but I couldn't stop.

Fuck. This was so much worse than I could have ever imagined.

"Mikey. Look at me." He pulled back a little and looked at me. His eyes got big when he saw that I was crying. He put his hand on my cheek and wiped my tears. "I am so sorry," I told him. "I am so sorry that I didn't know. And I am so proud of you for protecting your baby sister. But, it's my job to protect you. And no matter what anyone says, even if they try to scare you by saying something bad—like your mom saying she wouldn't let Maddie come home—I want you to tell me. Please tell me everything, so I can take care of you like I am supposed to. I don't want you to worry about making me feel sad, or mad. I love you and Maddie. You two are the most important people in my life. Do you understand what I'm telling you, Mikey?"

"Yes, but I'm the big brother. Big brothers protect little sisters," he whispered as his little chest heaved with a sob.

"And you're a great big brother. But I am a grown up, and I am your father. Fathers protect their children. Mothers are supposed to as well. Your mother didn't protect you, and I didn't see it. Promise me, Mikey. Promise you will talk to me. Is there anything else you need to tell me?"

"No," he sobbed. "It's okay, Daddy." He choked on the words. "It's going to be okay now." He breathed in a big shuddering breath, then let it out. I felt him relax against my chest as I rubbed his back.

"Yeah, we're going to be okay. I'm going to make sure of it." I felt him nod against me. And that was good enough for now. We could talk about this more when we went to our therapy appointment next week.

"You hungry? It's time for dinner." I asked when I heard his stomach growl.

"Can we have Happy Meals?" he asked.

"We sure can." I answered, and smiled down at him.

He grinned up at me. "I love you, Daddy."

"I love you too, bud. Never forget it."

I cleaned up the Oreo mess and loaded the kids up in my Jeep, then took off for Mickey D.'s. Happy Meals and the indoor playground was usually a great distraction.

As we ate, I did my best to create a happy mood for Mikey. Maddie was a great help with that, as it appeared nothing negative had resonated with her. I guessed between me and Mikey watching out for her, she had been untouched by Tara's bullshit. And Tara had been such an unmeaningful presence in her life that she was already over it. But Mikey? I wanted this burden he had been carrying to be completely off his shoulders. They wore themselves out on the playground, and later that night, we passed quickly through bath time, story time, and teeth-brushing time. We passed through "I'm thirsty," "I have to pee," and "I'm not sleepy" time, until first Maddie, then Mikey, crashed in their beds.

Finally, it was time to call Rose. I was going to do it before dinner, but with everything that happened with Mikey, time had gotten away from me.

I made my rounds of the house, locked everything up tight, and headed for my bed. I sat down and swiped to Rose's name on my contact list. My heart crashed in my chest when the phone rang in my hand. I rejected the call. It was from this area code, but I didn't know the number. It rang again, so I answered. "Hello? Who is this?" A hostile laugh was the only answer.

"Your wife knew me." My blood turned to ice in my veins.

"Who are you? What do you want?" I demanded.

"Money, of course. You're going to want me gone. And it's going to cost you." I saved the number, then I dialed it. No answer. A text came through.

UNKNOWN: WHEN I WANT TO TALK TO YOU, I WILL CALL. I WILL TELL YOU HOW MUCH. I WILL TELL YOU WHEN I WANT IT.

I called Lily. She told me she had already arranged for me to see Jane and get the DNA test done.

I called Ben, the chief, who was also Rose and Lily's father.

I called my parents.

What I did not do was call Rose.

Chapter 7
Rose

With a start, I woke up and rolled over into a sunbeam shining on my pillow. Blinking against the light, I stared at my cell phone with its blaring alarm taunting me from my bedside table.

He didn't call last night.

I picked it up to see if maybe he'd texted when I was asleep. *Of course not.* Bitter disappointment drove through me as the hope that had sprung up in the last couple of days died. I should have known better. These things just didn't work out for me. Love and Rose never mixed. Maybe I'd go to the animal shelter after work and get a dog. But with the luck I had, the dog would hate me just like that stupid squirrel outside.

I sighed and sat up. It wasn't worth it—having hope, chasing love. It hurt too much when it got away. Being lonely was easier and much less painful than being hopeful. I wanted Trevor—those feelings were real—but I couldn't count on him. But at least I could always count on myself, and maybe a cute cat. Or better yet, a guinea pig. They lived in a cage. It could never leave me. *Dramatic much?*

I sighed and kicked the covers off. My cell rang on my way to the shower, but I ignored it, not in the mood to talk to anyone. I needed coffee and Violet. She always took my side, even if my side was crazy.

All I wanted from life was what my parents had, or what Lily and Luke finally had. I wanted to be in love and have someone love me back. Why was that so hard to find? I would never lie. I would never cheat. I was kind of a perv in bed. And I was willing to put up with a lot of shit. Not bad shit like cheating or hitting or hating pizza, but reasonable shit like not putting clothes in the hamper or leaving the toilet paper on top of the holder. How was that not irresistible? Damn it, I was a freaking catch.

Wrapping up in a towel I swiped a circle in the condensation on the mirror. My sad face disgusted me, so I stuck my tongue out at my reflection. I started to worry about him. Then I got angry, and then I was back to sadness again. I could have called him myself, but he was so insistent that he was going to call me and so eager for me to agree to speak to him that I couldn't bring myself to do it. I still had some pride left.

I twisted my hair into a messy bun and stuck a pencil in to hold it. I applied pink lip gloss and some mascara and called it done. Mindlessly, I selected a sleeveless pink and white ombré maxi dress. Hmm, I was inadvertently dressing cute. Maybe I still harbored some hope. *Knock it off, stupid hope.* I added a fitted, short white denim jacket, rolled the sleeves up, and found my hot pink Birkenstocks. I looked at myself in the mirror again and tried positively affirming myself. But it felt ridiculous, so I stopped.

One more try. "You're cute and you're not a bitch," I said to my reflection in the mirror, " and you can rock a messy bun, and he can suck it." I strode determinedly out of my room to collect my things and go to work. The kids could always snap me out of a funk. Between the kiddos and Violet's magic coffee, I would have a good day. Even if I died trying.

The second my foot hit the front porch, I stopped and gasped. A beautiful potted pink hydrangea sat there. A card, tied with a bow, taunted me from a branch. Sitting there on the top step all gorgeous and apologetic with "Rosalie" printed on the envelope. *Hmph.* Since my mother was the only other person who called me by my full name, I knew it was from Trevor. It was too soon for my mother to try and cheer me up. There was no way she could have known that he was supposed to call me; she didn't even know we'd had a thing. Violet sort of knew, Lily suspected it, and I'd heard whispers at the Sunday dinners at my parent's house. But no one besides Vi and Lily had said anything to me directly.

I opened the envelope. It held a lovely white card with a red rose on the front. I flipped it open.

Rosalie,

I am so sorry I didn't call you last night. I tried to call this morning, but you didn't pick up. Please talk to me so I can explain. I'll be working all day. I'll call tonight. Please let me speak to you,

Trevor

I closed the card. Even his freaking handwriting was hot. I inhaled a deep, shaky breath so I wouldn't start to cry. I couldn't do this now. Call me a coward, but I just couldn't. I stood up, tucked his note into my tote and headed to my car. I would find somewhere to be tonight—without my phone.

I had a great morning. It was fucking delightful. I drank my hazelnut latte from Violet, ate my chocolate chip scone, and they worked a miracle. I got through the morning without crying. Or maybe I just got all hopped up on caffeine and sugar, so I didn't notice my heart was half broken.

Violet was supportive as usual. She got angry on my behalf and was prepared to embark on an adolescent tire-slashing, car-keying, house-TPing expedition with me. I said no to all of it because Trevor was renting Gram's house, she would get so mad if we TPed it. Plus, I didn't do stuff like that. Nope. I just ignore who I'm mad at like a normal human. But Violet's husband Tom was a dickhead of epic proportions. They were in marriage counseling for crap's sake, but I had my doubts that it would take. Could counseling make someone stop being an epic dickhead? I wasn't convinced. Therefore, I took most of what Violet said about love and men with several grains of salt. Though I did appreciate her blind loyalty.

I hadn't seen Lily yet; she was more apt to tell me to give Trevor a chance to explain. Therefore, I would be avoiding her right along with Trevor. I wished my sister Holly was in town. She would fall somewhere in the middle. Holly always gave good advice. She was a year younger than me and we'd always been close. But she was off on yet another adventure. She ran a successful travel blog, and was always gone.

At lunch, Violet and I sat in the tiny chairs in my classroom. We ate salad, sipped iced tea, and bitched about men, love, and life in general. We were in the same mood, pushing each other down a slippery slope made up of ice cream straight out of the carton, whiskey from the bottle, and sad old love songs. We were in a sorry state. "Violet, we need to snap out of this mood," I said.

"Fuck that. I've been in this mood for months, probably years. I think it's just how I am now," she said as she pulled a Snickers bar out of her purse. I pushed the remains of my salad aside and gave her an expectant look. She smirked and dug up another candy bar for me. We munched on chocolate and I listened to her bitch about Tom. I just nodded and gave appropriate sympathetic commentary. Violet got pregnant during her junior year of college, dropped out, and married Tom. She helped him graduate and stood by as he made himself into a snotty, rich, real estate guru. He was such a smarmy bastard. I couldn't stand him, but as a life rule, I didn't ever say bad things about someone else's man. I'd lost my best high school friend because her boyfriend was a cheater and I'd told her about it. Just one of the many times I fell into second place.

"Let's go for a hike after school. We could drive up to Robertson Lake and walk. No cell phones. No men. Just me and you and beautiful nature. Want to?"

She gave me a look and put her Snickers down. "Yeah, I want to. I've been hitting the chocolate hard. I think my ass is growing. At least that's what Tom told me." My eyes got big. It was hard not to say anything bad about him. So hard.

"Your ass is fine Violet. You are beautiful. And he—" I literally bit my tongue. Violet was gorgeous. I wasn't just telling her that to make her feel better. She had long, shiny dark brown hair, and big sparkling eyes. She was tall and curvy, beautiful, funny, and smart as hell. If she dumped that loser Tom, she could have anyone she wanted. Or no one, because that's okay too. Plus, she was the coffee queen of Sweetbriar, Oregon. Everyone in town loved her. Maybe

I should spread the word about Tom around town—threaten the beloved source of people's morning coffee, and there would be hell to pay. Right?

Violet laughed. "It's okay. I'm okay. My jeans still fit, so fuck him. But still . . ." Her eyes filled with tears. I hugged her, because what else could I do? Hiring an assassin to take Tom out was not practical. Telling my brothers what he said would land them all in prison—they liked to punch first, then ask questions later. And telling my mother would unleash the apocalypse. Damn it. I shook an imaginary fist at him and whispered, "Fuck you, Tom!" in my brain.

I managed to make it through the rest of the school day even though little Maddie was a constant reminder of Trevor. But eventually, I found that she was adorable and sweet, and so easy to like. I stopped thinking of him when I saw her and just enjoyed having her in my class. When I finally had a minute to check my phone, I saw that I didn't have any text messages or calls from him. Not a one. It was a relief. Sort of. Or not.

I drove home to change into clothes more suitable for hiking. I also turned my phone off and left it behind when I left to meet Violet at her shop. We stocked up on iced mochas for the drive and bottled water for the hike. We didn't talk on the drive up the mountain into the forest. We just sipped our coffee and sulked while the fresh air wafted through our opened windows. This was not a good start. I'd wanted to go hiking to improve my mood, breathe in the clean air, look at the pretty views, and all that stupid crap.

I slurped up the rest of my mocha, then unleashed a huge sigh. Violet turned and pulled into the little trail-type road that led to the parking lot. We didn't have to pay for parking since she had an Annual Northwest Forest Pass. Violet's sons were always taking off to go hiking or fishing.

At least, that's what they told her they were doing. I suspected they just drove up to deserted forested areas to make out with their girlfriends. Violet had sixteen-year-old twin boys, Finn and Nick. They were not identical; Lily and I were the only identical twins in the family. I was sure they could find something better to do up here than walk around the lake. Violet and I, however, *did not* have anything better to do. So, here we were, about to walk around a stupid, picturesque lake. We exited the car, then stood side by side.

The view of Mount Hood from here was spectacular. It stood tall in its snowy white glory, looming in the distance through the trees like a solid cloud pyramid. The sky around it was pale blue and the air was still. There were a few trees here and there full of colorful leaves, but the pine trees that surrounded the lake were green. We stopped when we reached it and stood at the edge of the water. The mountain reflected in it like a mirror, only distorting when ducks swam by and created shimmering ripples.

"It's so fucking pretty here," Violet said with a disgusted sneer. She kicked a rock into the water where it landed with a *plop*.

I burst out a startled laugh. "Yeah, we should have gone to a prison or a garbage dump to walk," I halfheartedly teased.

She looked at me sheepishly. "Fine, I'll try harder," she grumbled. "Let's walk." We started walking and stopped talking. I could tell Violet was hurting as much as I was. I hated it, for both of us.

I bit the bullet. "I don't like feeling like this," I said. "Look around. We're surrounded by beauty. We're breathing clean, fresh fucking air. And we're both miserable."

She stopped and looked at me. "Yeah I know. I just don't know what to say."

"All we did, Vi, was relocate our bad moods. I'm just sad, miserable Rose at a lake, instead of sad, miserable Rose sitting on my couch. And you, you're actually kind of scary right now." She laughed. "We deserve better Violet. Life is not just about dumbass men pissing us off, hurting our feelings, and letting us down. It's about . . . um, sisterhood. It's about pretty lakes, big-ass mountains, and drinking mochas in your Range Rover. We need to carpe the diem and all that shit, and quit moping around like losers."

"You're right. Let's run the rest of the trail. Race you!" She took off with her brown hair flying behind, and her laugh filling my ears.

"Hey! Cheater!" I hauled ass after her. We flew down the trail. Luckily, it was only a little bit crowded today. We dodged some power walkers, other joggers, and a few mommies with strollers, then left the trail to run in the woods for a few minutes to go around a couple of horses with riders. We were out of breath, red faced, and sweaty when we finally made it back to where we'd started—almost two miles later.

We stopped at the edge of the lake and stood panting together. Only this time I took it in. The sky shone with pinks and purples that swirled into pale blue as the sun began to set. The trees reflected like black silhouettes on the still water, framing the mountain, which shimmered with a lavender hue in the center. I grabbed Violet's hand and held it. We stood like that for a few minutes and tried to catch our breath before turning around to head back to the car, still holding hands.

Violet broke our silence. "Does this mean we are at one with nature now?" I nudged her side with my arm. She nudged me back. We nudge walked through the parking lot and laughed like loons until we got to the car. Who knew if we were at one with nature? What I did know was that I felt a little bit better.

Violet drove us to her shop, and I hugged her goodbye. "You deserve the best, Violet. If Tom doesn't want to give it to you, it's okay to move on," I whispered before I entered my car to drive home. I was starving, so I stopped at the food carts in town for a burrito. As I drove into my dark driveway, I saw something sparkle on my porch. I grabbed my dinner and crossed my lawn to get to the source of the sparkle.

Sitting on the table next to my porch swing was a huge bunch of red roses in a clear glass vase. Tiny lights filled it, surrounding the stems, making it glow and twinkle. I glared at it for a second, before picking up the vase and unlocking the door. I turned to scowl at that stupid hydrangea from the last apology for good measure before I went inside. I placed the vase on the coffee table and threw myself down in the corner of my sectional to watch TV and eat. Those stupid roses stared at me the whole time I was trying to enjoy my hoarded DVR *Game of Thrones* episodes. I was forced to appreciate their beauty and Trevor's thoughtfulness. Maybe I should give him a chance. Maybe I should go get my phone and call him.

Or maybe I should just go to bed and sleep on it. I showered and headed for bed. But I had to run back to the living room to get the roses first. I set them on my dresser so I could see them as I drifted off.

I did not turn my phone on. I still wasn't ready for that. I had spent almost an entire year trying to ignore the hurt I'd felt when Trevor took his wife back. A year of trying not to think about the pain it caused when I'd found out he was not even divorced before he started with me. Avoiding my feelings, downplaying them, or just denying that I even had feelings in the first place had led me to this point. And it wasn't a healthy place to be. I fell into a fitful sleep; dreams of Trevor filled my subconscious as memories and fantasies wrapped me up in a confusing web that I wondered if I would ever be able to untangle.

Chapter 8
Rose

I filled my Saturday with all the tasks that I always put off for "later." I did the laundry, grocery shopped, and gathered materials for my lesson plans. What I should have done was turn my phone on and dealt with my emotional baggage. So basically, I had a horrible day. I forced myself to ignore the doubt that plagued me every time I saw my phone. Deep down I knew that I was being a big baby. I wasn't being fair to Trevor, or myself, by avoiding him. I kept ignoring the nagging thought that he may have had a good reason for not calling me—that it might not even be about me. I did not like this side of my personality. This storm of self-loathing had been hovering over my head for as long as I could remember, and the clouds had yet to clear. But I couldn't find the strength to do anything about it. Every time I caught sight of the lovely roses he'd given me, it made me feel weak and unworthy. It kept me silent and at home, rather than reaching out to take what I wanted. Saturday was horrible, and I woke up Sunday afternoon in a miserable mood.

After turning my phone on, I found six missed calls

from my mother. My hand shook as that panicky feeling I used to get in my chest as a kid about to get in trouble rushed through me. I shook it off, knowing that if something serious had happened someone would have come over here and told me. I also had four missed calls and a text from Trevor. But he hadn't tried to call me today, not once. *I probably messed everything up by ignoring him for the last two days.* I tossed the phone aside and headed for the bathroom to stare at my bleary eyes in the mirror and brush my teeth. Looking at my sad expression was making me feel worse, so I smiled at myself. The toothpaste foam made me look crazy. I shrugged and spit; maybe I was crazy. I felt like blowing off the weekly Sunday dinner at my parent's house and going back to bed, but I didn't want to deal with the fallout if I missed it. My mother kept her apron strings tied up real tight. To her, missing a dinner was like missing her birthday, or worse, missing Mother's Day. I dressed in black leggings and a flowy purple tank top. After slipping into my pink Birkenstocks from Friday, I left for the day. I would be early for dinner, but maybe it would prevent my mom from getting mad about me not answering her calls. Wishful thinking, for sure.

My parent's house sat on several acres and sprawled in all directions. Squinting against the sunlight as I drove down the long driveway, I spotted my mother out front hanging pink and blue streamers across the porch. My grandma sat on the porch swing, filling balloons from a helium tank. Clearly, those six missed calls were meant to tell me something. I parked my car next to the rose bushes near the garage and got out. I braced myself when I noticed my mother had moved to stand on the porch, hands on hips. Great. I really didn't need a lecture about family togetherness right now.

"Well, hello there, Miss Rosalie. Nice of you to deign to acknowledge our existence. I called you at least five times, missy." Oh crap, I got the "missy."

"Chill out, Dahlia. She's here, and nothing has even started yet," Gram piped in. She was always good for reining in my mother.

"What's going on?" I asked.

"We're having a gender reveal party for Lily and Luke." Panic filled me. *Trevor will be here* . . .

I started to turn and leave, but it seemed Gram was also good for reining *me* in. "Calm down, sugar, Trevor won't be coming. It's his daddy's birthday today." I continued up the walkway and sat on the steps. I was relieved, but at the same time wondered how she knew about me and Trevor. Did everyone already know? I decided to ignore everything. After all, denial was one of my favorite coping skills. If I wanted to turn my phone off and be a hermit for a day or two, I was allowed. "There is coffee in the kitchen. Go and get some. You look like you need it," Gram added with a smile.

Jude and Levi, my twin younger brothers, were sitting in the kitchen shoveling scrambled eggs and toast in their faces. Did they ever go home? They rented a townhouse together just a few streets over from my house, but I didn't think they spent any time there. They were either at my house or here—for the food, I assumed. "Hey guys." I filled a huge mug with coffee. As I added sugar and half-and-half, I looked around for something to eat. I snagged a muffin out of the basket on the counter then sat at the table with them. This kitchen hadn't always been this big. My dad had added on to it a few years ago. It now had a big bay window that overlooked the pool and the patio where a table and chairs sat, centered in the middle. There was also a huge island, surrounded by stools. Opened French doors led out to the covered patio where balloons and streamers decorated the space. The upside to this day was that if there was going to be a party, there would be cake at some point. I could use some cake to eat alongside my feelings.

"You're in trouble," Levi informed me between bites. I shrugged. That was the least of my worries.

"Mom couldn't get ahold of you," Jude accused. "She's been calling the rest of us. Repeatedly. Violet told us we should all leave you alone. You okay?" I shrugged again and sipped my coffee. Jude was my sweetest brother. We used to cuddle and watch *Blue's Clues* together when we were little. I used to pretend he was my baby, even though I was only five years older.

"I'm okay," I finally responded. I could tell they were not convinced.

"I will punch someone in the face. Point me in a direction." Levi put his bacon down and pointed a finger at me. "Who hurt you? Was it Trevor?"

"Please, no face punching. But thank you." If I didn't stop him, he really would go punch Trevor in the face.

"You let me know," he said and returned to his bacon.

"Heads up, Violet is bringing Tom today," Jude informed me. My face must have shown my hatred because he laughed. "Finn and Nick are coming too. We have to be nice, so try to lose that expression."

I shook my head. "I hate that fucking guy. I'm in a bad mood as it is. He'd better not say anything mean, because I will not be held responsible for what I do, even if Finn and Nick are here."

"I'll punch *him* in the face. Is that okay?" Levi smirked.

"I'll let you know. But probably, yes. If I don't do it first. Also, what is up with the hostility, Levi?" Levi always made me laugh. He'd been a chubby little kid. Totally geeky, with glasses and braces. I had always thought he was adorable, but schoolyard bullies were relentless. That's when he learned how to face punch. He also developed a wicked sense of humor that was almost as fierce as his fists. Now, he was a six-foot, five-inch tall firefighter, who lifted weights and jogged for fun. Levi had to beat women off with a stick. Though, from what I heard, he didn't beat *any* of them off with a stick. Jude was a firefighter too. They both worked right here in Sweetbriar.

"I don't know. I just feel like punching someone and I'm not particular about who it is," he muttered.

"Becca has a new boyfriend," Jude spilled the beans.

"Shut up, Jude." Levi stormed out.

"Oh wow. He likes her?" Becca was his childhood best friend. She was his only friend back then, besides Jude. They drifted apart when he got hot, somewhere back in tenth grade.

"He won't talk about it. No use bringing it up," Jude said. I would *so* bring it up. It's what I do. I filed the information away for later. Lucky for Levi, I had enough to deal with for now.

"You miss a lot of stuff in this family when you turn your phone off for two days," I mused. "What about you, Jude? What's up?"

He shook his head. "Nope. What about *you*, Rose? Or, should I say, Rosalie? At least, that's what the card on the flower basket on your porch said." His raised eyebrow and sideways grin combo told me he knew my business and was going to grill me.

I looked out the window and shoved some muffin in my mouth. I chewed and glanced over at him. He just watched me with that expectant smirk. "What were you doing at my house?" His eyebrows got higher in response. "Fine. They are from Trevor," I admitted.

"I was there because I was supposed to have dinner with you, which you obviously forgot about," he reminded me.

"I'm sorry I forgot our plans. I went on a hike with Violet. We needed to get away."

"And . . ." he prodded.

I plopped the rest of my muffin to my plate and decided to fess up. "And, he was supposed to call me Thursday night, and he didn't, and I got all—"

"You got all 'Rose' about it," he finished for me. *What?*

"What do you mean I got all 'Rose' about it?"

"You think he's changed his mind about you, or got mad at you, or secretly hates you, or something like that. It's what you do," he informed me. I stared at him with big eyes as he patted my hand. "You do it with me, and I'm your brother."

"I've probably messed everything up then," I whispered.

"It's never too late to talk to someone, Rose." His eyes were full of sympathy. "I'm going to go help outside. Everyone's going to be here soon." He got up and headed out back. I sat there and thought about what he'd said. I couldn't call Trevor now; I left my phone at home. And I couldn't leave, because this was a party for Lily.

My lip curled when I heard Tom and Violet's voices coming from the living room. I took a deep breath and tried to uncurl my lip and smile. I couldn't do it. I tried to think of something happy . . . nope, still no luck. Then my mother came in through the back door carrying a huge pastry box.

Cake . . ....

My father followed her inside with another.

Even more cake . . .

I found a smile. "I'm glad you came, sweetheart." My

mother smiled back at me. I guess she wasn't in the mood to give me any more shit for not answering her calls.

"Hey, pumpkin," my dad added.

"Hi, Dad." I hoped he would not mention Trevor. From what I'd heard, Dad loved Trevor, and was super glad he'd hired him. *Please, please, please, don't say anything about him.*

Violet and Tom walked into the kitchen at that moment, saving me from a potential Trevor inquisition. "Hi, guys." I greeted them with my best phony smile. Violet had the look she got when she was trying to make everyone think she was okay, when she really wasn't. Her trembling smile made my phony one disappear.

"Hi, Rose," Tom said and sat at the table next to me. "Violet, would you pour me a cup?" He gestured to my coffee, then took his jacket off and held it out to her. *Holy heck, this was going to be so hard.* I blinked hard a few times and plastered my smile back on. I needed to maintain my generic expression and not blow raspberries at his stupid fucking face or flip him off. Tom was a good-looking guy. The trouble was, he knew it—and it made him act like an arrogant prick.

"How are you, Tom?" I asked.

"I can't complain." He grinned. "I just sold the old MacMillan place to a developer and I managed to make myself a few MacMillions." He bumped my shoulder with his and laughed.

"Well, congratulations," I said.

He nodded at me then turned to Violet at the counter. "Vi, my coffee?"

"I'm coming, babe," she answered distractedly.

He turned to me. "She makes coffee for a living. You'd think she'd be faster. Am I right?" He laughed again. My eye twitched. It literally twitched. I was going to die of a stroke from this fucking guy. I took deep breath, shoved the rest of my muffin in my mouth, and shrugged.

Violet came to the table with two coffees and some muffins on a plate. She sat next to me and took a sip of her coffee. Tom sipped his, then he made a face. "Violet, you put sugar in it. You know I went sugar free. Make me another one." He gestured to the muffins. "And babe, you don't really need a muffin, do you?" Both of my eyes were twitching. Could twitchy eyes kill a person? I grabbed a muffin from the plate and shoved half of it in my mouth in order to keep quiet. I chewed it and glared at Tom. I grabbed Violet's hand and squeezed it. She squeezed back. Then she stood up and headed to the coffee pot at the counter.

"How she manages to keep that stupid shop open, I'll never know." He muttered under his breath. I stood up to find Levi. I needed to see a face get punched. STAT. With a wave goodbye, I darted toward the living room.

Lily, Luke, and the kids came in the front door as I crossed through the arched living room entrance. I ran over to hug every single one of them. Dylan laughed when I swung him up and kissed his cheeks. "Baby. Gimme." I reached for Calla in Luke's arms. "I was just in there with Tom. I need baby cuddles to cleanse my aura," I said. He laughed, then handed her over. I sniffed her head as I snuggled her. She smelled so good. I swear I felt my ovaries drop an egg. I wanted a baby so badly. Tears filled my eyes and Lily put her arm around me.

"Rose, it's going to be okay," she soothed. I could only shake my head in response, or I would break down. It wouldn't be okay. I'd messed everything up and I knew it. "It's going to be fine," she insisted.

"I screwed up," I whispered. "He didn't call me, and I think I went kind of nuts."

"You thought he changed his mind or something, didn't you?" I looked away from her. "Did you even once stop to think that Trevor didn't call because something happened? That it had nothing to do with you?" I shook my head. She was right; I hadn't even considered that. It was always all about me. "You always assume the worst," Lily said.

"Not about other people. You always assume the worst about yourself," Luke added. I jerked back, cuddling Calla to my chest like a security blanket, or maybe a shield against his kind words. "You're smart, and funny." He pointed to Lily. "Obviously, I think you're beautiful." I laughed, even as I teared up, and shook my head. "You're fun to be around. Everyone loves you—"

"Stop it," I choked through the lump in my throat.

"No. Why can't you take a compliment? You're worth the effort, Rose. You deserve every good thing," he finished. I hugged Calla closer and she wrapped her tiny arms around my neck. A sob escaped, and Lily pulled me close.

"He's right," Lily said. "You deserve good things. Stop running from them."

"It's probably too late. I've probably already driven him away." I sounded so pathetic. I was even annoying myself.

Lily studied me. "Rose, what happened to you? Where is the piss? Where is the vinegar?" Levi entered the living room, just in time to hear her.

"I told you, point me in a direction. I will punch some faces. We'll get that pissy vinegar back for you." He wrapped his arms around me from behind and made faces at Calla in my arms. She giggled at him when he started using my hair to tickle her face.

"I promise you, Rose. It's going to be okay. Call him tonight," Lily said.

"Maybe."

"No maybe. Do it. Or I will come over and make you," she threatened. "You're going to be happy. I'm going to shove you into it, like you did for me." I didn't answer, I just laughed.

Mom popped her head through the arch that led into the kitchen area. "Is everyone here?"

"I've seen everyone but Asher. And Holly," I said.

"Ash is in back with all the kids. Holly is out of town, like usual. I'll call them all in, and then it's time! Head for the kitchen. I can't wait!"

As I looked at Lily, a metaphorical lightbulb popped on over my head, "They have two cakes in there. Does that mean . . . ?"

"I'm having twins. We just found out yesterday. You would have been the first to know if you had answered your phone," she told me with a huge smile lighting up her face.

"Oh, my goodness!" I was only ten percent jealous of her. The fact that I would have two more nieces or nephews to cuddle had cut it down from the fifty percent I had initially felt.

"Holy shit!" Levi said. "You are going to be like a round little ball. You're so short—how are you going to fit two babies in there? Rose, aren't you glad you won't be waddling around all winter like Lily's going to be?" I laughed with Levi, but my heart was not in it. I *wanted* to waddle around. I'd have two babies right now, if I could. Trevor had such beautiful kids. I wanted to make beautiful babies with him.

Lily grimaced. "I have no idea. It was so uncomfortable with just one at a time."

Luke put his arms around her. "You have me this time,

so don't worry. I'll carry you around if you want me to. I'll do everything you need. Anything you want, no questions asked." Now I was back up to fifty percent jealous, damn it. I wanted babies, and I wanted a husband to carry my miserable pregnant ass around too. *Stop it, Rose.*

We gathered in the kitchen. The cakes on the counter were each frosted with a thick swirly layer of white vanilla buttercream. The inside color of the cake would determine the sex of the babies. We counted to three, Luke and Lily each cut into a cake. One was pink, and one was blue. She carried a boy and a girl. I was fifty percent jealous about each baby, plus fifty percent jealous of her relationship. Did that make me one hundred and fifty percent jealous? I was also one hundred percent happy for her. Don't judge my math, it's how I felt. I was green with envy and filled with guilt about it, as well as overjoyed and happy for Luke and Lily. It was hard holding these tears back. My eyes burned from the effort. Violet put her arm around me and handed me a mimosa. We toasted to the babies with the rest of the family. But I was pretty sure she felt the same way I did: miserably happy.

Chapter 9
Rose

I drove home from the Sunday dinner-turned-gender-reveal-party last night determined to get my life back on track. I found my phone and checked for missed calls—there weren't any. My heart sank, but I decided to find my piss and vinegar and just call Trevor myself. It sank even further when my call went straight to voice mail. I did not leave a message. I wasn't that brave.

I had a miserable night full of tossing and turning and restless sleep. I woke up in a red-eyed snit. All I wanted to do was go back to sleep and forget my misery. I checked my phone; he hadn't called me. I had probably destroyed my second chance with him by avoiding him all weekend. I was already wishing the day was over before I had even gotten out of bed. I showered, then dressed for the day in a comfy, black maxi dress. I added a blue denim jacket, rainbow beaded lanyard, and a pair of black Converse sneakers. I did my pencil-bun-and-pink-lip-balm thing and left for the day.

I arrived at my classroom and found Violet waiting for me there with my usual hazelnut latte. She brought choco-late-almond filled croissants for our breakfast, and she didn't have to say a word. I already knew that she was just as happy as I was based on the breakfast she brought. We didn't even talk; we just sat and ate our junky breakfast in bleak silence. This was going to be the bright part of my day. Being able to commiserate with Violet made me feel less alone. I would miss her next week when she went back to her shop full time.

I tried hard to hide my mood from the kids. I smiled and sang my way through morning calendar, small groups, and reading centers. Violet was a trooper too; not one child noticed the internal pity parties we were both having. Finally, it was library time—break time.

We were quiet when we walked back to my classroom together after dropping the kids off. We sat silently in my tiny chairs and ate the Snickers bars that Violet had in her purse. It was kind of cool that I had another option for dealing with my bad moods—other than my backyard brooding. I had stress eating with Lily, and now chocolate therapy with Violet.

All this moping and misery was doing my head in. I needed an attitude change. Self-pity was bad for me. It felt like my heart was too big and burning a hole in my chest. I had lost my fight and I needed to get it back. I decided to change my lesson plan for the next hour to cheer myself up. It was time for the kids to learn the "Montherena".

"It's "Montherena" day, Vi. Are you ready?" I shouted. To Violet, it probably sounded out of nowhere—I mean, she wasn't part of my internal monologue—but she went with it anyway.

"Yeah, I'm ready." She laughed. "Let's go get 'em."

Basically, we were about to recite the months of the year to the tune of "The Macarena" and teach the kids the dance. It was impossible to do this lesson without smiling.

Violet and I could both use a laugh. Her husband was an asshole of epic proportions, and my man didn't call or answer his phone when I called. Okay, so he wasn't officially my man to bitch about. And Violet was worse off than I was. Yeesh.

Perspective.

I sneaked a peek at Violet. *Don't show any pity—she hates that.*

I smiled at her. I must have had some pity showing in my smile because she threw an eraser at me. "Quit it."

"I didn't say anything."

"You didn't have to. You've been surly since you got here." *I have been?* "You are mad at Trevor, and now you feel guilty because yesterday, you saw that my husband is worse." *And double yeesh.*

"I thought I was hiding it," I said.

"*Hmph.* The kids didn't notice, but I noticed. I am sorry he didn't call you, but don't let that ruin your day. I'm glad you're busting out the "Montherena." The kids will love it. Come on." She stood in the doorway and gestured for me to get my booty through it.

Violet and I strolled down the hall and down the stairs toward the library, chatting all the way about innocuous things. Both of us tried to avoid upsetting the other. Men could sometimes become conversational roadblocks—it was so annoying.

Lily stood in the library doorway with her back to us, lining up my class. "Line up kindergarten. Our eyes are on the door, our feet are on the floor. We'll get in line and say no more. Let me see your quiet foxes in the air so Miss Barrett can see how good you were today." My class was ready to go. They were in a straight line in front of Lily, their little fingers making perfect quiet foxes in the air: the two middle two fingers connected with the thumb to make the face, and the pinky and pointer fingers went straight up to make the ears. Adorable.

I had a class full of unicorns this year. It already felt like I was in movie—like *Kindergarten Cop*, but without all the kidnapping and criminal activity. The point was, these kids were fictionally well-behaved. As in, there was no way they could be real. I was just waiting for one of them to lose their shit and throw a tantrum. Or call me a bitch and tell me to shut up, like Jaden B. did last school year.

Their eyes lit up when they spotted me behind Lily. Kids were always fascinated when the two of us were together and sometimes made a game of trying to spot differences between us. One obvious difference right now was Lily's teeny-tiny baby bump that I was totally *not* jealous of at all. The kids stayed quiet in line and I gave them a proud smile.

"Mrs. McCabe, did my class behave today?" I asked Lily, and she played along.

"Miss Barrett, this was the best class I've had all day. In fact, they were such good listeners that next week they can each check out a book." We watched their eyes get even bigger, but still no talking. The achy, burning lump Trevor left in my chest disappeared as I beamed with pride at my class.

We walked down the hall and up the stairs to my classroom like a quiet train, with me as the engine and Violet as the caboose. We headed to the carpet and Violet started up the music. I demonstrated the moves in front of the class while Violet walked through and helped the kids who weren't catching on. It took a few minutes, but eventually they all got it.

Violet dashed over to answer the phone ringing on my

desk. Before she rejoined the class, she shot me big smile. With a huge smile back, I continued dancing with the kids, waving my arms, shaking my booty and doing the spin part of the dance. The kids were way into it, too. We were singing the names of the months and having a great time.

Something happened when we got to April. A throat being cleared in the doorway stopped me mid-hip swivel and I spun around to see Trevor with a huge bouquet of flowers in his hand and an even bigger smile on his face. He also carried a few big grocery bags slung over one arm. I spied goldfish crackers sticking out of the top. He had brought classroom snacks, his volunteer sticker was stuck right to his chest, and he had seen everything. Well, maybe not everything, but he'd absolutely seen more than I would've wanted him to see.

I stammered something about it being almost time for lunch. Violet stopped the music and I froze. Violet picked up my slack and reintroduced Trevor to the class. "Detective Hale is going to volunteer in our class today," she announced. "Come on over here and introduce your dad, Maddie."

Maddie ran to the doorway to hug her dad. "This is my daddy." Maddie made her own introduction and the kids were properly impressed. She eyed the flowers. "You got flowers for Miss Barrett?" she asked. There were some *oohs* and *ahs* from the kids. So much for being quiet.

"I did. I also brought classroom snacks." His answer was for Maddie, but he looked at me while he spoke. After a quick look around the room at Violet and the kids, I slammed my eyes shut. Everyone was smiling, except me. I didn't know how to feel yet. Well, my brain didn't know how to feel. My heart, however, was shooting sparks of hope and love tingles all throughout my stupid body.

"Why did you bring her flowers?" Maddie asked. I opened one eye to peek.

"I accidentally hurt her feelings, so I bought her flowers to say sorry." Again, he was answering Maddie but looking at me. I admit, I melted a bit. Okay, I melted a lot. Like, someone was going to need to mop me off the floor and carry me home in a bucket.

"Daddy, it hurts my feelings that you didn't bring me a present too," she announced, the clever little thing. I cracked a grin and Trevor winked at me and Violet laughed. Meanwhile, the kids moved their heads back and forth between me and Trevor and Maddie like this was a tennis match.

He looked down at Maddie. "Expect a new Beanie Boo on your pillow when you get home from school," he bargained. Some of the girls in class gasped and chattered quietly, speculating about which one she would get.

"I want a kitty cat one. And I want cupcakes for dessert," she added. *Well played, Maddie. Well played.*

"I'll go to Pixie Cakes—" Maddie's head bobbed enthusiastically as she beamed up at him. Trevor raised his eyebrows at her. "And Maddie—"

She cut him off, she already knew what he was going to say. "And I'll pick up my toys like I'm 'sposed to."

"Deal." They shook on it.

Violet took the bags full of snacks from Trevor, stored them in the cupboard, and lined the class up for lunch. I mouthed "thank you" to her. She winked and blew a kiss. I caught it with a laugh and stuck it to my cheek.

The class and Violet filed passed me to the cafeteria, which left me alone with Trevor. My nerves raced out of control. Even deep breathing didn't lessen the thunderous beat of my heart. It echoed in my ears and scrambled my brain.

"I owe you an apology, Rosalie." He handed me the bouquet. It was mostly Casablanca lilies, which I loved. Their vibrant green leaves provided a beautiful contrast against the creamy-colored petals and the fragrant beauty of the flowers was almost intoxicating. Interspersed among the lilies were a mix of blue thistle and other pretty little blue and white flowers. The bouquet was wrapped in brown paper and tied with white lace and raffia, and it was the most beautiful arrangement I had ever seen. There was no way he'd bought this at the grocery store. Trevor was thoughtful, smoking hot, sweet *and* a good dad. He was almost perfect. I peeked up at him over the blooms and he smiled softly at me. "I'm sorry I didn't call," he whispered.

"I'm sorry too." Suddenly, I was full of all kinds of clarity. And feeling a bit sheepish.

"You have nothing to be sorry for." His eyes crinkled at the corners adorably as he smiled with amusement at my apology.

"I'm sorry that I got mad at you," I insisted. "I'm sorry I avoided you. You not calling played right into some of my insecurities. And when I did try to call you and you didn't answer, I freaked out. But I know you better than that, Trevor. Something happened, right? Is everything okay?" I felt terrible about myself for being angry with him. He wasn't like the other guys I had dated in the past, and I wished I hadn't painted him with the same brush.

"Maddie was in the tub. I had just finished washing her hair. When I tried to answer your call, the phone slipped and landed in the water. It was a goner. Uh, Maddie also learned a new word and it's not a nice one. Hopefully she won't say it here." I smiled. "But Rose, more importantly, what insecurities? Tell me, so I don't hurt your feelings again." He was so earnest that I answered honestly without thinking about it first.

"Sometimes I feel like I'm second best. I lost my chance with you and she got you back and it fed into every bad thing I always think about myself and it's been festering," I admitted.

"She never had me—not like you do. I married her because I got her pregnant. I didn't love her, and she sure as hell never loved me. I tried, because of Mikey and Maddie, but she made it impossible. And I'm sorry I told you I was divorced when it wasn't final. It's just that I had finally gotten her to sign the papers. It was as good as finished for me, and it had been for years. We hadn't lived together since Maddie was born. At that point in my life, there was no way I would have ever taken her back."

"I get it, Trevor. It's okay. I guess I haven't had great experiences in the love department. Plus, I'm stuck in the middle of my siblings. Sometimes I feel like I'm invisible. I never really dealt with the feelings I had when we ended things last year, so it's no surprise any little thing was able to push me over the crazy edge," I added.

"I can understand all of that," he said. "My older brother lives in Texas and works for NASA. He is literally a rocket scientist. My younger brother lives in New York City, and he's a brain surgeon. He and his wife just adopted six orphaned siblings. Meanwhile, I'm a twenty-minute drive from where I grew up, a single father, and a normal, average, police detective. I almost went through a messy divorce from the wife who cheated on me constantly. My parents say they're proud, but come on . . ." He rolled his eyes and laughed.

I was indignant. "Trevor, you're the best man I know.

You're a police detective, and that takes bravery. You took your lousy wife back to take care of her when she was dying of cancer. Your kids are wonderful and adorable and it's all because of what a great dad you are—"

"So, you do still like me." He smirked, brown eyes twinkling.

"I never said I didn't like you," I insisted.

"I like you, Rosalie. I want to show you how much." He nodded once, like he had just made a decision. "I know what to do. I'm going to give you what you need, and then I will get what I deserve," he stated.

"And just what do you deserve? Tell me." I laughed. He took the flowers and set them down on the table next to me, then reached behind himself to close the door and twist the lock. His eyes bored into mine as he took my hands in his. I blinked up at him, already completely wrapped up in whatever he was going to say.

"I deserve a good woman. One with honor, kindness, and strength. I deserve to be first in someone's heart, and so do you. I want you to be the woman in my life. I will treat you like the beautiful princess you are, and you're going to finish falling in love with me." I gaped up at him like a dummy as he continued right on blowing my mind. "So, princess . . ." his voice got low and intimate as his eyes burned into mine. "Do we understand each other now?"

Thud. I just died. Rose's brain had left the building. I couldn't even nod to tell him that heck yes, we understood each other. I stood there staring up at him trying not to drool. My inner teenage girl twirled around her room and fist pumped the air because all her dreams had just come true. The items on teen Rose's love bucket list were getting checked off one by one.

He chuckled. How did he always know when I was flustered? And why did he like it so much? "Rosalie, will you have dinner with me Saturday night?"

"Yes," I whispered and nodded. Then I squeezed his hands in mine and kept on nodding. *Yes? Make that a hell yes.* I was going to eat the crap out of dinner with him Saturday night, or any other night, or every freaking night. I prevented myself from jumping up and down and making a bigger fool of myself. *Rose be cool, just a little bit.*

"God, you're cute." He grinned at me, and I got redder. My face was so hot, you could probably fry an egg on it. "I'll pick you up. Is six o'clock okay with you?" he asked. I nodded some more.

"Yes. Six will be fine," I murmured, completely lost in his presence.

He had barely touched me and yet I still felt him everywhere. In fact, he wasn't touching me at all anymore. He had released my hands and leaned forward, lips near my ear, breath tickling my skin. But it was so much more than that; I felt like I was lying naked with him. Like he was inside of my soul.

What is he doing to me? What is this feeling? Please let him be feeling this too . . .

I opened my eyes, and for the first time in my life, I wasn't scared to try to read someone. I had a feeling I wouldn't be disappointed. There was color in his cheeks and his eyes were still on me. Our breathing matched, and when I put my hand on his chest, his heart raced just like mine. I smiled. He immediately returned it and reached out to brush my cheek with his fingertips. I felt exposed, but it didn't scare me.

I wanted this. That nameless, faceless fantasy I had always had of the love I wanted.

Marriage and babies and family vacations. Skinned knees, sleepless nights and dinners around a table.

It had become Trevor; it was all about him now. I had no doubt that he was going to be it for me.

"Will you kiss me now?" I breathed.

He pulled the pencil out of my hair, my curls tumbled wildly over my shoulders. "Yeah baby, I'm gonna kiss you now," he growled softly. Hands drifted into my hair, pulling it away from my face while one big palm wrapped around the back of my neck and the other slid around to cup my cheek. My heart beat wildly in my chest, and I had the crazy thought that I might die if he didn't kiss me immediately. I felt like I was burning up, hot in a way I had never felt before.

As I gazed up at him, his expression grew serious. His eyes met mine before dropping to my mouth. My tongue darted out to wet my lips and his hand in my hair twisted gently to guide me closer. This was the moment I had been yearning for. I was right on the precipice of it, and when I stepped off, I would go from wanting him to *having* him.

My eyes drifted to half-mast as he lowered his face to press his lips to mine. It was gentle at first, then harder as our bodies melted together. Reaching high, I wound my arms around his neck and pressed myself against his tall, firm body from my lips on his, all the way down to my tip-toes. Our lips melded together—tongues meeting, faces slanting—and when I felt him grow hard against me, I shuddered with want. He towered over me, and I loved it. He grabbed fistfuls of my dress at my hips with both hands.

We had both been so hungry for this moment for so long. My half-hour lunch in my classroom was not going to be enough time to sate it. He pulled back with a guttural moan and I immediately wanted his lips back on mine.

Reaching up, I pulled him down with my hand at his neck and we crashed together again. His arms wrapped around my waist to lift me off my feet.

"Trevor . . ." I breathed. My body slid slowly down his as he loosened his arms. He pulled my face into his heaving chest and held me tight.

"God, Rosalie. I don't think I'll ever get enough of you," he whispered in my ear. I silently returned that sentiment and nodded against his chest.

I took a half a step back. But I held onto his arms because my knees were weak. *Weak knees from a kiss . . . are not a myth. Good to know.*

He pressed a fingertip to my lower lip, I kissed it and his eyes blazed into mine. I loved that he wanted me as much as I wanted him. Never had I experienced what it was like to have someone feel the same way I did.

"I'm going to go." His jaw was tight as he held himself back. "It will be too hard to stay here with you for the rest of the day like I had planned. I want you too much right now."

I nodded because I agreed. The chemistry between us was buzzing in the air. No way I could concentrate if he stayed. "Call me tonight?"

"I'll call you after I get the kids down for the night. No matter what." With promises in his eyes and a kiss goodbye, he left. I collapsed into the chair behind me. My hand drifted up to my touch my lips as a smile crossed my face. I could still feel him. The rest of the day loomed in front of me while the thought of his phone call lifted my spirits.

Chapter 10
Trevor

I didn't spend the day volunteering for Rose's class like I had planned, so I finally hit up Costco to stock up my house. Frozen pizza and McDonald's weren't going to cut it anymore. I was slacking in the nutrition department. The kids were going to have to get used to vegetables all over again. I stopped at Fred Meyer to find a Beanie Boo for Maddie, not wanting to see the look on her face if I forgot, and found a small Lego set for Mikey. Passing Rose's house right before turning onto my street gave me a smile that stayed on my face all the way home. I was about to pull my Jeep into the driveway, but stopped next to the curb because my front door was open. My smile faded. *What the fuck?*

Grabbing my cell from the console and called Cade. He was Rose's brother, and as I had found out this morning, my soon-to-be partner. I was off today, but I still carried my service pistol. I checked my weapon and headed to the door. Cade must have been close by, because he soon pulled in behind me and followed me inside. There was no sign that anyone had been here at all, except for the opened door. We made fast work of searching the house and the backyard. It wasn't until we got to Maddie's room that we saw an envelope, sticking right out from underneath her fucking pillow. I holstered my gun. Cade passed me some gloves, and I carefully opened it.

A birthday card with a purple-haired clown covered the front. I opened it. Under the generic happy birthday printed on the inside it said, "I'll see you soon baby doll. Love, your Daddy." My stomach sank as cold dread filled my veins. I bagged the card and the envelope, hands shaking with anger.

When I found this guy, he was dead.

"What the hell?" Cade muttered. He read over my shoulder. "What kind of sick fuck would leave something like this for a little girl to find?" I quickly filled him in on Tara, her cheating, the question about Maddie's true paternity, and the call I got the other night.

"I'll call this in. Then we'll unload your stuff. When are your kids going to be home?"

"My mother picks them up from school. I can have her keep them for a while."

"Good. We'll finish installing the security system. We should have done it before you moved in. I'll call dad." Cade's father, Ben, was the chief and my boss.

We unloaded. I changed Maddie's bedding and threw the old sheets in the wash. After remaking the bed, I placed the new Beanie Boo on her pillow. The chief showed up and together, the three of us finished installing the security system. Any thoughts I'd had about Cade getting the promotion to detective through nepotism were eradicated—he was smart, a good cop, and knew his shit. I was glad to have him as a partner.

"Don't worry, Trev. We'll get this sorted out," Ben said.

"I'll send a patrol through the neighborhood every couple of hours to make our presence known. Between that and the security system, you should be safe. Let the school know to keep an eye out. Maddie is in Rose's class?" He asked, but I got the feeling he already knew that she was.

"Yes, she is." Should I tell him I was interested in Rose? *Interested in her? More like half in love with her.* I decided honesty would be best and bit the bullet. "Um, Ben, I feel like I should let you know something—"

"Already know it," he said with a smile.

"You do? What do you know?"

"About you and Rose. Nothing gets past me in this family, son." He laughed.

"Oh, okay. I . . . is that okay with you? I feel like I should postpone our date Saturday because of what is going on with me, but I don't want to hurt her. I had to before, when —" I was going to explain about Tara and how I had to call off our divorce, but he interrupted me.

"I know all about that too," Ben said, making Cade laugh.

"He is all-knowing, Trevor. Better get used to it now," Cade informed me.

"Wow. How?" I asked. His dad skills were amazing. It seemed I could learn more from Ben than just police procedures.

"I keep my eyes and ears open. Rose rushed out of the house when I brought you to Sunday dinner that first night. That was when I figured it out. Details came later. I'm sorry you had to hurt Rose, but you did a good thing Trevor. Don't postpone your date, just bring the kids to my house on Saturday. Lily and Ash's kids will be there. The more, the merrier."

"I'll take you up on that. They'll love it."

"See? You all will fit right in. I like you for Rose. She needs someone steady."

Cade laughed. "Rose is going to love this."

"No, she won't. And you'll keep quiet," Ben ordered. Cade sighed and nodded.

After they left, I armed the extensive security system and I took off to get the kids from my parents' house. On the way back, we picked up some tacos from one of the food trucks in town. The kids were thrilled, but it felt like another parenting fail to me.

We ate the tacos, with cupcakes for dessert. The time flew by, like it always did. After tucking the kids in, I made my rounds of the house, grimacing as I passed the kitchen. It was clean—mostly. I hoped Rose was not a neat freak.

After locking my bedroom door behind me, I swiped to Rose's contact information and listened to it ring with an anticipation I hadn't felt in a long time. Back then, she had given me the feeling that my future had possibilities—of happiness and contentment, of a real love with someone I could trust. It destroyed me to put an end to it and I was almost giddy with the thought that I had earned a second chance with her.

"Hello." Her sweet voice sent goosebumps across my flesh. I fell back to recline against my pillows.

"I've missed ending my days with you," I confessed.

Her breathy sigh sent chills through my body. "Me too. I'm already used to having you around and it makes me nervous."

"Please don't be. I'm so sorry—"

"I wasn't fishing for an apology. Please don't."

"Okay. So, about that date. Saturday at six, right?"

"Yes. I can't wait, Trevor." I couldn't either. It meant everything.

Chapter 11
Rose

It was Saturday, six o'clock. Trevor and I were supposed to be out on a date. But instead I was home—alone.

He was also at home, knee deep in the stomach flu. Mikey had just gotten over it and was spending the night with his grandparents, but now Maddie had been hit. Trevor was too busy with barf bowls and the BRAT diet to go out with me.

But, let me be precise, this was the *fourth* Saturday at six o'clock that Trevor and I had tried to schedule. Something had gone wrong with every single one. If it wasn't Trevor's job keeping him busy, it was his kids. And one of the Saturdays was because of me; I'd had strep throat for the second one. Being a kindergarten teacher should come with hazard pay. I was always surrounded by germs.

I wasn't mad, and I wasn't hurting over it. He called me every night before bed, and we continued having our soul-baring conversations together. He had shared his fears about Maddie not being his with me and told me about the weird phone call and break-in so that I could be vigilant at school. Trevor still hadn't had the DNA test done. He confided in me that he knew it was stupid to keep putting it off, but he couldn't bring himself to do it. Lily was still gently encouraging him, but I decided to just be supportive. I understood why he was reluctant, and I felt the same way. I couldn't imagine Maddie not being Trevor's. The more I got to know her in my class, the more I fell in love with her.

I had only seen him a handful of times since. He had a crosswalk safety talk with the kids during a morning assembly and had volunteered in my classroom twice. I was dying to be alone with him, and from the frustration I saw on his face and heard in his voice over the phone, he was too. Which led to tonight and Maddie's stomach flu. I had considered going over there to help, but he didn't want me to get sick.

My ringing cell phone sent me scrambling through my couch cushions to find it. "Rose." Trevor's voice in my ear was like silk on my skin. I sank back into the pillows on my couch and muted my television.

"Is everything okay?"

"No. I miss you, I want you, and I feel like I'm never going to have you."

"Trevor . . ."

"I feel like I'm keeping you from living your life. All this waiting on me isn't fair to you."

My heart sank. "Stop it. I'd rather wait for you than be with anyone else. It won't always be this way. Don't give up—"

"That's not what I'm doing. I just feel terrible about tonight. About the entire last month. We're in the same town this time, and I still never get to see you. I never get to kiss you, to touch you. I can't get you off my mind.

Remember what we did when I lived in Tacoma and you were here?"

I shivered. "Yes, I remember," I whispered.

"Do you want to—?"

"Yes," I immediately replied.

He laughed, low and wicked, and the sound gave me goosebumps over my arms. "Where are you?"

My stomach did a delicious swirl as I stood up. "On my couch."

"Get in your bed," he demanded, but I was already on my way. "What are you wearing?"

"My robe. I just took a bubble bath," I answered honestly. I wondered what he wore—boxers, briefs? Or was he already naked, waiting for me?

"Don't tease me, Rosalie. I have been dreaming incessantly of what I'm going to do to your sweet little body when I get you under me. Tempting me now, when I'm this hard and nowhere near you, is cruel."

Anticipation zinged through my body. We were never in the same place when we both *needed it*. I had only kissed him a few times. We'd never been to bed together, or seen each other naked, but I needed him like nothing else. Trevor was the one for me, and I was sure I was it for him too.

"I want you, Trevor. I can't take this anymore." I sat on the edge of my bed.

"Touch yourself. Put your hand between your legs." I gasped as I spread my legs and did what he said.

He answered my gasp with a dark laugh. "I'll tell you what to do." His voice changed—it grew deeper, raspy. He was irresistible, and I was about to do whatever he told me.

"Will you touch yourself too?" I breathed into the phone.

"I already am. I had to. I want you so bad—it's killing me not to be with you now." Surprised at how turned on I was, I whimpered into the phone. "That's it, Rosalie, don't stop."

"God, Trevor. What are you doing to me?" I moaned.

"Making you come," he growled. "I wish I were there with you right now. God, the things I want to do with you—"

"What would you do if you were here? Tell me." I felt self-conscious but I wanted him too much and it felt too good to stop.

"What would you let me do, Rose? Can I taste you?" As I reclined back against my pillows my robe fell open. All sense of modesty vanished as the sound of his deep, sexy voice filled my ear. As I looked down at my hand on my body, images of his big, strong hands replaced my own. My skin tingled beneath my fingertips as I touched myself—rubbing faster, circling rapidly—exactly the way his whisper instructed in my ear. My cheeks flamed. The way he spoke to me fulfilled every dirty desire I had ever been too afraid to admit I wanted.

I remembered the shape of his lips: the defined cupid's bow on the top, and his sexy, slightly-fuller lower lip. I imagined what it would feel like to have those lips buried between my thighs. "Talk to me Trevor. And don't stop. I need your voice." I panted, breaths coming quickly. Could he tell my heart was racing for him?

"I can't wait to be with you, Rosalie. I dream of it. You're all I ever think about—your beautiful face, that gorgeous body, and your sweet heart—and everything about you makes me want you. I've never wanted any woman the way I want you. I haven't even been inside of you yet, but I'm still hard as a fucking rock over you."

"I like that." I shuddered, feeling the beginnings of an orgasm hit me as I pictured him in my mind.

"I bet you do. You like the thought of me desperate and hard—aching and crazy for you."

"I love it. Will you let me taste you too, Trev?" I'd never been fond of going down on a man, but my mouth watered for him. The thought of him, hard in my mouth, the power it would give me, drove me even closer to the edge.

"You can do whatever you want to me. I'm yours, baby. Fuck, I'm close. Are you going to come for me, Princess? Come all over those pretty little fingers. Let me hear it."

I let out a moan as I moved my fingers faster, wishing I could feel him inside me. His breath came faster, he groaned in my ear, and it amped me up even more. I called out as I came, "Trevor, my god." Sparks exploded behind my eyes and my body tingled from head to toe.

He laughed softly as his breathing slowed. "Is it sad that this is the best sex I've ever had?"

"No. I've never been like this with anyone else. I can't believe we did this again when you're just down the street from me." I felt curiously exposed, vulnerable, and nervous. He wasn't even here, and I felt like he saw me in a way no man ever had. I had completely let go for him. What would it be like in person?

"All these nights talking to you, and I never gave you what you needed. And to think it's this hot and we've never even slept together. I haven't even taken you out. I want you to know something." He went from teasing to suddenly serious. "I don't expect you to fall into bed with me—even though we just did this on the phone again. I want to date you. I want to build something with you, something that will last. It's important that you know it."

Could he get any more perfect? If I wasn't already

sprawled on my bed, I would have fallen over. "Thank you for that. I don't know what to say, other than I miss you and can't wait to be alone with you."

"I miss you, too. Should we plan for next Saturday at six?"

"Let's throw caution to the wind and shoot for Friday," I suggested.

"Friday it is. Let's get crazy and make it five. But remember, no expectations."

"I know, but don't get mad if I jump you," I teased.

"Trust me, you can jump on whatever you want, whenever you want. As long as you don't feel any pressure," he reiterated.

"You're perfect," I blurted.

His laughter filled my ears. "If I were perfect, I would have taken you out every Saturday night this month. Hell, we would have been together since I first met you. There would be no phone sex, because I would be taking care of you myself."

"Friday has to happen. I might go nuts if it doesn't," I blurted. *Way to be mysterious, Rose.* Desperation is so sexy.

"I'm already nuts without you. Would it be okay . . . if something comes up again . . . I mean, maybe you could just come over here for dinner? Or we could take the kids out together."

"Yes. That is absolutely okay with me, Trevor. I would love that so much."

"Okay. Friday at five then. Hopefully no one will get sick."

"I'll be crossing my fingers," I said.

"Do you want to have kids, Rose?" He asked, out of the blue.

I shot straight up in bed. "I do. Do you want more?"

"I always thought I'd only have two . . ." My face fell at his words.

"Oh. That's—" I was disappointed. No, I was crushed.

"Baby, let me finish. I only ever wanted two. But I can't imagine not having any with you. I would have one more with you. Or two, or even three, if that's what you wanted. Because with you, it would be right."

"Oh, Trevor." My heart was about to burst. "I hope so."

"I have no doubt. Maddie already loves you. She talks about you all the time."

"Your kids are great, Trev. I can't wait to get to know them better."

"Good. I'll talk to you tomorrow. I know it's only seven, but I'm going to crash. I was up all night with Maddie, and I'm wiped."

"Goodnight." I ended the call and double checked to make sure the phone had disconnected before tossing it to the bed. I let out an obnoxiously loud squeal accompanied by some graceful hopping around my room. He wanted me to have dinner with his kids! He thought about having kids with me! He really did like me. This was real.

Holy crap, this is real.

I was jolted out of my 1980's-teen-movie-bedroom-dancing by the sound of my doorbell. I stopped mid-fist pump, tied my robe closed, ran to the bathroom, washed my hands, and quickly ran to the front door. I threw it open and was disappointed to see three of my brothers—Cade and the twins. Levi and Jude were fraternal, not identical like Lily and me. Cade wasn't even a whole year older than me and Lily. He was our unofficial triplet, and we were close. Levi and Jude were almost five years younger and they loved it when I—in my five-foot-two-inch glory—referred to them as my baby brothers. They were huge, hulking, badass firefighters, yet I still wanted to pinch their adorable cheeks. The only one missing was Asher. He was the oldest. He was a single dad with two kids, and was always too busy adulting to hang with us.

"Oh, it's just you guys." I had Trev on the brain, and I idiotically expected to see him at the door. But he told me he was going to sleep—*duh*.

"Nice to see you too, Rose." Cade laughed.

"Let us in. We brought pizza," Levi chimed in from behind Cade.

"And Mom said to bring you some ice cream, too," Jude added, bringing up the rear.

"What? Why would she tell you to bring me ice cream?" I narrowed my eyes with suspicion as I glared at Cade.

"Uh, no reason," Jude answered, while Cade looked at his boots. That was even more suspicious, and I frowned.

"Bull crap. Tell me immediately or I'm locking the door." I shut it halfway with a threatening look.

Cade finally gave me a real answer. "She heard you were at home instead of out with Trevor, so she sent us to cheer you up. Lily and Luke are out and she's watching their kids, or she'd be over here herself. You should be thanking us." My mother was a nosy matchmaker. She was also a best-selling romance novelist, so love was her mission and meaning in life. I was surprised she hadn't yet butted in. Though she was doing it by proxy right now, and I had to respect it. That took skills.

"Yeah, we don't want to talk about your feelings," Levi said with a comically exaggerated shudder. "We just want to eat pizza and watch Netflix."

Sighing my resignation, I threw open the door for them to come in. They filed inside. Cade sat in the middle of my sectional and put the pizza on the coffee table. He opened one of the drawers below and pulled out a stack of paper plates and napkins. *Man cave décor is awesome.* Jude went to the kitchen to put the ice cream away. Levi noogied the top of my head as he walked by, so I hooked his ankle with my foot, causing him to fall to the couch. He played it off like it was intentional with a smirk as he spread his arms out over the back and crossed his ankles.

"Rose, where is that Sriracha Ranch dressing?" Jude shouted from inside my fridge.

"In the door. And bring me a Diet Coke. I'm going to change. I just took a bath. Don't sit in my spot this time." I ran to my room and put on some sweats, slouchy socks, and a blue Sweetbriar Grade School T-shirt.

"Why are you all up in my business? How did she even know about tonight?" I asked when I got back into the living room.

"Violet," they answered, and it was adorably almost in unison.

"She has a big mouth. But to be fair, I never told her to keep it to herself." I wasn't mad. I had a big mouth too, unless something was a secret.

I was glad they were here. I didn't feel like being alone. My brothers often came to hang at my house. I had a comfy couch, a huge TV, and I always had food in the fridge. They were like puppies—feed and water them and they were loyal for life.

"Dad already knows." Cade said. "And heads up, he loves Trevor. If you fuck it up with him, he might cry. But seriously, I like him too, he's a good partner. So don't fuck it up." I tossed a pillow at his head, but he ducked it and it hit the wall behind him instead.

"Shut up." I tried to be cool, but I couldn't stop smiling and it gave me away.

"Ooh, Rose doesn't need cheering up. She's sprung over Trevor. Look at her—she has heart eyes." Levi teased and fluttered his eyelashes at me.

"You shut up too." I threw another one of my toss pillows at him, but he dodged it and it hit Jude. Jude was the one brother that didn't tease me on a regular basis, so I felt bad.

"Sorry, Jude." He shrugged and handed me a Diet Coke. I took my place in the corner of the sectional and dug the remote out of the cushions. Cade snatched it out of my hand before I could even turn the TV on.

I responded to his remote theft with laughter. They all turned to stare at me. "She really is sprung. She didn't even hit you for taking the remote, Cade." Jude remarked. He was right; usually taking my remote earned a good smack on the arm.

"So, you really like this guy, Rose?" Levi asked.

"I thought we weren't going to talk about my feelings." I shot back with a smile. I hadn't stop smiling since I'd gotten off the phone. I'd never had this problem before. But—was it really a problem? Is this what it felt like to be in love? *Were we in love?*

"You're my sister. And you're here at home, not with him like you were planning on. I'll punch him in the face if you want me to. The offer still stands." Levi's face was like stone, but there was a twinkle in his eye.

"I appreciate your generosity, Levi. But I'm good. Maddie has the stomach flu."

"You let me know," he muttered, then shoved half a slice of pizza in his mouth. "Where's that Sriracha Ranch?" he asked Jude with his mouth still full of pizza. Jude was busy squirting it all over his slice. He finished, then passed it to Levi. They were going to use it all up. I had to drive all the way to Trader Joe's to buy that stuff, damn it.

"It should be called Sir-Rancha instead of Sriracha." Cade said with a laugh, causing them all to crack up. I rolled my eyes. They amused each other so easily, the big bunch of dumbasses.

"Did you invite him to Sunday dinner tomorrow?" Jude asked. My mother demanded that we all come to her house every Sunday for dinner. Almost all of us usually showed up. Mainly because we were all very close and we loved her. But also because it wasn't worth pissing her off. Plus, there was always delicious food. And she had a pool.

"I haven't, only because his kids have been sick. I should invite him. Just in case Maddie is better tomorrow," I mused out loud.

"I'm happy for you, Rose," Jude said. "He's a nice guy, and he has good kids."

"Thank you, Jude." My unending smile then morphed into the huge wonky smile that I was hardly ever happy enough to experience. Jude laughed at me and shook his head. Then we all stuffed our faces and binge watched *Game of Thrones* until it was bedtime and they all left to go home.

I climbed into bed with hope in my heart and a sense of blissful anticipation filled my thoughts as I drifted off to sleep.

Chapter 12
Trevor

The sound of my cell phone vibrating off the side of my night table and clattering to the floor roused me from my sleep. But I hadn't woken up in time to answer. I hadn't slept this deeply in ages and I was still exhausted. I rubbed my eyes and tried to focus. Maddie could be dramatic and needy when she was sick, especially when she had a stomach bug. Every time she threw up, she would cry, and it broke my heart. With a glance, I saw her sprawled out on her back taking up way more space than a five-year-old girl should be capable of. This king-sized bed was one of the things I'd switched out when I moved in this place. Sometimes, one or both kids had nightmares and it was just easier to let them sleep with me. Her barf bowl was still next to her head and the color was back in her cheeks. I felt her forehead. Her fever was gone, and she was no longer clammy. I breathed a sigh of relief and sat up.

I picked up my phone to check my missed call and my heart dropped. It was from a number I didn't know—was it the same man that called me weeks ago demanding money and making threats? It had been so long that even though I was still being vigilant with security, my panic had dissipated. *Fucking stupid, Trevor. You know better.*

How dare he threaten me? Maddie needed me. I'd always taken care of her, and I was going to keep doing so. I had to get that paternity test done—no more procrastinating.

I swiped to return the call. "It's the maybe-baby daddy," he answered.

"What do you want?" I bit out, stalking into the hall so I wouldn't wake Maddie. Mikey was at my mother's house, far away from the germs. I did not need to have two sick kids.

"A little birdie named Tara once told me you're a cop. I know you're trying to find me. But I have good news—I don't need money. I just want to see my daughter." He laughed and hung up. The *ping* of my phone notifying me of a text message made me jump.

UNKNOWN: KISS MY SWEET GIRL FOR ME AND TELL HER I WILL SEE HER SOON.

My stomach turned as I said a silent prayer that she would just be mine. What would make him change his game like this? Switching from blackmail, to wanting Maddie? And why wait so long to call again? I had to call Jeff. I had been putting off having a conversation with Tara's brother for too long. I always put everything off, and it was starting to be a huge problem in my life.

"Daddy? Where are you?" Sighing, I put my phone in my pocket and opened the door.

"Right here, sweetheart. Feeling better?" The smile that lit up her face sent a bolt of relief to my heart.

"Yeah, I want pancakes. My tummy is better. But only two little ones, not two big ones. And I want a bubble bath," she said.

"Anything else?" With a smile, I held my arms out. She shook her head and sat up. I carried her to the bathroom and sat her on the edge of the counter. After running a bath, I helped her wash her hair. It was long and curly, and she couldn't yet wash it by herself. I left her to finish and headed downstairs to make the pancakes, and coffee—lots of coffee. This exhaustion I felt was perplexing. Maybe the stress was hitting me.

I invited Jeff over to talk. He had moved to Portland to work as a security guard. It was a huge step down from being a police officer like he once was. After what he had done to Lily last summer, he was lucky he didn't end up in jail instead of fired. But he provided evidence and testified against the men who were truly responsible for Will's death and Lily's kidnapping in exchange for immunity. Plus, his motives for initially borrowing the money had been taken into consideration. It had all counted in his favor, and he'd avoided jail time.

Maddie came downstairs a few minutes later and sat on one of the mismatched painted chairs at the farmhouse table in the middle of the eat-in kitchen. I took the comb from her and fixed her hair in between flipping the tiny pancakes on the skillet and sipping coffee.

I was busy sorting my problems into the boxes in my brain. Compartmentalizing was something I had become too good at, it seemed. I had fucked up left and right. Locking boxes and putting them away had led me to this moment. I still didn't know if Maddie was mine, and I should have handled that months ago when Lily first brought the issue to my attention. Denial was a bitch. I didn't want to take that test. I wanted that bastard to just go away and leave my family alone. I slammed my mug on the counter, startling Maddie. She jumped in her seat and knocked the dolls she was playing with to the floor. She laughed and picked them up.

"Sorry I scared you," I muttered as I slid the pancakes onto a plate. I grabbed the maple syrup and passed Maddie her breakfast.

"It's okay, Daddy. Syrup, please," she requested with her eyes on the bottle. This kid would drink maple syrup straight if I let her. I poured a small amount over her pancakes. I refilled my coffee and smiled blankly at her as she sat eating happily.

A knock at the front door shook me out of my daze. "Uncle Jeff is here. I need to talk to him by myself for a little bit. You can go upstairs and play or watch TV in my room, okay?" She had finished eating, so I cleared her plate. With a nod, she went upstairs.

"Thanks for getting here so fast. Want some coffee?" Jeff followed me to the kitchen.

"I have news," he announced as he sat down. With a resigned sigh, I sat across from him. I'd had enough "news" lately. I did not need any more.

"My grandparents were rich. Did you know that?" I shook my head, surprised. "Tara and I each have a trust fund that would only be accessible once we turned thirty-five. My birthday was last week, so I got mine. Tara was only thirty when she died. I investigated, and it automatically goes to the kids with no age restrictions. You'll control it Trevor." I sat up straight with my gears spinning.

"I don't even know where to start," I finally answered. Jeff already knew the blackmailer was contacting me.

"I know. I've been racking my brain for so long, trying to figure out who was blackmailing Tara and hitting dead ends. This guy— I think he may have found out about the trust fund, and that's why he's changed his tactics. If he had Maddie, he would have access to her money. But he'll have to come forward. So far, there is no way I can prove he blackmailed Tara. I've been through all her stuff, and there is nothing to link him to her at all. I have no clue who he even is. This sucks, man. I don't like it."

It more than sucked. This news could devastate my life. "I have to get a paternity test done."

"Yeah, it's best you get that done right away. I have access to my money. But it will take some time before you can access the kids' share. Anything you need, and I got you," he offered. "We can get an attorney—a really expensive, mean one. I'll pay for it. Tara had her demons, but she wanted those kids with you. I owe it to all of you to make up for what I've done."

"Thanks, Jeff." I might actually need to take him up on his offer. At this point, I couldn't afford an attorney.

"How are the kids?" he asked hesitantly.

"Maddie is upstairs. She's just getting over a stomach bug. Mikey is with my parents. Want to say hi to her?"

"Next time. I'm sorry for everything, Trevor. I made some dumb decisions, and so did Dad. We didn't mean for anyone to get hurt—"

"I know." I decided not to tell him about Tara's mistreatment of the kids. He didn't know how far it went, and she was dead. Nothing would be accomplished by telling him about it, other than making him feel even worse.

"I'll keep in touch. Keep me in the loop, please? I want

to help." He held his hand out and I shook it with a nod. He left.

I finished my coffee while I cleaned up the kitchen. Then I raced to the bathroom and threw up. Looked like I was up next for the stomach flu. *Fucking great.*

I sat back against the wall across from the toilet and did what any grown man with the stomach flu would do: I called my mother.

I woke up much later huddled on the bathmat with the taste of vomit in my mouth and the sound of my cell ringing from the floor next to my face. I had lost track of time. All I knew was both kids were with my mother at her house and I had fallen asleep on my bathroom floor upstairs. I opened one eye to see Rose's name flash across the screen. "Rose. Hi." I managed to get out.

"You sound terrible. Did you get sick?"

"Uh-huh," I mumbled.

"Are the kids with you?"

"Mother's house."

"You're alone?"

"Mmmhmm." I needed to get into bed. I could tell I had a fever and I hoped I was making sense. Was I even awake?

"I'm coming over. I'll be right there."

"I'm okay. You'll get sick," I tried to argue. I didn't think it worked because she laughed at me.

"You need help. If you don't let me in. I'll just break in. I used to sneak out of that house all the time with Lily. I'm sure I could sneak into it, too." Her laugh was like little bells in my ear. I tried to smile but my mouth was so dry my lips just scraped across my teeth instead.

"Okay." I felt the phone hit my cheek before it hit the bathmat. I shut my eyes, because it hurt to keep them open.

I woke up this time to see Rose's face peering down at me.

"Poor baby," she whispered and helped me sit up. "Let's get you into bed."

Was she really here? I squinted at her. It had grown dark outside, and the light from the bedroom shone behind her, creating a halo around her pretty red hair. A fiery red halo—was that a thing? "Your eyes are green, and you look like a red angel." I told her as I pointed to her face.

She giggled. "My eyes are hazel. But sometimes they look green. Come on." She tugged on my hand. I tugged it back. I needed my hand. I couldn't give it to her. She felt my forehead. "You're hot, Trevor."

"Thanks," I said and tried to smile at her, but my lips got stuck again. I needed a drink of water. I lurched up to stand at the sink. I had to lean on the side of the tub to get there, but I did it. I turned on the tap and stuck my mouth under the running water. So good.

"Stop. Ew, Trevor. Get into bed and I'll bring you a glass of water."

"Rose. You're here. Hi." I smiled at her and it worked this time. I felt water drip down my chin and hit my chest. I tried to flick it off.

"Hi, Trev." She smiled back and it was the most beautiful thing I'd ever seen in my life.

"You're so beautiful. I love looking at your face." She turned red. "You're hot too, Rosalie." I informed her, making her laugh again. It sounded like little jingle bells. "Merry Christmas."

"Thank you, silly fever-boy. Now come on, let's get you into bed," she ordered. This time I let her take my hand. She could have it if she wanted it. I would give her anything.

When I woke up again it was daytime. I blinked against the sunlight shining in my face. My eyes finally focused on a glass of water on the bedside table. I sat up and took a sip. My head spun and I felt weak, like I hadn't eaten in a long time. Rose popped her head into my doorway with a smile.

"I heard the floor creak. It told me you're awake," she said.

"What?" I asked.

"The floor. This was my gram's room. We would spend the night here all the time. And we could tell when she got up by the sound right here." She crossed to the side of the bed and put her foot next to mine on the floor. "Listen." It creaked. "This old house is full of creaky things. Full of weird noises and memories." She laughed as she felt my forehead with the back of her hand.

I stared at her, not believing she was actually here. I thought I had dreamed her. "Your fever is gone, I think." She picked up a thermometer from the bedside table. "Open." I opened and she took my temperature. "Yep, all gone."

"Thank you," I whispered. I wanted to kiss her, but I didn't want her to get sick. Plus, my breath had to be the stuff of nightmares.

"You're welcome. Do you feel like coming to the kitchen? I can make you some toast." I nodded and stood up to follow her down. Then I thought better of it and headed to the bathroom to brush my teeth first.

"I'll be right there," I called after her. Brushing my teeth wasn't enough. I also took a fast shower and put on some clean clothes. Much better, except for the feeling like I hadn't eaten in a week. I headed downstairs and into the kitchen to find her at the table sipping coffee.

"Is it Monday?" I asked.

"Yep. Good thing it's a three-day weekend," she replied with a big smile.

"Did you spend the night? What happened? I didn't throw up on you or do anything that's a deal breaker, did I?" I asked and sat down across from her.

"Don't be silly. You were sick. I'm just glad I could help." She stood up and pushed the bread down in the toaster then passed me a tiny cup of applesauce with a grin. "Eat." She didn't have to tell me twice. I glanced at the clock; it was eight in the morning. I had been out of it for almost twenty-four hours.

"Your phone rang last night around dinner time. I wasn't trying to be nosy, but it was your mother, so I answered. I hope that's okay? She gave me her number and I texted her right before you came down. The kids are fine and she's making them waffles. I told her you'd call her. I wasn't trying to overstep—"

"Stop. It's okay—I appreciate it. I thought I dreamed you here." She passed me a plate of buttered toast, then sat down with her own.

"I'm really here. But there is something you should know," she said.

"Oh god, what is it? What did I do?" I groaned.

She laughed. "Nothing. Just . . . you are adorable when you're sick. So cute." She reached over and ruffled my hair. I grabbed her hand and kissed her palm. Cute, my ass.

"There is something *you* should know," I countered. She stared at me with those big beautiful hazel eyes and a gorgeous grin lighting up her face. She was so easy to fluster —it was irresistible—and I wanted to do it all the time.

"What?" she finally murmured.

"You're the most beautiful woman I've ever seen. But your inside, your heart, is even more lovely than your outside. I'm falling for you Rosalie, and I don't want it to stop." She melted at my words. Her emotions were always visible on her face and in everything she did. Her heart spoke to mine, and mine beat for her now.

"I'm falling for you, too," she whispered.

"I want to kiss you. But I don't want you to get sick. This was miserable."

"Hold me instead." She stood up and moved to sit sideways on my lap.

I held her close and kissed the top of her head. "How about Thursday at four?" I whispered in her ear. She laughed.

Chapter 13
Rose

It was Tuesday morning. I had primped, fluffed, and dressed in a denim shirt dress, black leggings and tall brown boots. I was at Violet's, drinking a latte and contemplating yesterday's awesomeness. Spending the morning in Violet's coffee shop was like spending the morning in heaven. It was beautiful and always smelled amazing. It smelled like coffee, of course, but also like chocolate and vanilla and the different spices from the baked goods she made. The floor was wooden and covered with pretty, floral patterned rugs and dotted with dark wood tables and purple painted chairs. Her décor was in varying shades of purple with a long piece of shining black granite forming the counter, and displays of whatever was on the menu for the day in cases on top and in front. I waved to Violet ,who was standing in front of the cash register taking orders and greeting her loyal subjects.

I thought of Trevor as I sipped my latte and imagined the future. I gloried in the fact that it felt good instead of scary. I had expectations instead of trepidations. I was no longer waiting for something to go wrong, I was waiting for *more.* I had thoughts of proposals, weddings, and babies. I was thinking of Mikey and Maddie and how to be a good stepmother. I was 1980's-movie-dancing in my brain again and it was hard not to squeal out loud. I was freaking joyful, and it was about time it happened for me. No more would I go into my backyard with only that rude little squirrel for company. I should buy a swing set or something for the kids.

He was falling for me.

I smiled into my latte as joy coursed through my veins, warming me up from the inside.

"Oh, gag." Violet shouted at me from behind the counter. "First Lily, and now you," she teased. I grinned back at her with the wonky smile—the one I almost never got happy enough to use.

"Aww, Rose is in *luuuurve.*" Her grin was huge as her voice sing-songed its way across the shop. I shook my head and took a bite out of my scone. I couldn't deny it; I was riding the high from yesterday and nothing would bring me down.

"Rose is in love? What? Did I miss it?" my mother called dramatically from the doorway. Violet's customers didn't react. Most were regulars and used to the light-hearted family drama that filled this place. Violet's coffee was amazing, but I was sure some people just came here for the sideshow. Following behind Mom through the doorway was Luke, Lily's hubby, and Liam, Luke's partner at work. Their offices were across the parking lot.

"Hey, Rose," Luke greeted. He knew better than to tease me. I'd been getting his goat since we were born—I'd win. Plus, he knew he owed me for stealing my twin sister.

"Where's Lily?" I asked Luke. "And why aren't you watching Calla?" I asked my mother. "Hi, Liam. I have no questions for you, so carry on." I teased with a smile. He laughed and headed for the counter to order.

"Lily is waiting for the bus with Dylan. Your dad has Calla because he's off today. And Liam and I have an early meeting, even though you didn't ask about me." Luke's brown eyes crinkled at the corners when he smiled at me.

"I missed you on Sunday." My mother said pointedly, pulling my focus away from Luke. Oops. I'd been at Trevor's house taking care of him on Sunday, and I'd neglected to call my mother to explain. My mom was a beautiful, eternally-immaculate vision of loveliness. She had long shining silver hair and blue eyes covered by black framed glasses, and was always dressed to kill. I wished I had inherited her elegance, but it seemed like my sister Holly was the only one out of all of us to get it.

"I'm sorry. Trevor got sick. His mom took his kids to her house and he was alone. I went over there to help." Her eyes lit up. *Here we go . . .*

"Oh, wonderful!" she cried as she sat down next to me. "I just adore him. He's a sweet boy. He was always such a good friend to Lily. He has polite, beautiful children, and he's so handsome. Your father has nothing but good things to say about him. Good for you, Rosalie." She glanced at me over the top of her glasses. "I trust that's who you are in love with?"

I sipped my latte and rolled my eyes at her. "It's too soon to say we're in love. I mean, we haven't even said it to each other," I stammered.

"Yet?" Mom pried, dragging out the word. I shrugged. "Oh, how exciting. Thanks, honey," she said as Liam handed her a coffee. "Sit down." She pointed to a chair at our table, and he sat. Luke came up behind him and he also sat down. I wished I could get my students to obey me the way just about everyone in the world obeyed my mother.

Mom pulled her laptop from her tote. She opened it on the table and looked at it, waiting. "What are you waiting for?" She usually just pulled it out and started typing away. She often worked here, claiming that people-watching got her creative juices flowing.

"Inspiration." She winked at me.

"Oh, okay."

"Wait. You'll see it too," she said strangely. I exchanged looks with Luke, who looked as puzzled as I was. He shrugged, as did Liam.

The door *dinged* as more customers came inside, including Trevor. He spotted me right away and came directly to our table with a big smile lighting up his face. "Good morning, Rosalie," he greeted me with a kiss on the cheek. Then turned to greet everyone else. I loved it that I was first.

"Hi sweetie. It's good to see you," Mom said. But she didn't start typing. She was being weird, and I was intrigued. Liam and Luke said hi, then continued their quiet conversation with each other. Trevor headed to the counter to order.

The door *dinged* again, and I was thrilled to see my sister Holly come through. I squealed and ran over to her and hugged her. Violet came out from behind the counter and joined us with a squeal of her own. Holly was beautiful—tall and blond and slim. She was the closest in looks to our mother, and had Mom's big, baby-blue eyes and naturally elegant posture. Her face was like a sculpture, with high cheekbones, a defined, delicate jawline, and full lips. I would be jealous of her if she wasn't as kindhearted as she was gorgeous. She was always off on an adventure, hiking and biking all over the place, photographing and writing for her blog and various magazines. She couldn't stay still. I loved her, I missed her constantly, and I wished I could help her find a way to be at peace.

"Holly Christina, come hug your mother," Mom ordered from the table. Her eyes were sharp as she stood there. I hung back to see . . . whatever was about to happen. What was Mom up to? Violet headed back to work behind the counter. Trevor, coffee in hand, made it to my side in the middle of the shop, and wrapped his arm around my shoulder.

"That's your other sister?" he asked.

"Yeah, Holly." I answered distractedly. I was waiting to see . . . *it*. I didn't notice anything until Liam noticed Holly. Then I saw it. I exchanged glances with my mother who winked at me, then sat down in front of her laptop. Luke smiled at Holly, then stood and pulled out a chair for her. "Oh crap," I whispered.

"What?" Trevor whispered back.

"I think my mother is going to try and matchmake Holly with Liam." I turned to the counter to see Violet shaking her head and watching my mother.

"That's bad?" he whispered.

"Yeah, kinda. I think. Not because of Liam though—he's a sweetie." I sighed and turned into his arm so that he either had to step back or pull me close. He chose pulling me close. *Yay!*

"Hi," I murmured as I gazed up at his handsome face.

"Hi, princess." His brown eyes twinkled as he grinned down at me.

"I'm glad you're better." I swayed in his arms, with weak knees and a dreamy brain fog.

"I'm glad you healed me. Thank you, baby," he said softly.

"Still on for Thursday at four? Or should we go for Wednesday at three?" I teased.

He shook his head with a frown. "I don't want to wait that long. I was thinking I could cook dinner tonight, can you come over? Kids will be there . . ."

I smiled, and yeah, it was the wonky one. He made me so happy I couldn't help it. "Absolutely. What time?"

"Come over when you get done at school and we'll make a night of it. But I gotta go now. Duty calls. I'll see you later." He cupped my cheek and kissed my upturned lips, before leaving with a wave.

I floated back to my table and sat down. Holly had gone up to the counter to order. Luke and Liam said their goodbyes and left. Liam gazed at Holly longingly as he walked to the door. Hmm. He was a sweetheart—a super tall, hot, buff sweetheart—but still.

"Don't do it, Mom," I warned.

"Do what?" she asked, the picture of innocence as she tapped away at her keyboard.

"Matchmake Holly," I hissed. "She's been through enough."

"Oh, I would never do that." She turned her computer so I could see the screen. "Look." Her face was proud as she beamed at me and my eyes got huge as I read.

What you never had can break your heart.

When the man Poppy was falling for tells her he has to go back to his wife . . .

I pushed the laptop back toward her with a huff. "That's me! You blurbed me! You're not allowed to blurb me!" I cried.

She was unaffected by my snit. "Too late. And it's not

exactly you and Trevor anyway, only sort of. I just wanted to see how he kissed you." She looked at me pointedly. "It was sweet. I'm happy for you, and I love how he calls you Rosalie. I gave you a beautiful name. You should make everyone use it," she added with a smile.

"Thank you. I'm happy too." I forgot to be mad for a second. Darn happiness, getting in the way of a good rant. "Don't put me in your book," I said sternly and tapped the top of her laptop with my finger.

"It's not you." She rolled her eyes from behind her laptop. "Her name is Poppy, and his name is Troy. He's not even a detective—yet. He's going to get promoted after he singlehandedly catches the serial killer that has been terrorizing the whole town." She beamed. "This is good . . . " she muttered and turned back to her work. I gave up. There was no breaking through when she was on a roll. And I didn't even care that much anyway. I knew she already had characters not-so-secretly inspired by everyone she knew. I guess it was my turn.

"It's time for me to go. Bye, Mom. I'll see you on Sunday, if not before," I said and gathered my things.

"Bye honey. Love you." She smiled at me and waved, then went right back to her book.

"Love you, too."

I put my mug in the mug bin, tossed my napkin in the trash, then headed for the door. "Bye Violet. I miss you already!" I called. She waved at me and blew me a kiss. "Later, Holly. Are you sticking around this time?"

"I'll be here until after Christmas. I'm starting a new project. I'll be working from home." I was surprised; it was only October. This was a long stay for her.

"Really? That's awesome. Girls night is imminent!" I shouted.

My day flew by and I was carried through it on fluffy, candy-colored clouds of awesome. Nothing could ruin this good mood. Not even when Mason M. came back from lunch recess with his hair full of alphabet soup did my mood break. I just picked out the noodles, washed his hair in the sink and carried right on with my best day ever.

I decided to go home and change into comfy clothes before I headed to Trevor's house. *But first*, I thought, *I should buy treats and presents for the kids*. I had no problem with buying their affection to start with. I thought of it as getting my foot in the door. I changed into my best booty-accentuating skinny jeans and a baby tee my mother had given me for my last birthday. It was black and said "Hello, my name is Hey teacher." across the chest. Truer words were never spoken. I added some cozy boots, collected my jacket and purse, then headed to Fred Meyer to search for stuff for the kids.

I was perusing the toy section, my cart already filled with those fluffy, frosted and sprinkled sugar cookies that kids loved—who was I trying to kid? I loved them too—when Lily and Luke cruised up to my cart with the kids.

"Auntie Rose! Are you buying me presents? And cookies too?" Dylan asked.

Yay! And my reasons for this "yay" were twofold:

1. I love my nephew.

2. He is Mikey's BFF and could tell me what to buy to earn the most points.

"I always have these cookies at my house, and you know where to find them, silly." He laughed and hugged me around my waist, and I kissed the top of his head. "I'm having dinner at Trevor's house. I am going to get Mikey and Maddie a present—what Legos would he like? If you give me good advice, I'll buy you some too." He beamed up at me and began examining the shelves.

"And what about you, my little sugar booger angel baby?" I cooed to Calla as I kissed her chubby cheeks. It was kind of awkward because she was strapped to Luke's chest in a baby sling thingy, but nothing stopped me from getting Calla kisses. Luke laughed at me, but so what? I was happy. If it involved giving him the upper hand in our battle of teasing each other, so be it. Though, he had been super sweet to me lately, so maybe our teasing battle was over.

I looked up from Calla's adorably kissable face to see Lily, standing at her shopping cart with a bemused expression. I braced.

"I once thought to myself, 'Self, Rose is hardly ever sweet,' but I see that I was wrong. All that smart-assery was hiding this." She pointed at me and waved her hand up and down. "This is great. You might be the sappiest, most sentimental out of all of us." I just shrugged and kept on smiling.

"Leave her be," Luke said, and I looked up at him surprised. He ruffled my hair. "Happy for you." And, yep, there would be no more teasing from me to Luke. And thus endeth the Rose/Luke banter for now and evermore. From now on, only sweetness and light would flow between us. No more snark.

"I'm happy for you too, Rose," Lily said. "Maddie loves Beanie Boos. Buy her one of the big ones, because Trevor always gets the little ones." She bent to the bottom of the shelf and handed me a huge white unicorn with a rainbow mane and rainbow glitter eyeballs.

"Oooh, get another one. I want one too," I said. She shook her head and tossed two of them into my cart.

"Here." Dylan handed me a Minecraft Lego set, and I added it to my haul.

"Pick one for you too." I handed him a twenty, then remembered it was Legos, and added another twenty. I grinned as his eyes lit up.

"Wow! Thanks, Auntie Rose," he said and hugged me again.

"You're welcome, sweetheart."

"I love Trevor like a brother. But if he does something to mess this up, I'm gonna kick his ass," Lily declared. "I've never seen you like this." Uh-oh, she had gone into protective mode. And don't let her size fool you—she *could* kick some ass. I could too. Having a cop for a father and growing up with so many siblings had made us both scrappy.

"Everything is perfect. No worries. See you tomorrow." I kissed her cheek, to her amusement, and went to check out.

Chapter 14
Trevor

As usual, I had acted without thinking. I couldn't believe I had invited Rose to dinner on a school night. *Crazy.* But that was my life. There was no use pretending it was something else.

Thank god I'd gone to Costco, so at least I had food in the house. I had to make a dish both kids would eat. There was no need to lead with how picky they were. I decided on spaghetti and meatballs. Mikey wouldn't eat the noodles, and Maddie wouldn't eat the meatballs, but at least technically, I'd only be cooking one meal.

On the car ride home from my mother's house I explained we were going to have company for dinner. I stopped short of threats, but they knew I expected their best behavior. When they found out it was the lovely Miss Barrett joining us, they were intrigued. I hoped that nothing they said would freak her out. I hoped Mikey would not tell any fart jokes. God, I just *hoped.*

"Help me pick up the toys in the living room when we get inside. I have to start the meatballs," I said after I pulled my Jeep into the driveway.

"Daddy, I don't like meatballs," Maddie answered.

I twisted back in my seat to smile at her. "I know. You can eat the noodles and salad."

"I hate noodles. Are you going to make garlic bread?" Mikey asked.

"Guys, I know what you like, okay? I just want you to clean up and be nice. Can we do that?" I twisted back and grabbed my keys and cell from the console.

"Yes, Daddy. I love Miss Barrett, I'm always nice to her." Maddie answered. There was no answer from Mikey, so I peeked at him in the rearview mirror. He wasn't even listening. He had two Minecraft toys out and was playing.

"I know you are, sweetheart. Let's go in." I unbuckled her booster seat and helped her down. Mikey was already at the front door.

"Can I push the numbers?" He liked entering the alarm code.

"Yeah. Go for it." He disarmed it, then raced upstairs, tossing his backpack and the toys on the couch on the way.

Great.

I reset the alarm, then hung my jacket on the hook by the door. "Mikey. Backpack."

"Just a minute," he yelled from upstairs. I saw his pants fly into the hallway.

"I hung my backpack up Daddy. See? My jacket, too." Her jacket was hanging sideways over the hook, and something had spilled out of the pockets.

"What's coming out of your pockets Maddie?"

"Oh! My graham crackers. And my rocks." She bent to eat a cracker from the floor.

I sighed. We were already off to a winning evening. "Pick it up, please?" She nodded and started to eat another one. "Trash, Maddie. Don't eat them."

I ran upstairs to change my shirt and get rid of my tie. We were lucky that there was no dress code in the department other than the ambiguous "business casual". Today I was wearing jeans and a sport jacket with my shirt and tie. I found a plain black t-shirt and an old pair of Levi's and put them on, figuring it was better to be comfortable and not try too hard. I glanced at myself in the mirror. *Should I shave?* Nah.

I yelled at Mikey as I headed down to the kitchen to start dinner. "Mikey, you have to wear pants today. Not just underwear!"

"Oh, man," he grumbled, then darted back into his room. I ran downstairs and started assembling my ingredients.

"Can I be your helper?" Maddie asked as she entered the room. She had put her pink apron on. I nodded, and she passed me a rubber band for her hair. I did a quick braid before she ran off to find her step stool in the pantry.

"Pick out some noodles while you're in there, Maddie. Mikey, do you want to help with dinner?" Maddie came back with some bow tie pasta. And Mikey didn't answer.

"Mikey! What are you doing up there?" I shouted.

"Playing Minecraft," he yelled back. Should I let him break the "no games until homework and clean up" rule and keep playing, thereby keeping him out of trouble? Or make him stop? Parenting was full of impossible choices. "Did you put on some pants?" He entered the kitchen in his underwear and a T-shirt, so there was no need for him to answer.

"Aw, come on. I'm at home. A man needs to be comfortable at home. I had a long day at school. Can I at least have a juice box first?"

I was forming meatballs and putting them in the hot

pan. Maddie was tearing lettuce for the salad. "Pants first, Mikey. Rose could be here any minute."

"You called her Rose, Daddy." Maddie's eyes were as big as her smile.

"That means he likes her," Mikey said in that sing-song kid voice.

"Is she going to be our new mommy?" Maddie asked. "Can she? Please?"

"How about we just have dinner and be nice. And yes, I do like her." There was a small smile on Maddie's face. I called it her planning smile, and it almost always preceded something that later—way later—I was sure I would laugh about. *Great*.

"I can be nice," Mikey said as he pulled everything out of the dryer, trying to find sweatpants. The dryer was in a small laundry room off the kitchen. I could close the door on that mess. I began to mentally assess the various messes in this house that would be visible to a guest. *Fucking great*.

"Mikey, I will give you five dollars if you go pick up the living room." I offered. Who said bribing your kids was wrong?

"Twenty," he countered. He reminded me of a poker player in one of those old-school Vegas gambling movies.

"You're not getting twenty," I replied.

"Fifteen then." I looked at him, raised my eyebrows, and didn't answer.

"Fine, seven," he huffed. "And that's my final offer." He crossed his arms over his chest.

"I'll give you five, and I won't ground you for starting the Xbox up against the rules."

"Okay, jeez." He stomped into the living room. Maddie ran after him.

"He's picking up, Daddy," she informed me loudly.

"Tattletale," he shouted.

"It's not tattling if I'm saying something nice, dummy." I glanced through the archway. She stood there watching Mikey, her hands on her hips, foot out and tapping. *Great.*

"Maddie called me a dummy," Mikey shouted.

"I have ears. Stop fighting. Maddie, get in here with me. Mikey, clean up." I had the meatballs browned, sauce poured over them, the lid on and a simmer going. The water for the pasta was almost boiling. I stared longingly at the fridge—it was too early for a beer.

The doorbell rang.

"She's here!" Maddie screeched and froze in the kitchen archway. She threw her hands straight up and jogged in place. I laughed; it was kinda the same reaction I was mentally having.

I washed my hands and crossed into the living room. Mikey had done a decent job picking up. It was as clean as a living room could be in a house that kids lived in. I stuck out my hand for a high-five. He smacked it and we did our secret handshake. "Thanks, little man," I said.

"No problem. Bros help bros," he answered, before flopping on the couch. He tilted his head to the Xbox with his eyebrow raised.

"Go ahead," I answered. He fired it up. I disarmed the alarm, then Maddie threw open the door.

"Miss Barrett!" she cried. But it wasn't Rose. I tucked Maddie behind me.

A man with a large manila envelope stood there. Sunglasses hid his eyes, a hat hid his hair, and everything about him was suspiciously non-obtrusive. "Trevor Hale?" I nodded and he passed me the envelope. "You've been served. Have a nice night," he said and took off.

My heart sank—and by sank, I mean it fell out of my body and I went cold.

"Daddy, who was that? If you got served, why didn't you dance?" Maddie asked.

I laughed, but it sounded hollow and wrong. I heard it like an echo, like I wasn't even on earth anymore, just floating above it. "I don't know. Go play, okay? Please." I moved to shut the door, then I saw Rose pull her car up to the curb.

I inhaled.

I exhaled.

I didn't know what to do. The end of my family could be in that envelope.

My eyes burned. I watched as she circled around the front of her car with Fred Meyer bags in her hands and a smile on her face. That smile died when she got close and saw me.

"Oh, god. Trevor, what's wrong?" she whispered.

I held out the envelope. "I don't know yet," I whispered back.

"What is that? Did you open it?" she asked.

"I just now got served with it." Her face got stony. She knew what was going on with Maddie, or most of it anyway.

"Give me that. I'll open it. Let's go in." I didn't even once consider asking her to leave. I didn't want to be alone. I stepped back, and she followed me inside. She locked the door and armed the alarm.

"Miss Barrett!" Maddie cried. She lunged at Rose and hugged her around her hips. Rose bent down and hugged her back.

"I brought presents." she announced.

Mikey shut off the Xbox and got up. "Hi, Miss Barrett."

"How about when we're not in school, you can call me Rose." The kids exchanged looks and smiled huge at her.

"Okay, Rose. What's in that bag? I heard the word presents, and that's my favorite thing in the world." Rose chuckled and ruffled his hair.

"Okay, Miss Rose," Maddie said.

"Just Rose, honey," Rose corrected with a smile.

I sat on the couch in a daze. Rose turned and sat next to me; thigh pressed along mine. She set the bags and the envelope down on the coffee table and took my hand.

I kept hold of her and drifted along in my fear. She was the only thing keeping my feet on the ground.

"Rose," Maddie said shyly. The shyness disappeared when Rose unearthed the elusive Pixi, the white Beanie Boo unicorn that I could never find, no matter what store I searched.

"Daddy!" she screamed. It was loud like only a five-year-old girl's scream can be. "It's Pixi! Rose found Pixi, and it's the big one!" She stuck it in my face, then hugged it and threw herself into Rose's arms. Rose hugged her back and laughed.

"I'm glad you like it. Here, Mikey." He was a bit cooler. But not by much after Rose passed him a Lego set.

He examined the box then held it reverently. "You bought me the Nether Railway Lego set. This. Is. Awesome." His eyes were huge as he smiled at her. "This box contains the top three of my ultimate favorite things in the whole entire world inside of it. Legos, Minecraft, and trains. I will never forget this moment. Thank you," he said and bowed his head.

"You're welcome," Rose said through her laughter. "I also brought cookies for after dinner, if it's okay with your dad," she added.

I nodded absentmindedly as my eyes kept drifting back to that fucking envelope.

"Um, how about you guys play with your new stuff in here, and your dad and I can go check on dinner." She took my hand, picked up the envelope, and pulled me into the kitchen.

"Wow, Trevor. It smells great in here. I want to help, but I'm a terrible cook."

I shook myself out of my fog and snapped back to reality. She was here. The kids were here too, and we were all safe. For now. And my meatballs were about to burn to the bottom of the pan. I had mentally freaked out before I'd thought it through. I wanted to kick myself. I had to quit doing that. "I got it. Have a seat." I kissed her quickly, then gestured to the stool at the end of the counter.

"I'd like to be one of those girls that insists on taking over the kitchen and impressing you with my skills, but I'd probably just burn the house down. And Gram would be so pissed if I did that," she said with an adorable laugh.

I winked at her and watched her cheeks turn pink. *Cute.* I loved how she reacted to me, always pink cheeks and smiles. But more than that, I loved how she knew what I needed, how she stayed around and didn't run off when I was upset. Rose was here for me. And something told me she always would be.

Chapter 15
Rose

He was making spaghetti. I could make spaghetti, if I had help from Chef Boyardee and my can opener, or Lean Cuisine and my microwave. I looked around, in awe that his house was so organized. He had two kids and his house was neater than mine. I would have to practice picking up after myself. If this thing between us kept progressing and we ended up living together, I didn't want him to know that I was a slob who couldn't cook. I could do other things, like mow the lawn and change my oil. I wasn't totally useless. I wished I could train my squirrel nemesis to clean my house like a Disney Princess; then I would have it made. Cleaning was the worst.

I was worried about what was in that envelope, but he seemed to have pushed it out of his mind, so I wasn't going to mention it until he did. We couldn't handle whatever was in there right now anyway. It was after business hours—attorneys and courthouses were closed. I imagined that hitmen and thugs were still open, but I doubted that Trevor would take that route.

I decided to be cute and distracting to keep his mind off the envelope until we could actually do something about it. I turned in my stool to face the side of the counter. When he turned around from the stove, I would be right in his eyeline. I put my arms on the counter and leaned forward using my arms like a push up bra and arched my back. Boobs were great distracters. I decided to worry about my personality when I was around the kids, and just use my boobs when we were alone.

"Would you like a glass of wine?" he asked as he turned around. His eyes got big for a second when he saw me. Then a lazy smile crossed his face and he looked me up and down. "Trying to distract me?"

I nodded and tilted my head. Oh, there was one more thing I could do: I could flirt. "Is it working?"

I stood up. He grabbed my waist and lifted me to sit on the inside corner of the counter. He was so tall that I was still looking up at him. Or maybe I was just too short, but it didn't matter. He was all up against me, and that was good.

"I'm glad you're here," he whispered before he kissed me. I cupped his face in my palms, and wrapped my arms around his neck while he ran his hands up my legs to my sides, lingering at the sides of my breasts—thus, proving that my boobs were on his mind and whatever was in that envelope was not.

"Ew, gross. I saw your tongue in her mouth. What's that taste like?" Mikey said with a voice full of disgust. I peered around Trevor and saw Mikey standing in the kitchen archway. Maddie was behind him.

"You kissed Miss Barrett. I mean, Miss Rose—um, just Rose. So, is she going to be our mommy now?" she asked while jumping up and down in the archway.

Trevor stepped back and grinned at me. He helped me

down and I kept quiet; that was Trevor's question to answer. But my smile said it all. I *wanted* to be in Maddie and Mikey's life. I knew that Trevor came with kids and I was ready to fall in love with them too. Heck, I saw Maddie every day in class. She was a little angel and I already loved her.

"Not yet," he answered them. "But I'm working on it." He winked at me and my wonky smile came out.

"Sweet!" Mikey exclaimed. "I want a brother. No more sisters. One is enough."

"Yes!" Maddie screamed.

Mikey shook his head at her. "Don't scare her away, dummy. Screaming hurts grown-ups' ears."

"I'm sorry I hurt your ears, Rose." Maddie whispered, all adorable and contrite. Yep, I loved this girl already.

"My ears are fine, honey. Don't worry. Let's set the table for your dad." They showed me where the dishes were and helped me gather everything while Trevor finished up with dinner.

Dinner was fun. We talked about our days. The kids told me all about their grandma's house and how they were glad they lived close to her now. I told them how this house used to be *my* grandma's house, and then I told them some of my best memories as a kid here. They told me all about their likes and dislikes, then Mikey told me everything he wanted for Christmas. Maddie said she didn't want anything so long as I was there, and my heart melted. We ate cookies for dessert and watched TV on the couch.

We did not mention that envelope.

I stayed through all the bedtime routines and helped tuck them into bed. I was honored that Trevor trusted me enough to let me into his children's lives.

"They won't take long to go to sleep," he informed me as

we stood in the hall. It was weird to be here and have it not be my grandma's house, or even Lily's, because I felt like I was at home. Did I have this feeling because of the house, or because of Trevor?

He crowded me back into the wall, placing his hands on either side of my head. I grinned up at him as he studied my face. "Stay with me tonight?" he whispered. My grin faded and I nodded. I would do anything for him, and right now, he needed me. As I followed him to his room, I knew right then that it wasn't the house making me feel at home—it was him.

This room was different now than it was when my gram still lived here. The bed was huge and covered with a dark blue comforter. My grandmother's quilts and flowery things were gone and replaced with Trevor's things, and I was glad. It would be odd to be in this bedroom and see reminders of my childhood. "I like it in here," I said lamely.

"I like having you in here," he said as he rifled through his dresser to unearth a blue Sweetbriar PD T-shirt. "You can sleep in that." I took it, then threw it toward the chair in the corner.

I turned and locked his door. "Thanks." I pulled my shirt over my head and tossed it to join Trevor's shirt in the chair. I reached back, unhooked my bra and with a shrug let it drop to the floor.

His eyes never left mine. "Are you sure?" I nodded. His body rocked toward mine, then he stopped. "Say it. Tell me you want this," he demanded, holding himself back.

"I want this. I want you, Trevor." With a lunge, he lifted me off the floor. His lips hit mine and my mouth opened under his. Finally giving into to the urge, I wrapped my legs around his waist and climbed him like a tree. He gripped my bottom and backed me into the door.

"We have to be quiet," he growled as he pressed his hard body against mine.

"I can be quiet." I gasped into his mouth before he kissed me again. With clumsy hands, I grasped at his shirt behind his back, fumbling to get it over his head. Chuckling against my lips, he leaned back a bit, leaving my back balanced against the door. With a reach behind his neck, he grabbed the material of his shirt and pulled it over his head before letting it drop to the floor. I was finally feeling his bare skin against mine. He had the perfect amount of chest hair, it tickled my breasts and I giggled.

"Baby, shh." His words were softened by his sexy, sideways grin. I leaned forward to kiss his neck. *Yum.* I licked it and he leaned his head back with a groan.

"You, shh," I whispered. He grinned that wicked grin again and I shivered.

"I guess I'll just have to keep my mouth busy somehow." He sank to his knees and kissed his way up the underside of my breast to suck a nipple into his mouth. I arched against him, my back like a bow, as he switched to the other side, pulling gently until my nipples were stiff peaks against his teasing tongue.

"Trevor, please . . ." I whispered on a moan.

Abruptly, he stood, lifting me under the arms as he turned away from the door and took a few steps to lower me to the bed. For a moment, he just stood there looking at me. "I've dreamed about this moment," he murmured before sinking to his knees. Big, warm palms slid up my thighs to undo my jeans. I shimmied them down as he took my boots and socks off, tossing them to the side. With a kick, my jeans joined my boots and Trevor untied the sides of my undies with a grin. "I like these," he murmured. I'd figured he would. What guy wouldn't?

I rose to my elbows and grinned at him. "Thanks," I breathed as he kissed his way up the inside of my thigh. My breath grew shallow as his eyes blazed their intent with a determined gleam.

He tugged until my legs and bottom were almost off the side of the bed. My body tingled with anticipation as he bent my knees up, so I was spread out before him with the soles of my feet balanced on the edge of the mattress. "Beautiful," he whispered right before he put his mouth on me. I immediately arched my back and moaned, then I covered my mouth with my hand as I trembled and writhed beneath his touch.

"Trevor," I murmured. "Please, don't stop," I said as my hips moved against his mouth.

"Baby, be still." He lifted—putting his hands under my bottom and my legs over his shoulders—so he could take his fill, rendering me powerless to move.

I looked up and was almost undone by the sight of his face, *right there*. "*Gumph*." I said—again with that non-word —and he chuckled against me. I panted instead of moaned; it was so hard to be quiet, but somehow, I managed. He held me firm as I came apart in his grasp. Gently, he lowered me to the bed, and I sat up at the edge. His eyes were intense as I unbuttoned his jeans and pushed them down his narrow hips, freeing him to my gaze.

I licked my lips with anticipation and leaned forward to take him into my mouth, but he had other ideas. "Next time." He stepped back, out of my reach and kicked his pants and underwear the rest of the way off. He was beautiful—all lean muscles and so, so tall. He reached into his bedside table, pulled out a condom and sheathed himself. Then he grabbed me under my arms and lifted me back to the middle of the bed to cover me with his body. I opened my legs and wrapped them around his waist while he buried his face in my neck. We held each other for a moment before he slipped inside. Both of us gasped at the feeling. *Finally.*

He pulled back to brace himself on his forearms and look into my eyes. I smiled up at him as he intertwined our fingers next to my head. Never was anything more beautiful than the feeling of him moving inside of me. I was meant to be here.

"Rosalie," he whispered against my lips.

"Trevor, yes." I breathed.

"This is real," he said as he pulled back to gaze into my eyes.

Before I could stop it, a tear fell from my eye and trailed into my hair. He let go of one of my hands and brushed it aside with his thumb, cradling my face with his big palm.

"This is real," he repeated.

I could only nod. There were no words to describe how I was feeling.

"You're mine now," he said.

Overcome, my eyes drifted closed. I was finally getting everything I'd always wanted, and I could barely believe it was true.

"Say it. Open your eyes and tell me you want me," he whispered into my ear.

"I want you. Please don't ever let me go." He thrust harder at my words, driving me closer to the edge.

"Never. I'll never let you go," he growled, and I gasped as his thrusts deepened and he ground himself against me after each one. I arched my hips up to get more and he gave it to me. Harder and faster, both of us panting, until we fell over the edge together. He collapsed on top of me before swiftly turning us so I was on top. I rested my head on his chest as he held me and stroked my back, sweeping my hair over my shoulder then tilting my face to his.

"Hi," he said with a sweet smile.

"Hi," I whispered back. Then he stood us up and carried me to his bathroom. Gently, he set me down, disposed of the condom, then turned on the shower. Taking my hand with a smile, he pulled me in to the warm water, wrapping his arms around my waist from behind. I relaxed back against him.

"Sleep here with me tonight. Don't leave."

"I'll stay," I answered. He leaned forward over my shoulder and kissed my neck.

"Thank you, baby." I turned in his arms and tilted my head back for a kiss. He smiled before pressing his lips to mine. He looked so adorable with his wet hair flopping into his face. I reached up and pushed it back, sighing as he trailed soapy hands up and down my back, and my forehead crashed into his chest.

"You're going to massage me to sleep in here, Trev." I warned sleepily. But I rallied and took the soap from him. It was my turn to feel him up. Absentmindedly, I ran my hands over every inch of his delectably hard body, relishing every muscle and plane I encountered. "You must work out a lot," I observed as I slowly moved from absentminded touching to mentally cataloguing what he liked best.

"I have to keep in shape. It's part of my job," he said with a chuckle.

"Yeah, I guess you need to kick ass sometimes," I mused. I was intrigued when various muscles flexed and released as I touched them. I looked up and saw he was watching me check him out with an amused expression on his face.

I shrugged. "You're hot," I said, and he laughed.

He quit laughing when I put my soapy hands on what

had to be in the top five of my most favorite Trevor parts. In fact, his expression grew more serious the more I touched it. I grinned and began to stroke it with intent. His eyes grew hot and bored into mine while his back crashed back into the tiles and his chest heaved. *Enough of this.* I stepped back so the water could rinse the soap off, then knelt on the shower floor in front of him. I made sure to watch his face as I kissed the glistening tip, then opened my mouth to slowly slide him inside. I sucked hard as I used my tongue to caress the underside of his cock. He was so hard and hot and I wanted him inside me again, but I needed a taste first. I was glad the shower was on and we were two closed doorways away from the rest of the house because he moaned, and it was loud.

"Fuck, Rose," he grunted. I hummed with delight when his head tilted back to crash against the tiles and his hips thrust gently forward. I loved this feeling—even though I was the one to kneel, he was under my control. My hair twisted softly in his grip and I placed my hand over his to let him know he could position me where he liked as I took him further into my mouth.

"Rose, Rose, Rose . . . I want you again. I need to be inside of you," he said. He stood up straight, forcing himself out of my mouth with a *pop.* He bent and helped me up, shut off the water, opened the shower door and pulled me through. He wrapped us in towels just long enough for us to be mostly dry, then rushed us into the bedroom, tossed the towels aside and picked me up under my bottom, forcing my legs around his hips. He didn't stop when he reached the bed. He walked on his knees until my back hit the head-board and maneuvered my body until I was at exactly the right angle to piston up inside of me. I threw my head back and held on, my arms wound around his neck as he thrust wildly into me. He fit me perfectly. He felt so good, so right. He was the best I'd ever had.

"Shit, I'm sorry." He suddenly pulled out to reach over toward the side table, opened the drawer and yanked out the box of condoms. They spilled all over the bed and I laughed. I crawled over and grabbed one, opened it with my teeth and slid it onto him. "Lie back," I ordered. He grinned, then leaned back against the headboard. I threw my leg over his lap and kissed him. He grabbed my hips and bucked up hard, filling me. "God, Trevor." I gasped because it felt *awesome*.

With his arm around my upper back, he lifted me and turned me onto my back, entering me with one hard thrust. Every ounce of sexual frustration we had built between us dissipated as he moved roughly inside of me, building us up to a crescendo I was sure would break me. I raised my arms over my head and placed my palms against the headboard. I had to, or he was going to fuck me right into it. I tucked my legs tight to his sides as he reached under me with one arm and held my booty up. He planted the other hand in the bed to hold himself over me. I'd never felt this way before: so completely taken, overwhelmed, and adored.

"You're so beautiful," he groaned against my mouth. I pushed at his shoulders until he turned to his back, then I climbed back on top.

"So are you." I gripped his cock, positioned, then slid down to take him back inside. He ran his hands up and down my body as I rode him, and I could tell that he had his own top five Rose parts based on the areas that got the most attention. When he got to what had to be number two and lingered there with lovely, swirly attention, I exploded over him and he quickly followed me. I collapsed onto his chest, exhausted.

"I'm glad you're here," he whispered into my ear. "With me, where you belong."

I lifted my head and kissed the underside of his jaw. "Me too," I whispered, hoping that this would never end.

"I'll be right back." He got up to head into the bathroom. And I sat up to brood. Already my heart was his. I couldn't bear it if he gave it back. I slid out of bed and found the T-shirt he'd tossed me earlier. After slipping it over my head, I waited at the bathroom door.

"My turn," I giggled as he passed me to head to the bed. With a soft smile, he kissed my forehead. I turned to watch him walk to the bed, because Trevor had a great ass. There was no way I was going to miss the sight of it walking away.

"Hurry, baby. I need you in my arms." *Thud.* If he kept saying stuff like that, I might drop dead. It was a real fear.

"'Kay," I murmured. I hurried and cleaned up. He held his arms out to me as I approached the bed and I crawled into them, pressing against his side. He reached down to cover us with his comforter, tucking us up tight in his bed. It felt like finally shutting the door after you'd gotten home after a long day. Safe, warm, right. The coziest feeling of peace washed over me and I sighed into it, letting it fill my heart.

"Let's go to sleep," he said and turned me to my side, tucking himself along my back like a big, warm, muscular spoon. He nuzzled his face into my neck. I let out a huge, contented sigh, and then I was out.

Chapter 16
Trevor

My alarm went off at four thirty. I shut it off, then glanced down at a sleeping Rosalie, tucked up against my side. She was lovely in sleep, with her beautiful hair spread out behind her and her face relaxed and at peace. My heart burst at the sight of her, finally at my side, where I had wanted her to be since the moment I first saw her.

I decided to wake her up with my mouth between her legs. I lifted the covers and crawled under them. I lifted one of her legs over my shoulder, parted her with my thumbs and dove in. So warm and soft, like silk against my tongue.

"Trevor?" She moaned softly, and her legs dropped to the sides, opening herself all the way for me. Her hips moved against me as her legs spread wider. She flipped the blanket back, uncovering me. I looked up at her as she smiled, then reached down to pull my face closer to her core. *Fuck yes.* I loved her uninhibited responses to me, how she was able to just enjoy herself and let go of everything, with no insecurities. I hummed against her and she made a little mewling sound in her throat. I would have to try harder; I was going for that adorable "*gumph*" she would say when she was out of her mind with lust. I gently thrust two fingers into her and stroked inside until I found the spot that would drive her crazy. I sucked her clit into my mouth and pulsed it with my tongue.

"*Gumph.*" There it was. I chuckled, then sucked harder, making her hips go wild against me. I switched it up and put my tongue inside of her while I circled her clit with my fingers. She drew her knees up to her sides, and I watched as she covered her mouth with her hand and bit down. *Damn.* I gave it a little pinch and circled faster. I wanted to taste it when she came. I speared my tongue inside of her, in and out, as she trembled beneath my hands.

"No more, no more. It's too much," she moaned softly. I licked her one more time, then kissed the inside of her pretty thigh. Her hands were in my hair, and she pulled at it until I started kissing my way up her body. I took a little bite under her breast before sucking a gorgeous pink nipple into my mouth. "Fuck me, Trevor. Make love to me," she whispered. More than happy to be inside of her again, I used a hand on the back of her knee to lift it over my shoulder. I didn't think I'd ever get enough of this, of her and her beautiful body. Her lovely smiles and beautiful heart. Her love, her care—just *her*. I reached for a condom—they were still all over the bed—and tore it open, wrapped myself up, then sank inside of her wet heat with a moan. Nothing felt better than this, and nothing ever would.

"Rosalie, will I ever get enough of you?" I moaned against her mouth.

"I hope not." Her breath tickled my lips. I kissed her, and she opened her mouth for me. I slanted mine over hers, deepening our kiss. We moved together with the soft early morning moonlight shining in through the window, illuminating her skin and making her glow like an angel beneath me.

I felt complete with her here, and happy for the first time in my life. Her warm body, so soft beneath my hands, trembled against me as I tugged her closer. I needed to hold her as we came down from this high. She rolled to her side, head thrown back, the red of her hair covering my pillow as I kissed that soft, sweet spot beneath her jaw. My hand drifted softly between her legs. "Are you okay? I was rough last night, I got carried away in you—"

Her head came up with a snap, eyes catching mine as her hands stroked up my chest to cup my cheek. I shivered beneath her touch. "I'm fine. I'm perfect, Trev. You weren't rough. It was beautiful, every single minute. Don't worry."

"Okay." Her heart beat against mine, pressed against me like she was. She was so close, but I had the feeling she would never be close enough.

I grew up wanting to be a family man like my dad. I wanted a wife and kids, a house, and a yard for a dog to run around in. I had accepted my life as a single dad. But then I met Rose, and everything changed. I started to have hope for my future again. Dreams I thought had died were within my reach once again. But why now, when everything could fall apart so easily?

I had to open that envelope. I had to take that fucking paternity test. And if necessary, I would fight for my daughter.

Sensing my changing mood, Rose propped herself up on an arm and snuggled against my side. "I'm going to go home to shower and get ready for the day. The kids shouldn't catch me here yet. But before I do, should we go downstairs and open that envelope?"

"Yeah, I need to prepare for whatever happens." She

kissed my cheek, got up, and gathered her clothes. After quickly donning them, she headed for the door.

"I'll meet you down there." I knew she was going to open the envelope before I got there. It may have made me weak, but I was glad. I'd rather hear it broken gently from her, then read it for myself. I dressed quickly and followed her down to the kitchen. The expression on her face after I entered caused me to drop into a chair at the table.

"He is suing you for custody of Maddie." I stared at her as my heart left my body. I dissolved into the chair as cold filled my veins. "But this letter doesn't name him, it's from an attorney in Portland. There is a demand for a DNA test, and a clinic named that will perform it. I think you should go to Jane and have her run a test. You can trust her." I could trust Jane. She was Will's little sister, and that made her family.

"You're right, I will. Lily has already called her for me. She knows what's going on," I said.

"Good. You have an attorney, right?" I nodded. "Okay, well, I'm going to have Violet call Jake to have him check your attorney out. Make sure you have the best you can get."

"Okay." I didn't know who Jake was, but Rose seemed to believe that he was an attorney expert. And I trusted Rose.

"It will be okay," she declared. "We can move to—I don't know, somewhere he can't get to us if she's not yours and you lose custody. But I don't see why that would happen. Something feels off about this whole thing. You are on Maddie's birth certificate, plus you were married to her mother. Everything is in your favor so far. No matter what the test says, we're not going to lose Maddie. I'm not going to let it happen."

"We're not going to lose Maddie." With her words, I came out of my fog. I wasn't alone with this anymore. I stood up and stalked over to her to lift her up onto the counter, so we could be almost eye to eye.

"I'm going to get through this because of you." I looked into her gorgeous hazel eyes. The determination shining out of them soothed me.

Her eyes smiled into mine. "This will pass, and it will be okay."

After a quick kiss, I stepped back and helped her down. "Text me when you get home, so I know you're safe." After gathering her things, she blew me a kiss and left.

Somehow, I managed to get through the rest of the morning without losing it. But my mother knew something was up the second she saw me. "Should I take them home with me? Should they even go to school?" she whispered after she read the letter.

"I think they should probably stick to their routine. I don't want them to know anything is wrong."

"You're probably right. I just can't stand this Trevor. Our little Maddie—" Tears filled her eyes, but she managed to keep it together after a second.

"I'm going to take Maddie to see Jane after school. I don't have to do what that prick says. I'm on the birth certificate. I am her father. All he wants is the money."

"How much money? Can't we just give it to him and make him go away?" she asked.

"We don't have that kind of money, Mom. The kids are going to inherit a couple million dollars, whenever the will goes through. Jeff is helping me handle it."

"You trust that guy?" She looked skeptical.

"I do. He texted me the name of the trustee, so I can set up the kids share myself. He offered to pay for my attorney. He's not a bad guy. He was just an idiot about Tara, is all."

"Okay, honey. But if he doesn't come through and you need money, you come to your dad and me."

"I love you, Mom." She hugged me and patted my cheek. I had already said goodbye to the kids when I woke them up, so I headed out the door for work.

I wanted to stop at Violet's before I went into the station. Rose was usually there in the morning and I needed a fix of her. It had only been about two hours and I already missed her. She was vital to my state of mind, like an anchor keeping me here on earth when I was threatening to float away in my fears about Maddie. I parked and headed inside. I looked around, but I saw no sign of her.

Disappointed, I headed for the counter to order. I felt like I was back in high school, hanging out and waiting for my girl to walk by. Only this time, the girl was so much more than a crush. She was becoming the center of my world, and I had to find some way to show her what she meant to me.

I found a table by the window and sat with my iced mocha and blueberry muffin. Violet was swamped with customers today, so I barely even got to say hi to her, let alone grill her about where Rose was. The door kept *dinging* as people kept entering the shop, and my head started to feel like a jack-in-the-box popping up every single damn time. I wanted to text her, but I didn't want to crowd her, or make her feel pressured. Unable to restrain myself any longer, I took out my phone to call her right as she came through the door. My breath left me; she was so beautiful. A huge smile filled her face when she saw me, and I knew it had to be as big as mine. We beamed at each other as she headed my way. I stood up and she entered my arms. I sat back down keeping her sideways in my lap as I kissed her sweet mouth.

"Oh, gag." I heard Violet shout from the counter, followed by a laugh. "No making out in my shop allowed." I was impressed when Rose shot her the finger without breaking from our kiss. How could I be this happy and this worried at the same time? Being with Rose was changing me. Before, I would have been dwelling on the paternity test and what the results would be. Now, I had hope.

A few minutes later, one of Violet's baristas came to our table and passed Rose a coffee and little bag full of tiny scones, then rushed back to the counter. Rose turned from me and saluted Violet and the baristas at the counter. "Perks of being Violet's sister." She laughed and took a sip.

"I should have texted you again to meet me here. I—" Why was I afraid of saying what I wanted to say? I used to be sure of myself. I used to go after what I wanted, hard. I used to let nothing stand in my way. Tara had messed up my head. I studied Rose's face, open and honest, looking up at me. "I want to see more of you." I blurted. Her eyes softened, filling me with relief. "And, if it's too soon to wake up with you in my arms every morning of every day, then I want to at least wake up and hear the sound of your voice on the phone."

She placed her cup on the table and melted into my arms, head on my shoulder. "Whatever you want, Trevor. I want it too. I just want you." I hugged her closer, then let her go so she could sit in her own chair. A moment longer with her in my lap and I would end up having a problem walking out of here without attracting attention. She settled into her chair and took a bite of a scone.

"Good. I still have to take you out. Did we miss Thursday at four?" I joked.

"Not yet. It's only Wednesday. Don't worry, there is still time for something to ruin it. We could change plans to Saturday at six, but that seems to be bad luck for us." She laughed. "We don't need any more vomit or strep throat."

"Hmm, today at three is out. I'll be taking Maddie to Jane at that time. Tomorrow at four will have to be it. I can't wait until Saturday at six to see this beautiful face." I cupped her cheek and kissed her forehead. She blushed, like I knew she would. I loved her reactions. There was honesty in her face, and I craved seeing it.

"How long will it take to get the results?" she asked.

"Not long. Jane said by the end of the week, we should know."

"God Trev, I'm hoping so hard."

"Me too. I'm so lucky I have you. You're keeping me sane. Giving me another focus. Thank you, Rosalie," I said.

"I'm just glad I can be here for you. And for the kids. Whatever you need."

"Just you, princess. You're what I need." She swayed toward me and I almost forgot we weren't alone. All the noise in this busy coffee shop didn't pull my focus from her and I was about to be very inappropriate. I wanted her naked, I wanted inside of her again. I'd never felt anything like this before. It went beyond all my natural inhibitions. I watched her eyes grow hot and I was about to go for the *"gumph"* when Cade slapped me on the shoulder. I jumped in my seat and Rose let out a nervous giggle.

"I got here just in time," he said as he plopped in the chair across from me. "One more second and you two wouldn't have just been eye-fucking. You're welcome."

"Shut up, Cade," Rose said with a red face. I winked and watched her blush even redder. She was adorable, and I

was going to enjoy cataloguing all the different shades of red
I could turn my Rose.

Chapter 17
Rose

I wanted to smack Cade for interrupting. But then again, I *was* about to jump Trevor right here in Violet's shop and that would have been embarrassing—eventually. I decided to be grateful instead.

"I have to go, or I'm going to be late." I said with a sigh. I would much rather take my clothes off and sit on Trevor's lap all day, but I had to go and educate the youth of Sweetbriar instead. "What are you two doing today?"

"We'll be solving crimes and kicking ass, like usual." Cade answered, his cocky grin in place as he lounged in his chair.

"That sounds about right," Trevor agreed. "Then after all the crime solving, I have the thing with Maddie. Will I see you tonight?"

"Come to my house when you're done. I'll make dinner," I offered.

Cade choked on a laugh. "Don't do it, man. She can't cook."

"I can heat stuff in the oven, Cade. Anyone can do that." I glared at him before gathering my things.

"Except you burn almost everything. I'm not trying to be a dick, Rose. You know it's true." I stuck my tongue out at him because he was right. No matter how hard I tried, I could not cook, not even toast. I was a curse in the kitchen.

"Don't worry, I don't want you for your cooking." Trevor said it with that smile that was just for me. My face heated and he winked at me again. For some reason, he seemed to like getting me all hot and bothered.

"Okay, okay—I don't want to know why you want her," Cade said. "All I'm saying is, order Chinese food, Rose. Or pick up a pizza. No one likes food poisoning."

"Thanks for the advice, big bro." I kissed Trevor as I stood up and noogied Cade as I hurried off.

"Later, Violet. Thanks." I shouted from the doorway.

My workday flew by. I burst through the school's entrance with a smile on my face and a lightness in my heart that I hadn't felt—well, ever. It was a glorious October afternoon in Sweetbriar. All golden sky, fiery sunsets and crisp fall air. Colorful leaves were like confetti in the trees; waiting for a brisk wind to let them fly and decorate the sidewalks with shades of red and yellow. I walked toward the parking lot, crunching through the pretty leaves that partially covered it on the way to my car.

I went to Imperial Dragon and picked up Chinese food. I had already stopped at the store for treats and if the rain stayed away tonight, we could all make s'mores on my patio together. With haste, I rushed into the house. I had to clean up before Trevor got here with the kids. Luckily, I was messy and not dirty—meaning, I dusted and mopped and swept and vacuumed. I kept my kitchen and bathroom clean. What I did not do was put stuff away when I was done using it or keep up with my laundry. All my hampers were crammed full of dirty clothes, but the floor was visible, so that was good. I emptied the dishwasher and set my table. I set the food out then hurried to my room to change. I decided on black yoga pants and a cute, flowy, knitted, hooded shirt. Dressing up would be weird, like I was trying too hard. I added some pink lip gloss and a ponytail. I glanced around my room, cataloguing the space. I always made my bed, so my room looked clean once I picked up all the clothes. But I doubted he'd stay here tonight with the kids. It felt too soon for that.

Plopping into my bay window seat, I tucked my knees under my chin to gaze out into the front yard. Sometimes I sat here and watched the action that happened on my street. Before Trevor, I would sit here and watch the kids playing in their yards and riding their bikes. It wasn't just watching; it was also wishing and yearning. Sometimes there was even pining involved. This was what I had always wanted—a husband, some kids, a yard for a dog to run around in, and maybe even a mini-van with DVD player in the back. Crap like that. I wanted my own family. This relationship with Trevor and his kids meant everything to me. But I didn't have a chance to start worrying, because there he was, pulling up to the curb in his Jeep.

Would he like to buy a mini-van with me? We couldn't fit any more kids in that Jeep, and my Beetle was already too small. I hopped up and ran through my house like it was on fire. Mikey started laughing when I opened the door before he even knocked. Too eager? Don't care. If eagerness was a turn off, then Trevor was dating the wrong girl. Mikey held out a bouquet of flowers.

"For me? Thank you, Mikey."

"Yeah, for you. These are the first flowers I ever gave to a babe." He leaned an elbow against the side of my porch railing and winked at me. I buried my face in the flowers and gave them a sniff so I wouldn't laugh. This kid was adorable.

"That's so sweet of you, Mikey. Want to come in?" I stepped back and he rushed through the door.

"Hi, Rose! Hi!" Maddie shouted and waved from the Jeep as Trevor helped her get out of her booster seat. He turned and grinned at me as she ran up my walkway. I scooped her up and kissed each one of her cute cheeks. She hugged my neck, then I put her down and she ran inside the house with Mikey.

"Do you like the flowers?" Trevor asked.

"I love them. These are the first flowers Mikey has ever given to a babe. He's got your wink Trevor." I laughed.

"God, that kid." Trevor sighed. He looked hot in his jeans and white T-shirt. His shirts had a magical way of always staying tight across his chest and biceps, while fitting perfectly loose everywhere else.

I tried not to start drooling as I stared at him. "He is something else Trev. Lily would tell me stories, and I always thought she was exaggerating."

"Nope, I have to watch him every second. In fact, we should probably get inside." I grabbed his hand and led the way.

"Dad, this is the most comfortable couch in the world. You've got to buy us one." Mikey said from my corner spot on my sectional. He had wrapped himself up in the afghan my Gram had knitted and had my remote aimed at the TV. Maddie, on the other hand, perched daintily on the edge of my club chair in the corner. She had found my Pixi the unicorn and waved it around excitedly before hugging it to her chest. I grinned at her.

"Mikey, we talked about manners in the car. Did you forget already?" Trevor asked exasperatedly.

"It's fine, Trev. I want them to be comfortable here," I whispered.

"See? She wants us to be comfortable. Can I take off my pants?" Mikey asked.

I shot Trevor a look and tried to hide my laughter. He could answer that one. "No. Pants stay on," he said with an exasperated sigh.

But Mikey was in the mood to push his luck. "Okay, then can I have some of the M&M's that she has in that drawer?" He pointed at the coffee table drawer. Yeah, it was where I kept my M&M's. Unless it was summer—then I kept them in the freezer.

I could tell Trevor was getting frustrated, so I spoke up, "I have s'mores stuff for after dinner. And I bought Chinese food, since a little birdie told me you like chow mien."

Mikey sat up straight. "What bird? And what else did they tell you about me?" His eyes narrowed with suspicion as he studied my face.

"Lily told me what you guys like." I choked on a laugh.

"Did she tell you I like spring rolls?" Maddie asked.

"She sure did. Are you hungry? The table is all set."

We headed into the kitchen. I could tell Trevor was worried about this evening, and I wanted him to relax. "It's going to be okay. I got sake," I whispered as an aside.

He hugged me around the waist and kissed my cheek. I tilted my head to the side, so he'd kiss my neck, my favorite spot for kisses, especially when he was sporting that yummy stubble on his face—like right now. We both sat down, and I saw the kids were watching us with smiles on their faces. Could this be going any better? Maybe, if we were married, and all of us lived here. That would be better. I started filling the kid's plates and passing Trevor food so he could fill his.

"I gave you the little forks that I have for Dylan. He hates big forks. Is that okay with you guys? Oh, and I have these cool *Lego Movie* plates too, they are all divided up, so your food won't touch." I smiled at the kids.

Mikey looked impressed. "Rose, you might just be the perfect girl for my dad. I hate my food touching, you have M&M's in your living room, plates and forks I can work with, and I see a bunch of different kinds of Goldfish crackers on the counter over there. I love to watch Netflix and enjoy a flight of Goldfish crackers." Laughter burst out of me. This kid was too much.

"Mikey watches the Food Network with my mother," Trevor explained somewhat sheepishly.

Mikey sighed, then turned to Trevor. "Rose has kid DVDs on her shelves. I saw them with my own eyes." He turned back to me, "It's important to have kid stuff around. Especially for Maddie. She breaks things."

"I do not!" she said, just as she dropped her cup on the floor. "Oopsie." She hunched her shoulders. "I'm sorry, Rose." Trevor picked it up and patted her head, while Mikey smirked and shrugged.

"It's okay, baby. It was empty, and plastic. I drop stuff all the time in here. At Rose's house, we relax." I assured her. Then I poured Trevor and I some sake. "After dinner, we can go out to my patio and have s'mores, maybe my squirrel will be outside," I added as an afterthought.

"Oh my gosh. Dad, she has a squirrel." Mikey said through a mouthful of sweet and sour chicken. Maddie just looked at me with big eyes. She was having a hard time with her noodles.

Trevor watched me talk to the kids with a small smile on his face as he sipped his sake. "Well, Mikey, he's not actually *my* squirrel, but he comes to my yard pretty much every day and I feed him corn. He throws it off the table some-times. He's kind of a jerk, now that I think about it. He's very demanding." I took a bite of egg roll, then leaned over to help Maddie swirl some chow mien noodles on her fork. I also cut her chicken into smaller pieces while I was at it.

"Thank you, Rose," she said, then took the bite of noodles. Only a few noodles came out of the swirl. I passed her a napkin, then helped her wipe her mouth.

Mikey watched me as he ate with a thoughtful expres-sion on his face that matched his dad's. I looked down at my shirt. *Did I drip sweet and sour on myself?* Nope, and no boob snacks for later either. My cleavage was all clear of crumbs.

"She's helping Maddie," Mikey informed Trevor.

"I see that," Trevor answered but his soft eyes were on me. "Thank you, Rosalie."

"You're welcome," I answered, bemused.

The rest of dinner went smoothly. We talked about Halloween next week. Maddie wanted to be Rapunzel, from *Tangled,* or Elsa, from *Frozen.* She was a different Disney princess every year. Mikey wanted to be the Incred-ible Hulk. Last year he was a Creeper from *Minecraft.* He told me he liked green things that blew up and then laughed his ass off. I shook my head and my brain whispered, "that kid". I told them I usually dressed up like Ms. Frizzle from *The Magic School Bus.* I had a collection of the different dresses from the show. I was horrified when I found out that Mikey and Maddie had never seen it. We made plans to remedy that ASAP with a binge watch this weekend at my mother's house for Sunday dinner.

We got lucky and it hadn't started raining during dinner, so we headed out to my patio for dessert. I removed the cover and lit the firepit while Trevor cautioned the kids to be careful around it. We skewered the marshmallows and I taught Mikey and Maddie the way of the s'more. After we had indulged in the sticky goodness and cleaned the kid's faces, they asked if they could play on the lawn and wait for my squirrel. I said sure. The kids were running around my backyard, and I was all cuddled up on Trevor in my hammock—top to toe, lying up against his chest, his hand on my booty. It was cuddle perfection. My heart sighed because I was finally living the dream.

"Where is the squirrel?" Mikey shouted.

"He probably won't come around because you're noisy. It probably freaks him out." I hollered back.

"Come on, Maddie, let's be quiet," he yelled and climbed into the hammock with Trevor and me. Trev opened his arm, and Mikey stretched out next to him. I extended my arm and lifted Maddie to my side. We were all four cuddled in my hammock with the golden, right-before-sunset light shining through my trees on us. I was so freaking glad I'd bought this giant hammock.

I pointed to my little picnic table squirrel feeder, mounted up high in the tree, with its fresh corn cob sticking up off the table. He didn't usually come out this late though. I was afraid the kids were going to be disappointed. But then— "Oh, shh, you guys, there he is." I whispered and pointed at the back of my fence. Maddie and Mikey gasped, and Trevor laughed softly.

"What's he gonna do, Rose? Is he gonna eat the corn?" Maddie whisper-spit in my ear.

"I don't know, sweetie. Watch and see." I hugged her closer to my side, which only made me squish further into Trevor's hard body next to me. Bonus.

We watched as he crept along the fence line and scurried up my oak tree to the feeder. He sat on one of the tiny benches and stared at us. Then he picked off a piece of corn and ate it. Then another. Then he started chattering and tapping the table.

"Oh crap. Watch out." I whispered as he started sliding the corn off the table. "I usually buy a different kind of corn. They were out," I explained.

"I think he hates this kind, Rose." Mikey said. And Trevor laughed. I felt it, that laugh rumbling in his chest. I was glad I could give him a nice evening in the middle of all the stress he had been going through. I kissed the side of his neck and he squeezed my waist.

"I told you he was demanding," I said.

"He's rude too," Maddie agreed.

We cuddled and rocked gently in my hammock until the sun set and Trevor took the kids home to get ready for bed.

Chapter 18
Trevor

As I tucked the kids into bed, their smiles had matched my smile. This might have been the best night I have ever had, and I was pretty sure the kids felt the same way. It was all because of Rose. She was magic. Funny, sweet, and so full of love. She made an ordinary night at the dinner table fun. She entertained the kids with s'mores and a squirrel—no TV, no video games—and her sweet sense of humor. Nothing would get in my way now. I wouldn't be able to live without her, and I didn't want to try.

During my bedtime rounds to check the locks, I spotted a rolled-up paper stuck through the mail slot, balanced half inside and half outside. Someone had to have placed it there within the last ten minutes. I looked through the peephole; no one was out there. On the way to the front window, I grabbed the baseball bat out of the umbrella holder next to the staircase. I shifted the curtains to peek outside—no one. I darted to the back door to check—nothing. I sent a quick text to Rose to let her know what happened, and that I might not be able to call tonight. I called Cade to come be my backup, then took my gun out of the safe and sat down on the stairs to wait. I was not about to leave my kids in here alone to go outside to have a look around.

Blue and red lights shone through my front window. With a dash through the entryway, I threw open the door to let Cade in, surprised to see Ben and Rose had joined him. "Trevor, I'll stay here with the kids, so you can find out what's going on," she said as she ran into my arms. Cade waved before heading around the side of the house followed by Ben.

"I'm so sorry all this crap keeps happening," she said against my chest. I reached behind her to shut and locked the door. She pulled away and slipped out of her coat. "Aw, Gram's bat is still here."

"It was in the umbrella holder," I informed her.

"It's good some things never change." She took it from me. "I'll go sit upstairs. You go do what you have to do."

"Thank you, Rose." I kissed her, then headed to the back door

"There's no sign of anything back here. Let's go back inside." Cade grumbled after I found him in the trees at the rear of the yard.

Ben was in the living room. He had unrolled the note I'd found and placed it in a plastic bag. "If it's like that clown card from the other day, there won't be prints on it." I took it, and read it. It didn't say much.

She ruined me, and now she's gone.

"What the fuck is this supposed to mean? Maddie couldn't

ruin anyone—she's only five." I froze as realization hit me. "What if this is about Tara?"

"It makes sense," Cade agreed.

Ben nodded his agreement. "He may have been in love with her or something?"

"If he wasn't fucking with me, I'd feel sorry for him. She was a piece of work." I said.

"If this is about Tara, maybe he wants to punish her—or punish *you*, Trevor. I mean, she refused to sign the divorce papers, right? She was still married to you when she died." Cade and I had gotten close over the last two months, he knew all about Tara and the many ways she had fucked my life up.

"Maybe she was messing with this guy too? Maybe I've been looking at this from the wrong angle. I mean, this guy is screwed up in the head, that's obvious. But maybe he loved her, and she broke his heart. I never loved her, but if I did, I'd be a mess too. She ruined enough of my life without me ever being in love with her," I said.

"And there is still no idea who he is?" Ben asked.

"No clue," I confirmed.

"We'll take this to the station. Maybe there will be prints this time," Cade suggested.

"Thanks," I said as they turned to leave.

"See you tomorrow," Cade said.

"And I expect to see you on Sunday at the house for dinner," Ben added.

"Yep," I answered, then shut the door.

The unexpected silver lining from all this bullshit tonight is that I had Rose upstairs. I needed that woman like I needed the air in my lungs. I relocked the door, rearmed the alarm, then hurried up to get to her. A quick peek into their rooms as I passed by confirmed the kids were still asleep.

She sat on the foot of my bed, waiting for me. "I heard them drive off," she murmured. I nodded as I closed the bedroom door behind myself, twisting the lock with a grin. She wore tight yoga pants and a long fluffy pink sweater, and my hands itched to be on her. I stalked toward her, grabbed her under the arms, lifted, and shifted her up the bed. Planting a knee on the bed, I spread her out underneath me. "Rose," I whispered against her lips before I kissed her.

"Hi," she gasped, grabbing me by the neck to pull me down for more kisses. I could endure all the stress in the world if I got to end every day like this.

She pulled back. "Trev, what happened? Did you find anything?" I didn't want to talk about it—about how stupid I'd been for so many years, or how I didn't fight harder to remove Tara's toxic hand from my life. Or how blind I'd been when I let the kids spend time with her, how I gave her chance after chance, but I had to get it out, and Rose deserved my honesty. She deserved everything I had to give. I rolled to my side and pulled her close. She rested her head on my chest and looked up at me expectantly. I wasn't looking forward to seeing the inevitable disappointment when I told her how weak I had once been.

"I think we have a new theory. Maybe this whole thing isn't even about Maddie and it's about Tara instead." I told her what the note said and explained everything we'd discussed downstairs.

"It sounds plausible. What about the paternity test? When are the results going to be ready? Did Jane say anything? I'm sorry, I didn't want to ask my million questions at dinner in front of the kids." She laughed, no trace of disappointment.

"She took mouth swabs, and blood. She said only one test was necessary, but I want foolproof results. We'll know by Monday."

"Monday," she whispered. "We will have to find a way to keep your mind off this whole thing until then."

"Aren't you going to say anything about how badly I screwed up? About letting the kids down by even letting them near her?" I didn't want her to pretend that she was okay with it. I was determined to have every card on the table before we went any further.

She moved from my chest to and sit next to my side, surprise suffusing her features. "You didn't screw up. You were trying to give your kids what they needed—their mother. It's not your fault that she was a good liar. Is it terrible that Mikey didn't confide in you? Yes. But how else would you have known? Did they have bruises? Did they act scared? Did they ever say they didn't want to spend time with her?"

"No. None of that."

"Well, again—how else were you supposed to know? Don't do this to yourself. It's not your fault, Trevor. You were mixed up with a bad person who took advantage of your goodness. Don't let her take any more pieces of you."

"Come here." I sat against the headboard and held out my arms, needing to feel her next to me. She crawled forward to stretch out at my side. "What would I do without you, Rosalie?" I whispered in her ear, then I kissed a trail up and down her neck. It had not gone unnoticed by me that neck kisses drove her nuts. She arched her neck backward and I nuzzled in, kissing and tasting her sweet-smelling skin. "I'm sorry," I murmured.

"What for?" she murmured, her breath tickling my skin and raising goosebumps in its path.

"That you went and got mixed up with a guy with so much baggage. I haven't even taken you out. Never bought you dinner. Never took you to the movies, or dancing, or for a walk under the stars, or whatever," I felt her laugh against me.

"I don't need all that stuff, Trev. You have all I need, right here." She patted my chest. "You have the best heart. You try to take care of everyone, and then you beat yourself up when you can't do it all. You're funny and kind, your kids are awesome, and you make good spaghetti. You always remember what kind of coffee to get me at Violet's. Plus, you know where my favorite spots to be kissed are . . ." She tipped her head back and I chuckled as I kissed her neck again, "See?" she continued. "Oh, and you make me come every time. That's a very important trait for a boyfriend to have." She giggled when I buried my face into her neck; the giggling stopped when I slid my hand down her pants to rest against her soft warmth.

"Every time?" I said against the soft skin of her neck.

"Oh yeah," she breathed. "Right there, right there—" Her voice was soft and dreamy in my ear—exactly how I liked to hear it. With a hand wound in her hair, I pulled her head back and gently bit her neck. I traced over the delicate line of her jaw with kisses until I reached her lips.

She tried to touch me back, but I cupped my hand between her legs and held her still. "No, let me make you come." She relaxed back into the bed, then turned her body to the side, to hook her leg over my hip.

"Okay, Trevor. Whatever you want."

Whatever I want. "I want you." Slamming my lips to hers, I claimed her mouth. She kissed me back with the same wild desire that burned through my body whenever she was near. I took her with my fingers and watched as she came apart at my side, trembling, gasping, and more beautiful than I deserved. With a sigh, she rested her head on my chest. "Sleep here?" I asked. I never wanted her to leave.

She nodded against me. "I have my pajamas and my toothbrush in the car."

"You won't need the pajamas, and I have extra toothbrushes in the hall bathroom." I tugged at the waistband of her pants. She wiggled them off her hips with a grin, then sat up to watch me. I liked the way her eyes felt on me. I grinned and winked at her, flexing my abs when I lifted my shirt because that's where her eyes seemed to be, she blushed and looked away. *So fucking cute.* "Take your sweater off, princess." She rose to her knees on the bed to yank the sweater over her head, tossing it at me with a smirk. Then I was the one to blush. Well, maybe not blush, but she made me feel hot, and that is for certain. She had on the tiniest white lace bra I had ever seen. I could see through it; I could see *everything*. My mouth started watering.

"*Gumph*." I said, making her laugh. I stood there staring like a fool at her in that amazing bra and almost non-existent panties. I had felt the panties when my hand was in them, so I knew they were there, but *seeing* them was a whole different experience. They covered, and they didn't. I was experiencing some kind of underwear science and it was turning me stupid. She crawled toward me on her knees and I lost my damn mind. She had turned from my sweet, shy Rose into a living fantasy. I know, because I'd had this fantasy before, so many times.

"Aren't you going to touch me, Trevor?" she asked with that sweet smile on her face that I loved so much.

Fuck. Yes.

All I wanted to do was touch her, but I didn't know where to start. All that creamy pale skin, those pretty, pink nipples peeking through the white lace, that gorgeous red hair falling down her back. I don't think my dick had ever been this hard in my entire life. "Tell me what you want." Her sweet smile turned kind of naughty as she ran her hands up my bare chest.

Never mind. I came to the conclusion that our desires were in alignment and decided to start at the top. Seizing her face between my palm, I kissed her hard, thrusting my tongue into her open mouth as her hands went to my forearms to hold on. I placed my knee between hers and walked her back to the middle of the bed.

The whole entire time away from her, when I'd had to let her go to care for Tara, I'd thought of nothing but this. Nothing but being with her, fantasizing about what it would be like to touch her, to taste her, to have her available to kiss, to pleasure, to love. Those thoughts had been constant, and they'd *hurt*. I didn't hurt anymore, because the reality was so much better than the fantasy.

I grabbed two handfuls of her gorgeous ass and pulled her up against me. Those panties were hot, but they had to go. I needed in. She sat, straddled across my bent knees, so it was easy to let go of her and rip the flimsy strings holding the sides together. We both gasped. I lifted her up, then slid into her with a groan.

"Shit, shit, condom." I said and pulled out of her. She leaned back and reached into my bedside table. After tearing the package open with my teeth, I rolled the condom on. I let out a loud groan, but it felt so good.

"Shh. The kids will hear . . ." She moaned softly as she moved her body up and down over mine. My hands traveled over her hips, up her delicate spine, then up and over that soft white lace that covered her perfect, rounded breasts.

"I don't know if I should take this off of you or keep it on." She looked hot in it, but I also wanted to get my mouth on her bare skin.

"You can have it both ways." Pulling the cups of the bra down, she let her breasts spill over the lace. She was a fucking genius.

"God, you're amazing." I bent her backward and put my mouth to a nipple. She collapsed backward on the bed with a laugh. I followed on my knees between her spread legs and pulled her bottom up my thighs. She lost the laugh when I plunged back inside. Her back arched, her neck arched, everything archable on her body arched as she whimpered and moaned. She managed to do it quietly though—and it might be ridiculous, but it made me want her even more.

"Touch yourself. I want to watch you do it." I had heard the results of it when we talked on the phone, and I wanted to see it for myself.

She opened her eyes, watching me as she ran her hands down her body, over her breasts, tweaking each nipple on the way; down her flat stomach, over her navel, then back around her curvy hip. Her body was like a treasure map. Her hands traced the path to the spot that I was dying to watch her touch. I almost had to stop watching. It was so hot, and I didn't want this to be over too soon. With every swirl and tap of her fingers she tightened on me. Then she moved her hand downward to spread her fingers out where we connected. I felt her hand between us, stroking me every time I entered her.

"That feels beautiful," she whispered. She was right, it

did. Everything about us together was beautiful. We lost control together, gasping and panting for breath until we both went over the edge.

"Will it always be this way?" she asked, still breathless as we lay side by side.

"Yes." I turned to face her. "I've never felt anything close to this before."

"It's the same for me too, Trevor." Smiling, we kissed and whispered together before drifting off to sleep. We woke up together with the early morning sun shining through the window. Our bodies had stayed intertwined, even while we slept. I knew this because I had lost all feeling in my arm and her face was stuck to the side of my chest. She smiled at me as she sat up and rubbed her cheek. Her hair was a mess, and her cheek was red, but she was still the most beautiful thing I had ever seen.

"I'll see you today?" she asked.

I propped my hands behind my head and watched her as she stood up. "I'm not going to have any more days where I don't see you."

She gathered her clothes and with a laugh she threw her torn panties at me, "You owe me, Trevor." Her face scrunched up as she appeared to reconsider. "I changed my mind. You don't owe me. It was worth it."

"Text me when you get home." I said, and watched her put her clothes on. Watching her slide those yoga pants on over those gorgeous curves—with no underwear—then bend over and put her breasts in that bra, was almost as good as watching her take it all off. It was making me wish we had woken up earlier and had time to make love before she left. I put my hand under the sheet tent I had just made to adjust myself.

"I'll text. And Trevor, we need to wake up earlier tomorrow. I hate letting all that go to waste," she said as she gestured down at the sheet with a frown. I burst out laughing as she turned, blew me a kiss and left.

Chapter 19
Trevor

I hadn't felt this way in so long, I almost didn't recognize the feeling. I was happy. I smiled through my shower, and I was still smiling when I woke Mikey and Maddie up. I made coffee and breakfast. The kids ate, I sipped, and all the while the smile stayed on my face. It must have been infectious, because Mikey smiled back at me.

"Why are you happy? Are we getting a dog?" he finally asked.

"We're getting a dog?" Maddie piped up. "I want a white fluffy dog. I want to name her Princess Vagina Sparkles."

I choked on my coffee. Damn, it almost came out of my nose. "What did you say?" I managed to ask through my coughing.

"I want a white dog," she absentmindedly answered as she twirled her hair and ate her cereal.

"She wants to name it Princess Vagina Sparkles," Mikey said through his snickering laugh. Of course, he would remember. And of course, he would repeat it. Probably often.

"Okay, okay. Okay." What the hell was I supposed to say? "First of all, we aren't getting a dog. And second, vagina is not a good name for a pet," I explained.

"Vagina is a bad word," Mikey told Maddie.

"Vagina is a pretty word," Maddie insisted. "I think it's beautiful and it sounds nice. I like the letter V. V is my favorite letter."

Mikey just sat there and giggled while he ate his cereal.

I shook my head. "No, you can't name a dog after a private part or a bathroom word." Parenting books did not address crap like this—why didn't books talk about stuff like this?

The doorbell rang. Thank god. "Hold on a sec, it's probably Grandma." I ran to the front door, disarmed the alarm and opened it.

"Hello, honey," she greeted with a smile.

"Hey, Ma."

"Maddie wants a dog and she wants to name it Princess Vagina Sparkles," Mikey shouted from the kitchen. "Hi, Grandma," he added, as an afterthought. I ran my hand over my face and into my hair while my mother just stood there and laughed.

"Grandma, do you think Vagina is a pretty name?" Maddie added with a shout.

"My gosh, sweetie, you sure were blessed with unique children," my mother finally said after she finished laughing.

"Unique, huh? Is that the word for it?" I chuckled. She patted me on the shoulder.

"Come on, kids. Time for school," she called. They

gathered their backpacks and kissed me goodbye. I ran upstairs to finish getting ready for work. On the way up, my phone rang. I stepped into my room and sat on my bed to answer it. It was early morning, I expected it to be Rose. I swiped to answer without paying attention. I mindlessly answered, "Hello?" But it wasn't Rose.

"I saw your girlfriend leave this morning. She's real pretty. I love her red hair. I like her house, too. Small and cute, just like she is."

"She's not my girlfriend. I just fuck her sometimes," I blurted. Maybe if he thought I didn't care about Rose, he'd forget about her.

"Is that why Tara was so damaged? You fucked around on her?" he shouted, sounding crazy.

"No. That was the other way around. You should know. What's your name?"

"No. No, no, no, no. I have no name. I'm nothing. But you—you—you are a terrible person, Trevor Hale. This is all your fault."

"What is all my fault? I haven't done anything to you." Sick of this shit, I lost my temper.

"She wouldn't leave you. She wouldn't let me take care of her. I wanted to be the one. But it was always you, you, you. Maybe I'll take *your* girlfriend," he threatened.

"I already told you. She's not my girlfriend. If she were my girlfriend, she would have had breakfast with my kids this morning." Hopefully he would buy that. "She's just my friend. Sometimes we have fun together. That's it. Ask her out. She does what she wants. I have no claim. But if you hurt her or try to force her into anything. I'll arrest you. I'll arrest you *after* I'm done with you."

"I don't hurt women," he yelled. "I loved Tara. *You* hurt

women. You're the one." He sounded indignant. Like I had insulted him by what I said about hurting Rose.

I couldn't take that chance though. I just couldn't.

I sent a text to one of the guys on patrol tonight asking him to keep an eye on her house. He texted back that they would put her on their rotation.

Chapter 20
Rose

It was unseasonably hot today. I could see the heatwaves radiating off the asphalt that covered the nearly deserted parking lot. I had been so busy in my classroom that I was one of the last to leave the school. I crossed the lot in a hurry, because deserted parking lots gave me the creeps. I was beeping the locks open on my Beetle, so I could put my tote and file boxes away when I heard footsteps behind me. I jumped and whirled around, prepared to stab someone in the eyeball with my cat ear keychain. I relaxed and smiled when I saw that it was Trevor. But I tensed up immediately when I noticed the expression on his face. It reminded me of the one he had when he dumped me to take care of his wife. I placed my things in my backseat and braced for whatever bad news I was about to hear.

"Rosalie." The tone of his voice told me all I needed to know. It was remote and full of pity.

Oh god, here we go. Not again. Please not again...

"What is it?" I asked, already distancing myself. I could tell he didn't like that—my distance—but did he want me to hurt? His expression was tender, as if he wanted to comfort me before lowering the boom on my heart. No, *no*. I would keep my pride. It looked like that was all I was going to be able to keep at the end of this anyway.

"Please, don't be like this," he implored. Seriously?

Don't be like this. Gah! Men. Trevor was just like all the rest of them.

"What is it? I have a lot of work to do when I get home. Everyone thinks that teachers are done for the day when they're off. Newsflash—they aren't." I laughed. I had a lot of practice dealing with a broken heart. In fact, I'd been practicing a lot over the last year or so. Starting right after Trevor dumped me the first damn time. Sarcasm and jokes got me through before, and they would do it again.

"I don't want this to be ugly, Rose. I hope we can stay friends. I just have a lot going on, and it's bad timing for me. It has nothing to do with you. I want to do right by you, be fair to you. I don't want to drag you into everything—"

I cut him off. I had to. Listening to his sorrow filled words would destroy my composure, and I would not cry in front of him. "It's fine, really. I will be fine. I mean, I was fine when this happened before."

He flinched and looked to the side, away from me. I watched his jaw clench—he really didn't like that. Well, too damn bad. I was sick of being concerned with what men liked. What about what *I* liked? I would like a man with a fucking spine, that's what I would like.

"I'm not fine. I'm sorry, Rose. So sorry that I have to do this to you again," he finally said.

"You don't *have* to do anything Trevor. What is it? I'm not good enough to be involved in your life? Everyone has problems. We all have baggage. You just don't trust that I'll be able to handle yours. And that's on you, not on me."

Pain flashed across his expression. I felt bad, then I remembered that he was the one choosing this. Not me. I would stay with him forever, if he let me.

"I do trust you. I don't want to burden you. There is a difference. I don't want to put you in danger. I don't want to drag you down with me. I don't *want* to do this. I *have* to do this. I was serious before when I said I wanted to try again with you," he shouted. He was so defensive that I knew I must have hit on the truth.

"But deep down, you really don't. Do you? You keep leaving me Trevor. You keep opening my heart, then telling me to close it right back up. I need someone that will stay. I need someone I can trust. I deserve that." I felt tears burning in my eyes, about to form, about to fall. I blinked them back. I didn't want him to see me cry. He lost the right to see my vulnerability and he didn't deserve to see how much losing him again was hurting me.

He dragged his hands through his hair, then threw his arms out to the sides. "It's not fair to you for me to stay with you. I just need to explain, then you'll understand—" he was frustrated with me and that pissed me off.

I cut him off, sick of his excuses. "Stop. I don't want to talk about what's fair. I want to talk about *feelings*, but you aren't capable of that. I don't understand why you think there is anything left to say. There is nothing to explain. And I'll *never* understand this." I finally shouted back. "Not. Ever. So, don't bother trying to explain it to me."

"It's not about how I *feel*." His palm hit the center of his chest. "It's about what you deserve. It's about your safety. It's about the mess my life is," he insisted.

"Love *is* mess." I stood up on my tiptoes and shrieked in his face. He drew back with a sharp inhale. Regaining my composure, I added. "Love doesn't care about what someone is going through. I don't care that you have problems, baggage, whatever it is that you don't want me to know about. I care about *you* Trevor." I poked my finger right into the center of his chest, ow, damn it. "I would have been there for you no matter what. Why can't you see that? Do you even know me at all? All that time talking, and it's like you *never heard a word*." I shook my head and took a step back. "God, never mind." I couldn't stay. I couldn't stand there and listen to anymore of his bullshit reasoning, that whole "*it's not you, it's me*" nonsense. I did deserve better than that. I deserved to be with a man who listened and cared about what I had to say. Not one who dismissed my feelings because he thought he knew what was best for me.

"Do you love me?" he whispered. He looked stricken. For a moment, I wavered.

Yes. So much.

I love you Trevor.

"You'll never know," I hissed and whirled around. I got into my car, started it, and took off.

The tears started falling before I got to the first stop sign. I was sobbing by the time I pulled into my garage. I broke down when I got inside. Safe inside my house, finally alone, I curled up on my bed and let it all go. My biggest fears and my worst insecurities about myself had slapped me in the face with this man. And not just once, but twice.

Was I so unlovable?

Was I not worth fighting for?

No more. I would give myself tonight, then after it was over, I would not cry over any man ever again.

Not ever.

Chapter 21
Trevor

I watched her drive away and I couldn't shake the thought that I had just made the worst mistake of my life. What had I done? I couldn't escape the feeling that I'd completely blown it. Destroyed the last chance I had to be happy. I could have protected her a different way.

I do know her.

She was kind and beautiful. She was funny and sweet, and she deserved so much more than what I could give her. She didn't understand what I was trying to do for her. I didn't mean to hurt her. I didn't know I was going to break her heart.

I should have known.

The person I did not know was me.

Over the years with Tara—while trying to build a family with her when she didn't want any part of it, dealing with the lies she told, the cheating, the deception—I had lost myself. She left stains on my heart and tears in my soul. Tara left me feeling worthless and full of doubt. All I had to cling to during that time was my kids. I tried to be the best father I could be. I left myself no time to heal, to regain my sense of self. I just hurried through each day, consumed with the minutiae of life. I never thought of the damage left in my heart. Not once. Until right now.

When I first met Rose, it was easy to pretend. She lived so far away, and the distance allowed me to live in a fantasy. A fantasy in which I was whole, and worthy. A place, in the dark of my bedroom at night, where I could talk to someone and fall in love with a voice whispering their secrets in my ear. A woman who listened to my own secrets and made me feel safe to share them. It was almost unreal. It felt too good to be true.

Then it was over. Destroyed by the person in my life who had consumed and annihilated every good thing I ever grasped for.

When I'd moved to Sweetbriar and had seen Rose again, I'd wanted her. I'd wanted those feelings back. Except this time, *it was real*. I was not talking to her at the end of my day, with my problems shoved aside. She was in my life, in my space. She was a woman who deserved the world. The more I was around her, the more she drew me in. But at the same time, I fought against the compulsion to get away from her, to protect her from my disastrous life. Wanting her made me feel selfish.

I thought I was doing the right thing. But her words still haunted me.

Love is mess.

My god, I love her. What have I done?

I drove home in a fog, spent the evening by rote, going through the motions and trying not to break down.

I went to bed, sick with the feeling that I had completely fucked up. I had no idea how to fix it. I didn't sleep much. I woke up with the same crushing grief sitting like a weight on my heart. How in the world I would ever get her to trust me again? I'd won her trust again and just like she'd said, I'd opened her heart—then broken it. I'd worked so hard to get her back, and I'd thrown it all away.

That phone call had put me into a panic. I'd reacted before thinking everything through. I could admit that sometimes I don't make the best choices when I'm under stress. And right now, I felt like I was buried under more shit than I'd ever thought possible. I reacted like a short-sighted idiot. Aside from Rose, I also had to worry about Ben and Cade, and her other face-punching brothers. *Shit, they should hit me. I deserved it.*

Flowers and sweet words would not fix this. But I could start with that. My only hope was that *she knew me.* On some level, she had to understand why I'd reacted the way I did. Getting her to listen to me and let me explain would be the hard part.

I dragged myself out of bed and headed downstairs to start the coffee before I got the kids up. They would be so disappointed if I couldn't get Rose back.

I'd screwed this up on every level.

I went online and ordered flowers, lots of them. I paid extra so they would be on her porch when she woke up.

I went through my morning in a daze. Lack of sleep and worry about, well, everything, consumed my mind. I said goodbye to the kids, finished getting ready, and headed to the station.

Cade was in my office when I got there. I took a deep breath when I saw the look on his face. Obviously, he'd heard. The fist slamming against the side of my face confirmed it. I stumbled to the side and landed on the couch in my office.

"Can I explain before you hit me again?" I adjusted my

jaw and stood up. I heaved in a huge defeated sigh while he stood there glaring at me.

"This better be good." He had a stone face and clenched fists. I took a deep breath.

"I got a call from the guy. He watched Rose leave my house and he must have followed her because he knew where she lived. I convinced him that she wasn't my girl-friend and I am pretty sure he bought it. I broke up with her without thinking everything all the way through. I thought I was doing the right thing. I thought it would keep her safe. I fucked up. I hurt her. I want to fix this, and I have to get her back."

He shook his head. "What were you thinking? Did you even call it in? Get her protection last night?"

"Of course I did. I texted Matt on patrol. They drove by and gave me updates. No sign of the guy. That's all clear for now."

"Well, that's good. At least." We both turned around when Ben entered my office and shut the door behind him.

"He explained," Cade told Ben. "Don't hit him."

Ben laughed. "I'm not gonna hit him. I talked to Matt and Lily, so I know what's happening. Trevor, what are you going to do about this?" I should have figured that Ben would already know everything.

"Fix it. Somehow. Get her to listen so I can explain? Perform a miracle? I really hurt her. I don't know what I was thinking other than I had to get her away from me, so she would stay safe."

"I hear you. It was stupid, but I understand. I'll call Levi and Jude. They're on their way here. Asher too, and Lily . . ." Ben trailed off as he pulled his cell phone from his pocket and walked out of my office.

"I won't hit you again, man," Cade announced as he plopped onto my couch.

I crossed behind my desk and sat in my chair. I sat back and sighed. I had a moment of relief when I realized that her family might not end up hating me. Hopefully that would help influence Rose to let me talk to her.

"There's always hope, Trevor. Rose can be stubborn, especially when she gets hurt. Don't give up. Once she understands the why of what you did, she'll come around. But, getting her to listen? Have fun with that. And if this happens again . . ." Cade's raised eyebrows told me I would be in for it if I hurt her again. I expected nothing less.

Chapter 22
Rose

I woke up, sick with the grief of yesterday still rolling through my mind and heavy like an anvil on my chest. I went through my morning routine and stepped outside. Rose petals of all colors decorated the porch and spilled down the front steps. Two beautiful potted rose bushes sat in white wicker baskets on either side of my step railings, their pink and white beauty like a slap in the face. *Damn him.* I scowled when I saw a card on the table by my porch swing. I picked it up and opened it. It said, *"Please let me explain."* I wadded it up, threw it behind me, and stomped off to my garage. I got in my car and headed for Violet's.

She was waiting for me with my favorite hazelnut latte and double chocolate muffins. With a smile, she ushered me to a table in the corner, near her office and partially hidden by a half wall and a huge potted plant. No one would spot me here, and if Trevor dared to come in here, I could avoid him easily. Violet sat with me, passed me the goodies, and sighed.

"Rose, you're not going to like this, and it goes against

everything I always talk about—but you're going to end up forgiving him." I gaped at her because *the fuck I was.*

"What? Are you nuts? I'm not going to forgive him, just so he can crap all over me again. This hurts." I said over the lump in my throat. My eyes started to fill, but I blinked furiously to stop the tears from falling.

"I know it hurts." She reached for my hand and managed to hold it before the sting of betrayal forced me to yank it from her grip. "Just listen to him. Let him explain. He thought he was protect—"

"I can't believe you, Violet. I can't believe this. I thought you were on my side."

"I am, Rose. I'm always on your side. That's why I want you to hear him out. Or at least just remember what you already know about him and let that guide you. He has good reasons for what he did—"

"Stop it." I got up, grabbed my coffee and the muffin and with a glare at Violet, I stalked to the door. Unbelievable. There was *no* good reason for what he did. It still burned, and I couldn't let it go. I might never let it go. I might never get married and would die alone, just to spite him.

With my normal temperament nowhere to be found, I huffed and snarled and stomped all the way through the parking lot to my car. I called in sick and ate my muffin and drank my coffee as I drove up the mountain. I stopped at the resort my friend Harper worked for and rented a room. I booked a massage and a facial and bought a bathing suit from the gift shop. After I felt sufficiently pampered, I headed for the hot tub by the club house and soaked. Harper came out with a glass of wine, handed it to me, and sat in a deck chair.

"Man trouble." She grinned.

"Please, don't tell me you know about it too," I groaned.

"I don't know all of it. I only know that Jude and Levi are *not* going to punch him anymore. Your dad intervened, but not before Cade took a shot at his face." I perked up, not because I wanted anyone to hit Trevor, but because Cade was on my side and so were Levi and Jude. "But even if I didn't already know the story from Jude, you're displaying all the classic symptoms. And you're not in school today. Bella is going to be disappointed. I'm not saying that to make you feel bad," she added when she saw my guilty expression.

"I couldn't handle it today. His daughter is in my class. I couldn't face her. I'll be better tomorrow."

"Maddie? Bella has a playdate with her after school at their house." My eyes widened. "We've all been there, Rose. Heartbreak is a bitch. Take all the time you need. Is one glass going to be enough? How about a margarita? Or a bottle of vodka?" she offered with a wink.

"No, thank you. This is plenty." I held the wine glass aloft, like a toast.

"I'll send some lunch up to your room. Chicken salad?" I nodded. "I'll have them put it in the fridge. See you tomorrow when I volunteer. You take care of you, Rose. Text me if you want to talk and I'll be right over."

"Harper, you're an angel. And by the way, Bella is too. I'm glad she's in my class." Harper beamed with pride and it made me smile.

Settling back into the hot tub, I sipped my wine. I waved as Harper walked back to her office in the club house.

My phone rang from the deck next to the hot tub and I scowled when Lily's picture, labeled "Wonder Twin," flashed on the screen. I set down the glass and dried my hands. "Don't tell me to talk to him," I grumbled.

"I'm not going to tell you that! Are you okay? Do you want me to drive up and be with you? Luke will take the kids. We can veg out and watch TV, I can bring pizza for dinner and we can talk, or bitch about Trevor's dumb ass, or just do our nails or something. Whatever you need."

My jaw dropped. "Oh, I was expecting you to tell me to talk to him like Violet did."

"No, her heart's in the right place, but no way. Trevor was a colossal idiot, and I'm mad at him too. He really needs to use his brain instead of freaking out and making panicked decisions. I mean, come on! When I see him, he's going to get a piece of my mind," she huffed.

Tears filled my eyes. "I expected you to take his side."

"No way. I'm on your side. Always, Rose. No matter what."

"Thank you, Lily. And no, you don't have to come up here. I'm in the hot tub. I had a facial, and I'm feeling better already. I'm just going to head to my room and maybe take a nap."

"You're sure?"

"Yep." It was all a bunch of lies, but if she came up here —on my side and full of sympathy—I would lose it, and I was trying so hard to keep it together.

"I love you, Rose. Call me if you need me, and I don't care what time it is. Promise me."

"I promise."

After hanging up, I drank my wine and did not think about Trevor. I didn't remember his handsome face and sweet smile. I didn't think at all about his gorgeous body and beautiful eyes. I forgot all about the way he kissed me and held me close all night. Lies, all lies—everything about him filtered through my mind until I had to get up and go back to my room. I took a shower and went to bed.

When I woke up it was dark outside. I panicked for a minute, forgetting where I was, until I turned the light on and remembered I'd checked into the resort. *Way to run away, Rose.* I quickly dressed and headed to the front office to check out. I had to get home. No more calling in sick. No more running away like a big baby.

It was dinner time, so I stopped and picked up some tacos on the way home. I drove into my garage, and hurried through the side door, deciding to eat on the patio before heading inside. Usually I was more observant. On a normal day I would have realized that the side gate to my fence—the one that was between my garage and the side of my house—was open. I always kept it closed. I jumped a foot and screamed when I saw a man standing on my back porch.

"You're Trevor's girlfriend," he stated as he leered at me. My father raised me to trust my gut, and my gut said to get the hell out of there. I threw my tacos at his face and rushed back into my garage. I slammed the side door and locked it. I got in my car and got the hell out of there, not stopping until I pulled into my parent's driveway. My dad was sitting on the front porch drinking a beer and talking on his cell phone. I must have looked as freaked out as I felt, because he set his beer down and rushed over to my car.

"What's wrong?" he demanded.

"I got home. There was a man on my back porch. I threw my tacos at him and came here." I panted. Everything started to hit me, and I started to shake. That man was bad— I'd felt it. My dad hugged me and guided me inside the house as he pulled his phone out and called Cade.

"Cade. Go to Rose's house. There was a strange man on

her back porch. She's here with me and she's staying the night." He turned to me. "Your mom is out back in her office writing. I ordered pizza. It's in the fridge. Jude and Levi are upstairs. I'm going to meet Cade. You're staying here tonight." I nodded. No way I was going home. Not until after I got a new taser, at least.

"Thanks, Dad."

"It's going to be okay, honey. And that guy on your porch? He's the reason Trevor did what he did. He was trying to protect you. Was it stupid? Yeah, but maybe give him a chance to explain. Even if you don't forgive him—which would be understandable—it might make you feel a bit better if you knew the whole story." I stared at my dad. Wow, okay.

Did I overreact? Probably. It's what I did best, or so I'd often been told.

But I was not the only overreactor or jumper to conclusions, or whatever, in this relationship. Trevor flew off the handle a couple of times too—like yesterday when he dumped me.

I stared out at the patio as I ate my pizza and watched the moonlight reflect off the pool. It reminded me of all the nights I'd spent talking to Trevor on the phone. Staring out my window or sitting on my patio in the quiet dark, talking about life, sharing our hopes, and realizing our dreams were the same.

I knew him.

I knew his heart.

What a mess we had made of this.

I smiled as my mother rushed through the patio doors, arms out and ready to gather me into a big hug. Jude and Levi's footsteps down the stairs further buoyed my spirits as I was enveloped in the comfort of my family.

Chapter 23
Rose

I woke up late and I did not have enough time to go to Violet's for coffee, but I felt bad about storming out on her yesterday. I felt bad about so many things that had gone wrong lately. Most of which had to do with my tendency to get butthurt and pouty and go into hiding. But the time for feeling bad was over; it had to be. Now was the time to take control of my life. No more running. No more hiding. I pulled into Violet's parking lot, because I at least had time to apologize to her.

I had spent a year drowning in my bad attitude, using jokes and denial to cope. Using sarcasm and cynicism as my main methods of expressing myself. I had let go of who I was, and what I wanted—*what I needed*. I had forgotten how to fight, to care, to love. I was a mess of wussed-out feelings buried under rage and Dorito cravings. Being with Trevor again had been like a bandage. It had only covered the mess beneath the surface, without fixing anything. It felt good, it felt right, but unless we talked through our issues, it would never work. He would freak out about something, and I would run away. Rinse and repeat until we broke each other's hearts again. No thanks.

All my life I'd been greedy for love. And whenever I'd thought I finally had it; it went away. But I'd always let it go. I was sick of *letting* stuff happen and I was so, so sick of being alone.

I breezed through Violet's door with purpose. I spotted her behind the counter and ran to her. She caught my hug with a surprised smile. "I'm so sorry, Vi." I murmured as she hugged me back and stroked my hair.

"Oh, Rosy Posy, it's okay. I understand, and I'm sorry too. It wasn't the right time for what I said yesterday," she whispered in my ear. "I made triple chocolate doughnuts today, just for you."

"I'm so lucky to have you, Violet. And not because you feed me coffee and breakfast every day. I'm lucky because you always take care of me. You're always here for me. And when you need me, I'm going to be there, just like you always are." I pulled back and looked her in the eye. "I promise, Vi. I'm here for you. I love you." I watched her face scrunch up. She blinked a few times then that smile she used when she wanted us all to think she was happy flashed across her face for a moment.

"I love you too, Rose."

One of her baristas broke the moment by passing me my coffee and a doughnut in one of Violet's purple pastry bags. I took it with a thank you, gave one last squeeze to Violet, then headed out to my car.

Harper was standing by her car waiting for me when I pulled into the parking lot at the school. She waved at me maniacally and rushed over to my door before I could even get out of my car. "Girl, I've got news for you," she said without preamble.

"What is it? Is everything okay?" Then I remembered. Her daughter Bella had a play date with Maddie at Trev's house last night. My mouth dropped open.

"Everything *will* be okay. For you. I saw Trevor last night. That man is miserable. I have never seen a hot guy be so sad. He was in sweats, hair a mess. And Rose, I would swear on my daughter's life that he'd been crying. And everyone knows when a man cries over a woman, that means he loves her." She pointed a finger in my face. "Don't argue, you know it's the truth."

"Did he say anything?" Hope was blossoming. I could feel it spreading throughout my body and blowing the dread away.

"He didn't have to. I took one look and it was obvious. He's a mess over you. And can I say, between us girls? He was in gray sweatpants. I tried not to see it. Hand to god, I tried. But, I mean . . . you go girl. Get it. If that hottie was all broken up and crying over me, I wouldn't be here right now. I'll tell you that right now. I'd be all over that man. Epic make-up sex is on the docket for you." She finally took a breath.

"I was going to try and talk to him when school gets out," I said.

"Do it. I approve. And be sure to *not* tell me the details. I haven't been lucky in that department." She laughed.

"What about you and Jude?" *Did I just say that out loud?* Shit, I didn't want to piss Jude off.

"Oh, Rose. You know we're just friends. He's been my bestie since second grade." She rolled her eyes at me. But then she looked away and it seemed like a wistful look away. Her denial came too quick and it made me suspicious. Hmm. I filed that information away to use later, once I had my own shit together.

"Okay, Harper. Just friends." I let the Jude subject drop. "Don't forget to stop in the office to sign in and get your volunteer sticker, then come on down. We're starting with journals in small groups today. Do you want to run one?"

"Really?"

"Yep. All they're going to do is get their journals out, write a sentence about something that happened yesterday and draw a picture of it. You just guide them and help with words they don't know yet. Oh, and encourage them to use the heart words. Easy."

"Okay, I'll do it. That sounds way more fun than filing your papers." She laughed.

"Awesome, I'll see you there. And thank you for volunteering. You don't know how much it helps." Harper headed for the front office and I headed for my classroom.

My stomach dropped when I turned the light on. There were flowers on my desk and bags of snacks for the kids sat next to my closet by the door. *He sure knows the way to my heart.* I sighed and stepped into the room. I jumped in fright when I heard someone behind me in the doorway.

"Trevor had me drop all this crap off for you this morning," Lily grumbled and rubbed her back. She crossed to my desk and sat in the one adult sized chair in my classroom—my chair. "You two are a couple of drama queens, I swear. Dammit, I mean, how are you feeling? Do you need a hug?"

I couldn't help but laugh. "I'm going to be okay. I see your mood swings are back."

With raised eyebrows she said, "You're not mad at me? This pregnancy is making me bitchy. I try to be nice, but everything comes out all mean and nasty. I'm sorry Rose."

I chuckled. Lily's pregnancy grumpiness was not new. This was her third go-around, and I'd been expecting it.

"Nope. I've been doing some thinking. I won't speak for Trevor, but I can admit that I overreact from time to time."

Lily laughed. "Time to time? Okay. Shit, I mean—it's understandable, he fucked up huge and I don't think you overreacted at all. I would feel the same way. I'm covering for Miss Lawrence for small groups today. I'll be here for a few hours. Lucky you." She turned around in my chair and started perusing the contents of my mini fridge. I broke my doughnut in half and passed her a piece. "Ohh, doughnut. Mmm . . ." She stuffed her half in her mouth and moaned while she chewed it. I handed her the other half. She was pregnant; she needed it more than I did. Plus, she sounded like Homer Simpson and it was hilarious. I pulled out my phone to take a video of her and her new lover: the doughnut. She flipped me off, but it didn't stop her from shoving the other half in her mouth and moaning just as loud.

"You're welcome." I chuckled and shook my head at her.

"So, do you want to talk about it?" Lily had been back in town for almost a year, so our twin mind meld was back. Her eyes got big and she nodded her head at my unspoken request. "Okay, but whenever you want to talk, I'm here for you," she promised before turning back to my mini fridge to rummage around. I had pickles and beef jerky in there, just for her. Pregnant Lily was easy to deal with; just distract her with food and ignore her crankiness.

"I'll wait here. You get the kids," she said with a mouth already full of pickle. We both smiled at Harper when she entered with a wave.

The morning dragged on and on. I needed this day to go fast so I could find Trevor and see where we stood. But for now, the kids were at PE and I had prep time. I was going through their journal entries from this morning. I froze in my seat when I got to Maddie's. She had drawn Trevor, sitting on their couch. He was even wearing gray sweatpants just like Harper had said. But the part that struck me were the big blue colored tears coming out of his eyes. She had drawn herself sitting by him, giving him a hug. She'd written, "My dad is sad. I am sad." Tears filled my own eyes as I set her journal aside. *I will fix this, for all of us.*

The afternoon took forever to pass. I was antsy as all heck. Maddie kept looking at me questioningly and I kept smiling at her with what I hoped she knew was reassurance.

Hurry up three o'clock . . .

Finally, the last bell rang. I walked my kids upstairs to the gym, and then I was free. No meetings or lesson planning would get in my way today. Except—I didn't know where Trevor was. I could keep my business to myself, like usual, and drive all over town like an idiot and waste time. Or I could text Cade. I decided to stop by Trevor's house before I did anything else.

I passed my house on the way. *Should I change?* No. I just wanted to see him. The thought of him upset and crying made me want to cry. But what if he wasn't crying about me? He did have a lot going on. What if he found out the results from the DNA test? Oh god, what if Maddie wasn't his? *Gah!* None of that mattered.

I used to be—until yesterday, but so what?—the kind of girl that expected my man to figure me out. To give me what I needed without having to tell him exactly what that was. Sometimes, even *I* wouldn't know what I needed. How unfair was that? Trevor was the only man who had ever come close to that ideal. What I failed to do was give him what *he* needed. He was the one in turmoil now. He was the one whose life was in disarray. He was the one *in need.*

I used to be obsessed with *finding the one.* I should have

been more concerned with *being the one*. In other words, being the best Rose I could be and not just for the man in my life, but for myself too. How could someone make me happy, if *I* couldn't even make me happy?

When Trevor and I first met, he was finally heading in the direction he wanted to go. I thought he was divorced, and he wasn't—that's true. But in his heart, he was already divorced, and it was finally going to be legal. He was free, and he was happy. That's when I fell in love with him, with his best version. I missed the time that he took care of Tara, but I am here now for the aftermath of it. I am here to watch the pieces of her mess litter his life and cause him to question the things he once held true.

I needed to lift him up. Because I believed, down to my bones, that he would do it for me whenever I might need it.

I knocked on the door.

As I stood there waiting for an answer, I thought of all the ways he had been there for me during the months we'd reconnected. Even our brief separation was one of them; he'd only broken up with me to protect me.

"Rosalie," he whispered upon opening the door. He looked terrible: tired and unshaven, rumpled and bleary-eyed. I knew it wasn't all because of me. I had finally gotten over myself enough to realize that.

"Can I come in?" I asked. He stepped aside. I headed for the couch in the living room.

"Would you like a drink or something to eat?" So polite. He sounded tired and formal, so fearful and so *not Trevor*.

I had to fix it. "No, I just want to talk to you."

He collapsed backward onto the couch. "Okay . . ." he sounded resigned.

"I'm sorry, Trevor. I keep running away and you keep pushing and we keep going around and around. Causing pain and breaking each other's hearts. I'm not going to run anymore. I'd like to fix this."

He sat up straight. "You mean that?" A startled laugh escaped him. "I was sure you were here to tell me to leave you alone."

I shook my head. "I'm not. I don't want that."

"I would have left you alone—if you really wanted me to. I'm not some alpha male creep who would force myself on you. I know I kept sending you flowers and trying to get you to talk to me, but . . ."

"But what?" I questioned. *Please, please, please . . .*

"But, I love you. I'm in love with you Rose. I only want what is best for you. And if that means that I have to leave you alone, then that's what I'll do," he answered.

"I don't want you to leave me alone. You're the love of my life Trevor. What we have is worth fighting for. I love you too."

He smiled softly. "I sense we're not done talking and I can't just carry you up to my bed."

"You sense correctly. See? You *do* know me." I grinned at him.

He chuckled at that. "And you know me. I was blessed the day I met you."

I sucked in a breath. "Don't you go and muddle me now Trev, we have to talk. First."

"Then second?"

"We'll see."

"I react before I think," he confessed.

"I always think the worst, then I run and hide," I said.

He smiled sadly. "Sometimes I think I don't deserve you."

I grabbed his hand. "Sometimes I think the same thing— that I don't deserve you."

"Well, aren't we a pair?" He chuckled and laced his fingers with mine.

"It's almost like we deserve each other. Maybe we are meant to be." I laughed.

He turned serious. "We *are* meant to be, Rose. We deserve to be happy." He leaned forward and touched his lips to mine. I kissed him back, then fell into him. We tumbled back on the couch, him on his back, and me tucked along his side. We settled there and just held each other, letting it sink in that we would be okay.

"Promise to talk to me before you make decisions," I whispered.

"I will. Promise to talk to me if you feel hurt or insecure. Please don't run away from me again," he whispered back.

"I promise. Please don't ever let me go again."

"I'll never let you go," he answered and pulled me closer. I could feel his heartbeat, steady against my cheek. I let the rhythm calm me. I relaxed into his body and he held me tighter with a sigh.

We almost fell off the couch when there was a banging on the door followed by the bell ringing over and over. He shifted me to the side and stood up. "Stay here," he ordered. With a hurried nod, I sat up. He rushed to the door, while I tried to see who it was in the mirror in the foyer, but I couldn't. I peeked out the front window and saw Jane's car.

"Oh my god, Trevor. I have been trying to call you all day. I finally just decided to drive over." It was Jane at the door. She obviously had news.

"Do you want to come in?"

I scrambled up and almost tripped over my own feet in my rush to the foyer. There was no way I would let him hear this news alone.

"I can't," she said. "I have to get back to the hospital. I

didn't want you to wait any longer than necessary. Maddie is yours. Trevor, you don't have to worry anymore. She's yours."

I had never heard a bigger sigh of relief in my life. It was like his whole body deflated when he let it out.

Jane laughed and hugged his neck. "I am so happy for you. I have never looked forward to giving test results more. This is a beautiful day." She looked over his shoulder and smiled at me. "Hi, Rose!" she cried. "And it just got better. Everything is good between you two now?"

My eyebrows raised, and I shook my head with disbelief and a bemused smile. News traveled fast in this family.

"Girl, you know Lily told me everything." She laughed.

I smiled back at her. "Everything is fine. And it just got better. Thank you, Jane."

"This is all my pleasure. Take care of our boy here." She pulled out of his arms and patted his shoulder. "I'll see you later, Trev."

He hugged her again. "Thank you, Jane."

"You're welcome. We'll all have dinner together soon. I miss you guys—it's been too long. Give Mikey and Maddie kisses for me. Later Rose! Call me." She waved at me then turned around and headed down the driveway to her car.

He shut the door, then turned to me. Tears formed in his eyes, then spilled down his cheeks. "I don't know what I would have done if she wasn't mine."

I took the three steps that separated us and looked up at him, "You don't have to worry about that ever again. No one can ever take her from you."

A sob shook his body. He held his fist at his mouth to hold it back. He took a step then stopped, like he didn't know where to go, or what to do.

I cupped his cheeks and wiped his tears with my

thumbs. "Baby, she's yours." Another sob shook him. "Come sit down." I took his hand and led him to the couch. He sat down just as we heard footsteps running up the walkway and the pounding of tiny fists at the door.

He glanced behind himself, out the front window. "It's my mom with the kids," he choked. Then a laugh escaped him.

I beamed at him. "I'll let them in. Stay there." I ran to the door, unlocked and opened it. The kids let out a whoop when they saw me, and I sat down on the floor to hug them both. "Trev has good news, in there," I whispered and waved his mother to the living room.

Tears filled my eyes when I heard her excitedly squeal, "Oh, Thank god. Oh, Trevor."

At least one of Trevor's worries disappeared today, and I was glad I was here to see it happen.

Chapter 24
Rose

After he broke the awesome news to his mother, she insisted that he drive me home and "take all the time he needed". I did not even care that I would be leaving my car at his house. I just wanted to be alone with him. I could worry about getting to work in the morning later. We drove to the food truck lot in town and meandered around trying to choose something to take to my place for dinner. He held my hand the whole time and I couldn't stop smiling. Holding hands in public and being that gooey couple that annoyed everyone—that was on my love bucket list.

We finally decided on the Greek food truck. We ordered and sat together at one of the picnic tables while we waited for our dinner, smiling at each other like giddy teenagers. We almost didn't hear our number being called to pick up our food. We held hands when we collected our food, even while we ate it, and all the way back to his Jeep. On the way home, he only let go when he had to use both hands to drive.

"I got to drive you home, and I paid for your gyro. This

is almost like a date." His eyes crinkled as he smiled at me from across the console. The light from the ceiling of my garage shone into the car, like a tiny spotlight on his handsome face. I leaned to the side and caressed his cheek. He leaned into my touch, and his smile softened to the one that I knew was just for me.

"Kiss me," I whispered. He reached over and unfastened my seatbelt. He pushed his seat all the way back and grabbed my hand.

"Climb over," he ordered and tugged on my hand. He didn't have to tell me twice. With zero grace, I clambered over the console to sit sideways in his lap. He laughed softly before pulling my face to his. His hand sunk into my bun, loosening it, then undoing it completely, until my hair spilled over. He wound it around and around his hand and kept me still so he could kiss me how he wanted: hard and demanding. His hand at my waist slid around my back and down to my bottom so he could pull me farther up his lap. I turned my body, pressing my chest to his. He groaned into my mouth, then placed biting kisses on my lips, my cheeks, along my jaw, then down to my neck, where he lingered. Heat pooled low in my belly, sending delicious tingles throughout my body.

He gripped my hair and continued plundering my mouth while he slid his other hand up my leg and under my dress. I was out of control. No, I was under *his* control and it was amazing. I drove my hands up his shirt, needing to feel his skin under my palms. I pulled it up and over his head, dropping the shirt into the back seat. Then I ran my hands over his chest. I gasped when his wandering fingers reached the apex of my thighs.

"Can I?" he whispered against my lips. I didn't answer, at least, not with words. I bent my leg and rested my foot on his knee, opening myself for whatever he wanted to do to me. He pulled the gusset of my panties aside then sunk two fingers inside. I moaned as he thrust them in time with his tongue in my mouth. I rocked my hips to his rhythm as much as I could in this cramped space. "You feel so good." He pressed his thumb against me, while his fingers continued their merciless, magical torture. "You're so soft. You're so perfect."

I reached my hand between us, cupping him and pressing his hardness with my palm. "I want this. I want it now Trevor." I said and grabbed his hand. He gave me one last swirl, then I shifted up to straddle his legs. He lifted his hips, lowered his sweatpants, and freed himself. I held my panties to the side and started to sink down on him. "I love how you feel." I groaned as he gripped my hips and started to thrust upward before suddenly stopping. I tried to sink down, but he held still.

"No condom?" he questioned.

"I'm on the pill. I'm clean. I trust you. I don't want to stop. Can I?" He nodded and let me go. I slammed myself down on him, and he grunted. Loud.

"Fuck. Rose. Fuck me," he demanded. I did as he asked. I rode him hard. It was a good thing we were in his Jeep; my beetle would have been rocking and bouncing all over my garage. He put his hands to the sides of his seat to brace himself, so I could take him as hard as I liked, which was just as hard as he gave it to me with his fingers and tongue a few minutes ago.

My hands were on his shoulders, holding on as I bounced up and down. I added a little twisty grind, so I could rub against him every time I took him back inside. I had never felt anything like this. I was in control of what we were doing, but also out of it at the same time. He stared into my eyes with a smile and I grinned back as I rocketed us both to the explosion our bodies demanded.

"I'm close baby. Hurry," he ground out. I went faster. "God, I need to fuck you." I could tell he wanted to be the one in charge. His hips kept thrusting up, even though he was trying to be still for me. "Harder Rose, harder," he growled. I slammed down again and again, as hard as I could. I wanted to give him what he needed. I wanted to drive him as crazy as I felt right now. I started squeezing as I rode him, and I smiled as his head fell back against the seat. I kissed the underside of his jaw, then sucked on his neck as I started to come apart on top of him. I felt him tense up beneath me as he started to come. I slid down and stayed, because I wanted it all. He let go of the seat and held onto my waist, then wrapped his arms around my back, to keep me there as he shuddered to his release. His head came up and I kissed him softly, then rested my head on his chest with a huge sigh.

"That wasn't even on my list, but it should have been." I said without thinking.

"What list?" He asked. *Oh crap.*

"What?" I tried to play dumb, but I knew it wasn't going to work.

"List. Rosalie, what list? I think I need to know about this list." I felt his laugh rumble in his chest beneath my cheek. My cheek, which was turning redder by the second. *God, I have a big mouth.*

"I have kind of a bucket list. A love bucket list."

"Like a sex list? I can get on board with that."

"No, not all of it is about sex, Trevor. And some of it you've already done."

"Have I now? What boxes did I check for you, baby?" he teased.

"You held my hand earlier when we were getting food. Holding hands in public. That was on the list," I admitted, and he chuckled.

"I want that list. I'm going to check all your boxes." He was suddenly serious.

I raised my head. "It's not written down or anything." Lies, lies, lies—I totally had it written down in my N*Sync diary from tenth grade that no one would EVER see. "It's just things I think about sometimes. Like, you gave me flowers to apologize, that was on the list. And we made out in your car just now, that was another one. I really loved those flowers, by the way. That was the prettiest arrangement I have ever seen. I took a picture and set it as the background on my phone," I added.

"I'll give you a better background." He reached for his phone in the console.

"Oh no, please don't send me a dick pic. I've had enough of those to last a lifetime."

"I'm not going to send you a dick pic," he said after he finished laughing, "Kiss me," he ordered while he stretched out his arm. I kissed him, and he snapped a picture. He turned the phone back and we looked at the photo. It was hot. My hair was a wild mess, and I could see his tongue in my mouth. Wow, it looked as sexy as it felt. "A just-fucked pic. Put that on your phone." He grinned.

"You're a nut, Trev." I giggled.

"You can feel free to send me a pic of your tits though. I promise I won't set it as the background on my phone." He winked at me.

"No way. It would probably end up on your cloud or something. Then one of your kids will go on your tablet and see my boobs. No thanks," I said through my laughter.

"You're probably right. They're better in person

anyway," he said as he gave one a squeeze. "I wish I could stay with you tonight. I hate leaving you. We have to do something about that. Soon," he said.

Did men not understand that dropping little bombs like that drove some women crazy? Like me. He was driving me crazy. "*Do something about that.*" LIKE WHAT?! Get married? Get engaged? Live together? Where? When? Why? How? And what the heck? *ARGH.*

"Okay," I murmured delicately, instead of letting my ranting thoughts get out.

He kissed me again. And, it must be said, that this entire conversation took place with him still inside me. It also must be said, that I needed to create an adult version of my love bucket list. Tenth grade Rose had *no clue* of the things she should have been writing down.

"I've got to get the kids." He sighed. I rose up, setting him free. We both gave a little moan at the loss. His eyes took on that intimate look that he always gave me after we made love, sort of a sleepy and sexy you're mine and I just had you again smirk. My god, I could have lost that look. I slid my panties back in place and felt the warmth of what we'd done together. "Keep it. For tonight, keep it for me." He cupped me between my thighs. It felt kind of strange and primal and claiming. And weirdly, sort of beautiful.

"I will," I promised, and he kissed me hard.

"I'll walk you in." I opened the door and climbed down. My dress fell around my legs as I stood. He pulled his pants up, found his shirt, then exited the car. He slipped his shirt back on and held my hand as he walked me to my front door. We stopped at my lighted threshold, and I had visions of being in Trevor's arms as he walked through it. Someday, I hoped.

"Key." I handed him the key, he unlocked my door,

opened it, then kissed me in the doorway. "It feels wrong to leave you here," he murmured, and held me close.

"So, don't. The kids are with your mom, probably having way too much fun. You could text her?" I suggested. They would be safe with her. The security system in that house was epic. My dad believed in overkill when it came to home security. Trevor looked contemplative for a second, then pulled his phone from his pocket. He sent off a text, and almost immediately I heard the ding of the returned text.

He grinned. "I can stay. And I can give you more of this." He cupped me again, over my dress, and my knees went weak. His eyes were hot on mine and they grew hooded as looked me up and down. My hair was in total disarray from his hands in it and I knew my dress was askew. He bit his lip. *Yum.* I could feel my own lips were swollen from his kisses. "We're not done."

It was a dark promise, And one that he fulfilled over and over until the sun was barely up and we crashed together in a sweaty heap on my bed, and into an exhausted sleep.

"Baby wake up." I felt his breath tickle my ear as he whispered against it. I also felt his hard chest pressing against my back, his hard thigh pressing between my legs, and his even harder cock pressing against my ass. *Holy crap, this is awesome.* The only thing better than all that magnificent hardness up against me, was the even more magnificent fact that we were completely alone in my house. No kids. No interruptions. I reached behind me to see which hard thing my hand would encounter first. Hmm. The outside of his thigh; I could work with that. I ran my hand over his warm skin, lightly dusted with hair, and he groaned into my ear. "Okay, one more time before I have to get home to the kids," he said, and I giggled. I had lost count of how many times we were together last night. My bed was a wreck, my bathroom floor was probably still wet, and I'm pretty sure the tub was still half full of water.

I gasped as Trevor bit, then sucked, on the back of my neck while reaching around to pinch and pull on my nipples. Holy wow! All night long he had been shocking me with the creative and ingenious things he could come up with when we didn't have to worry about being quiet or running out of time. Trevor was a deviant, in the best way. When I was with him, I was just as bad. Or good? I guess that depended on one's perspective. Or maybe it was just the two of us together that made it so explosive. Make up sex was almost worth starting a fight to have it—almost.

He held me still when I tried to turn over, and I decided to just surrender. Wrestling for the top was fun, but letting him get his way was even better. I went limp, and he growled into my ear and bit the lobe. All thought left my head as my body succumbed to his, and what it could give mine.

"You're going to let me have my way with you." It wasn't quite a question, more like a demand. Still, I didn't answer. I just nodded my head. He grabbed the ends of my hair and tugged it to the side, twisting my head back so he could kiss me. He released my hair, but not my mouth. He continued kissing me, and it felt like he also grew a few hands, because they were everywhere. Around my throat, cupping my breasts, between my legs, inside of me. I had never felt so consumed. With love, with lust, with him, by him. It almost bordered on obsession. I was his. I loved him with my whole heart, with nothing held back. If I lost him, it would devastate me. I would never have anything like this again. The way he made me feel was addictive, and I never wanted it to end.

"God, I love you, Rose. I love you so much," he said as he pulled my leg up and back across his hip, and entered me with one savage, hard thrust. I gasped with a scream. It didn't hurt, it was the most beautiful thing I had ever felt. "Never leave me. Promise me," he demanded. He pushed me to my stomach, covered me with his body and continued fucking into me. I couldn't speak. He overwhelmed me, and I loved every minute of it. "Say it, Rosalie. Tell me you're mine."

"I'm yours. Only yours, Trevor," I managed to gasp.

"Always, Rose. Forever," he promised, and somehow he went impossibly harder after those words. He pulled me to my knees and up to straddle him backward over his lap. He held me there as his hands wandered over every inch of my body, and he continued his brutally beautiful thrusts up into me. My head fell back to rest against his chest and I reached back to hold onto his waist. This was his ride, even though I was on top. I felt his breath on my cheek and heard his panting moans in my ear.

Suddenly he slowed. He started to glide in and out of me with smooth, fluid movements. One of his arms encircled my body, his hand rested over my breast, as the other hand went between my legs. I felt his fingers split and rest at the sides of our connection, "Do you feel it?" he whispered.

"I feel it. I always feel it," I whispered back.

"I love you, Rosalie." I felt his body tremble against my back.

"I love you, too." He held me so tight, it almost hurt. I gripped his forearms and held on, as he increased his tempo again, driving us both higher until we fell together, drifting off into shared bliss.

We lay side by side for a moment. After he had caught his breath he turned to his side. "Good morning," he whispered.

"I'm still sleepy," I confessed.

"We didn't sleep much last night." He smirked, then stood up. "I have to get home. Do you want to get ready? We could get coffee together, get your car from my house, and you could head into work from there?"

"We should take a shower together first." I added to the plan.

He grabbed my hands and hauled me to my feet. "Good idea."

Chapter 25
Rose

After the best morning of my life, I had the best day ever at work. Trevor and I had coffee and breakfast together and made out in his car in his driveway when we got to his house. I finally felt completely secure in our relationship. But the best part is that we did it together. We solved our problems, fifty-fifty. Not one of us giving a bunch of stuff up to make the other one happy. And to top it off, today was Halloween. It was one of my favorite holidays.

I loved Halloween, especially when it happened on a non-school night. Have you ever been in a school the day after Halloween? I don't recommend it—a late night combined with copious amounts of candy made for a bunch of wackadoodle kids the next day. Luckily, today was Friday, school was out, and I was getting ready to head out for the evening. I looked in the mirror one last time to tweak my Ms. Frizzle bun and smooth down my outfit. This year I decided to rock the solar system dress, with a stuffed version of Liz, her chameleon, sewn to the shoulder. Lily and I were taking her kids, Trevor's kids, and my brother Ash's kids trick-or-treating at the Sweetbriar Trick or Treat Trail in town. Trevor was on duty tonight, and Asher was busy on a big project with Luke, so Lily had brought Trevor's kids and Asher's kids all home with her after school to dress in their costumes. We'd planned to meet at my house, then trick-or-treat our way down the street to Jude and Harper, who were joining us with Bella. From there, we would all head downtown to the trail. I usually volunteered at the police or fire station on Halloween. I would pass out candy and help with the decorations. This would be the first year I'd experience the whole parental trick-or-treat thing. It would be the first of many. *I hope.*

The doorbell rang, and I hurried through the house to answer it. Lily stood there, dressed as Hermione from the *Harry Potter* books, with the kids. Dylan was Harry, decked out in Quidditch gear, complete with a broom, and baby Calla was Dobby the house elf. I laughed when I saw her, because Lily used to get so mad when Dylan told her Calla looked like Dobby. Unfortunately, Dylan was right; Calla had resembled Dobby when she was born. The other kids followed them inside. Mikey was dressed as the Incredible Hulk, Maddie was Rapunzel from *Tangled*, Mara was Elsa from *Frozen*, and Mark was Dr. Who, with the TARDIS as his candy bag. Mark looked me up and down admiring my costume. "You know, Ms. Frizzle was probably a time lord," he informed me. "I read about it on Reddit."

My eyebrows went up, because I had indeed heard of such rumors. "Aren't you too young for Reddit, Mark? I'm telling your dad." He rolled his eyes at me. Seven years old, and he had already mastered the eye roll and had discovered Reddit. My big brother Ash had his hands full with this one. He was lucky that Mara was such a sweetheart. For now, anyway.

"Oh, come on, Auntie Rose. I only look at *Dr. Who* and Minecraft stuff on there." Mark was precocious, and we all helped Ash look out for him. I raised my eyebrows pointedly. "Okay, fine," he grumbled, then headed to the huge jack-o-lantern candy dish on my coffee table with the other kids to pre-load their candy bags.

"Ready?" I asked as I held my door open. They all jumped up with varying affirmative answers and ran outside. Lily passed Calla to me and gestured to the bathroom, the poor thing. All she did lately was pee and throw up. It was a seemingly endless cycle. I stepped out to my front walkway and strapped Calla into her stroller to wait. It didn't take Lily long, and we were off. I lived two blocks from downtown Sweetbriar. We strolled down my street, then the next, letting the kids knock on the doors and trick-or-treat as we headed downtown.

We passed the townhouses where Levi and Jude lived, just as he was exiting with little Bella from my class in tow. She was beautiful as Belle from *Beauty and the Beast*. He joined us, and we all laughed as Maddie, Mara, and Bella did their little girl squeals and hugs upon seeing each other. The three of them held hands and skipped along, kicking up and crunching the colorful fallen leaves as we continued down the street.

"Harper had to go in to work?" I surmised. Jude nodded. "You're a good friend, Jude." He just shrugged. Jude's feelings for Harper were stronger than he let on. They had been friends since grade school. Harper's boyfriend had taken off when she got pregnant, and Jude had always been there when she needed him. He was almost like a dad to Bella.

We turned the corner and stood at the start of Main Street. The kids' excitement ramped up as we paused there for a moment and took in the sight. Sweetbriar was a small town full of people who loved holidays, all holidays. If there was an opportunity to decorate in any way, be it wreaths, flower barrels, or twinkly lights, then you'd see it throughout town.

Halloween meant hay bales with jack-o-lanterns and colorful gourds on top, and barrels of orange and yellow flowers placed here and there along the street. Purple and orange lights wound up in the branches and up the trunks, making the trees that lined the street sparkle in the early evening dusk. Over our heads, strung across the street from light pole, to light pole, were pumpkin luminaries, smiley ghosts, and bats on strings. Spooky silhouettes and haunting displays decorated the windows of every shop, and the owners were all dressed up to pass out candy.

Each shop did their own thing inside, but the best one, every year without fail, was Violet's. My sister was an indiscriminate holiday lover. For Halloween, her place transformed into a cute little haunted coffee shop with cotton spider webs with googly eyed spiders hung in the corners, black and purple organza ribbons festooned with dangly bats and ghosts tied to the light fixtures, and bright orange flowers in black pots were on every table. Violet dressed as a witch every year. Sort of like Morticia Addams, but with a pointy hat. In other words, sexy, but also kid-friendly. Her sons, Finn and Nick, dressed up every year and helped her pass out goodies. This year she was handing out little cups of apple cider, and black and orange frosted donuts. Her shop was where the kids wanted to go first, and they didn't care about skipping other shops on the way to the tiny shopping center off the street and across from the park where Violet's coffee shop stood.

"Happy Halloween!" she shouted when we opened the

door. She waved excitedly when she saw it was us. "Oh, gimme that baby." She ran over from behind the counter, leaving Finn and Nick with a couple of her baristas to handle the customers and trick-or-treaters. She picked Calla/Dobby up from the stroller and cuddled her. "I saved you guys a table." She pointed to a table by the couch and the kids and Jude headed over. Nick followed them from behind the counter with a tray of treats.

"Oh, thank you, Violet. I need to sit down for a minute." Lily said as she joined the kids and sat with a plop in a chair.

"I'd take a sore back any day if it meant I'd get a little snuggle bug like this." I said and booped Calla's nose with my finger. Calla giggled, and my biological clock's alarm went nuts.

"Me too," Violet agreed. *Huh?*

"You want a baby, Vi?"

"Tom doesn't. I don't think he ever even wanted the ones we have." She looked sad. I hated seeing her like this. I felt bad that I was glad I wasn't in her shoes. She had settled down with Tom because she was pregnant. They were not a love match. I wanted love, and I wouldn't settle for anything less. I missed Trevor already, and hoped we'd see him when we passed the police station.

"You don't have to stay with him. You can start over with someone else. Ooooh, like Jake, maybe." Jake was Tom's best friend since high school. He was also the finest-looking man I'd ever seen, except for Trevor of course. He'd put himself through college as an underwear model. I had a huge pre-teen crush on him. Pretty sure I still had the binder I'd filled up with magazine ads of him somewhere in my house. I should get rid of it—Trevor didn't need to see that, or even know it existed at all.

Violet rolled her eyes at me.

"Or not." I shrugged. "The point is, you're only thirty-six. You can have another baby if you want." She ignored me and continued cooing to Calla. We both looked at the door when the bell *dinged*. Levi walked in, followed by some kids and adults in costumes. I cringed when I saw a creepy clown with purple hair among the trick-or-treaters. Ever since I had read *It*, I'd had a fear of clowns and visions of Pennywise had joined me in many nightmares over the years. I quickly turned away from him and Violet laughed at me. My fear of clowns was not a secret among my siblings.

"Hey, Levi," I shouted. He was already ordering at the counter. He didn't even say hi when he passed us—rude. "Do you want to trick-or-treat with us?"

He turned and smirked at me.

Guess not.

"Yeah, I'll go." He let out a huge sigh as he left the counter with his coffee. "Someone's got to protect you from that weird clown."

I stuck my tongue out at him and he laughed. Secretly, I was glad he was coming though. That clown gave me the heebie jeebies. I kept feeling like he was watching me—my coulrophobia would not quit.

"Ready guys?" I waved to the kids, who were finishing up their doughnuts and throwing away their trash. Lily and Jude joined Levi and me at the door. We said goodbye to Violet, then headed out.

"Ohhh, look kids, it's getting darker. Is anybody scared?" Lily said in an ominous voice. "You'd better keep on holding hands girls, you don't want to get lost."

They grabbed hands and giggled.

It wasn't fully dark yet. The sun still hovered low in the sky, burning with red and orange fire. The streetlights had turned on, and the trees were twinkling with their purple and orange fairy lights. I cracked glow stick necklaces and hung them around the kid's necks. It felt magical outside; the lights and decorations made us all feel like we were in another world. The light breeze stirred the leaves and rustled our costumes, unearthing a few candy wrappers as well. The pumpkin luminaries started to glow above us, and the jack-o-lanterns had lit up to grin with malevolent, flickering glee.

"I'm not scared," Mikey announced. "I can Hulk Smash any scary bad guys." He started grunting and waving his green foam rubber Incredible Hulk fists around.

"I'll stick with you then, Mikey. You can protect me." I grabbed onto his Hulk fist. He smiled up at me with his green painted face, and we were all off again, this time stopping at each store front to trick or treat. With bags filling fast with candy, we walked the crowded street, laughing along the way. Lily pushed Calla in her stroller, and my brothers and I made sure the big kids stayed near.

Main Street ran through the entire town, with turn-offs to neighborhoods all along the way. The city buildings sat in the center: city hall, the police and fire stations, and the library. The buildings surrounded an open-air court-yard. Every season featured different decor. For Halloween, they had an area staged for parents to take pictures, and we were headed to the picture stage next. The crowd was large, as usual for Halloween, but it was important that I got some good pictures for Trevor since he had to miss tonight. Even though I knew he was working, I still had my eyes peeled, hoping to see him in town. I cringed when my eyes passed over that yucky clown again. I could swear he was looking right at us. Levi laughed at me, and my little Mikey the Hulk growled at Levi when he noticed. *Aww, so sweet.* I leaned over and kissed his little green cheek.

Lily and Calla held our place in line for pictures while Levi, Jude and I took the kids around the courtyard in the loop of city buildings and small vendor booths for candy. Through the window of the police station, I saw Cade and Trevor talking at the reception desk. My stomach did a yummy swirl and my heart flipped over in my chest. I hoped I never quit having this reaction to him. He caught my eye and grinned at me, gestured to Cade and they headed our way.

"Hey, Ms. Frizzle," he said as he swept me into his arms and twirl-hugged me. *Oh my god.* Getting twirl-hugged in public was on my love bucket list. He really would end up checking all the boxes. Then he kissed me, and it was a kiss of instinct—I was there, so he kissed me. My heart fluttered and I kept hold of his arm for balance. Every time he touched me, I got weak in the everything.

"Hey, Hulk." He held his fist out and Mikey bumped it. I was beaming from ear to ear. Getting over myself and taking a chance on Trevor was so worth it. I could have been home by myself, passing out candy to kids and wallowing in my miserable aloneitude. Instead, I was with Trevor's adorable children and being twirl-hugged in public.

I shook myself out of my love trance to see my brothers looking at me. They stood in a row and were all giving me a look that told me that I was in for some teasing later. But I didn't even care. It was all worth it. Cade reached out and tugged one of my Ms. Frizzle curls. "It's good to see you happy, Rose. It's about time." Maybe I wouldn't get the teasing I expected after all. Then Levi smirked at me. Alright, maybe I would . . .

I had the feels. My heart felt too big for my chest. Just

like the Grinch at the end of the story, it was three sizes too big. It's funny—finally getting a little bit of happy in my life made me realize just how *unhappy* I was before. I had shut my heart down, only letting scraps of love inside to feed it. From my family and my students, from those who were unlikely to hurt me. Maybe my heart wasn't three sizes too big; maybe it was just back to the size it was supposed to be. Maybe letting Trevor into my life was like putting water on a flower, and I'd bloomed. There had always been something about Trevor. From the moment I'd met him, he felt safe and comfortable and *mine*. It had intrigued me. I guess that's why I fell for him so fast.

"Guys, it's our turn!" Lily shouted from the line. We hurried over to the spooky backdrop. I cringed yet again when I saw that clown standing behind the cotton candy booth. I should reread *It* or watch the movie. Maybe some flooding therapy would make me get over this ridiculous fear. We shuffled the kids up to the platform and encouraged them to say "cheese."

I was startled out of my clown-induced wariness when Trevor suddenly and abruptly grabbed my arm. He reached out for Mikey and picked Maddie up. "We need to go. Now," he said. Cade rounded up Mark and Mara, holding their hands, gathering them close. Dylan rushed over to Lily when he noticed the change in mood.

"What's going on?" Levi asked.

"What's happening?" Lily said at the same time.

"We need to get the kids out of here," Cade hissed quietly. "That clown. We need to catch him," he whispered to Levi, so the kids wouldn't overhear.

"Jude and I can take them all to the fire house. We can give them a tour, distract them. We could take them to

Lily's house after. We'll keep them all safe." Jude nodded his agreement as Levi whispered.

Trevor's eyes were intense on mine. "Will you go with them later, to Lily's house? I don't want you to be alone at your place, Rose." Turning to my brothers, he asked, "Will you take them home, Levi, Jude?"

"I'll go with Lily," I agreed. "I'll stay there until I hear from you. Luke should be home soon too. We'll be safe," I whispered while Levi and Jude nodded their agreement.

"We'll drive them all to Lily's, and we'll stay there as well. I have my truck parked behind the firehouse. Don't worry, Trevor," Levi said.

"Do what you have to do. We got this," Jude confirmed. Trevor kissed me quickly, said goodbye to his kids, then took off with Cade.

"Come on, kids. Who wants a tour of the firehouse?" Jude asked. The kids looked interested, but what put them over the top was when Levi added, "I heard that Jude keeps a secret stash of Twizzlers and Skittles in his locker. Let's go and see." We hustled the kids into the firehouse and all the while I kept my eye on that clown. It was disconcerting to see that he too was keeping an eye—on us.

Chapter 26
Trevor

We watched as Jude and Levi finished escorting Lily, Rose and the kids into the firehouse. Rose turned back and blew me a kiss. I reached out and caught it with a small laugh. Cade and I turned our backs and pretended to head back to the station.

"My god, man. We've got shit to do. Quit making eyes at my sister." Cade hissed at me as we walked.

I couldn't help it. The pieces of my life that Tara had ripped apart were finally fitting back together. That clown freak was most likely the last piece. I could be happy and still go after this guy. I didn't need to be miserable to catch him, for fuck's sake.

"I'm good. Text your dad," I hissed. "Don't let on that we notice him. We need to surround him before we go after him."

Cade nodded and did what I suggested while I kept my eye on the clown. He didn't notice me; he was too busy staring into the windows of the fire house, the dumb bastard. I glanced back through the front window of the station. Ben headed our way with a determined stride. My eyes swept the courtyard. I saw some of the patrol guys entering the area from different points along the perimeter. They had gone around the backs of the buildings to slowly swarm the area and surround him. I wished it wasn't so crowded. It was a complication we did not need.

Sweetbriar was a small town and there were not a lot of officers on the force. This is one time that I missed being in a large city. Where I came from, there was always a lot of back up.

"Do you think the clown on the card in Maddie's room is him? Or did he copy the card? I mean, this has got to be the guy that broke into your house. There is no way this is a coincidence. We need to see him without the clown make up. Maybe it was him in Rose's backyard. She could ID him," Cade said quietly.

"Shit." I hated the idea that I'd left her alone to be scared in her own home. "I'm going to find out. I don't care what I have to do, I'll get him talking."

"Did he think we'd forget that creepy-as-fuck card? What an idiot," he continued.

I shrugged. Him being an idiot was working for me now. I was about to put an end to his weird obsession, and he was making it easy—too easy. It made me antsy. There was something off about this. Something about the way he watched the fire station and ignored me and Cade.

"Something is wrong," I said.

Cade looked around, he sensed it too. "Yeah, this feels weird."

I pulled out my phone to call Ben. "Go to the fire station. Go through the back." I was pleased to see him turn around in the lobby and head for the back of the building.

"What are you thinking? Do you think he has help?"

I shook my head. I had no idea. Everything that had

happened up until today would make me think that he was alone. But this eerie feeling would not go away.

I heard a whooshing sound, like something out of an echo chamber. Cade heard it too. I saw him turn quickly around, trying to determine where the sound originated.

"Cade," I grit out.

He turned back to me.

"I . . . think I've been shot," I wheezed, clutching my chest.

"The fuck?" he said, looking me up and down.

I pulled my hands back and looked at them. There was no blood, but there was a bullet hole in my shirt.

"Gun! Get down!" we heard someone shout, along with screams from the crowd. I scanned the crowd and the previously hidden patrol officers were attempting to get control and find the shooter. I assumed it was the clown, but there was no way to know that for sure.

"Go, Cade. I'm okay. Just . . . need . . . to catch . . . my breath," I huffed.

"I'm not leaving you here, dumbass." He put his arm around my waist. I sagged against him. It felt like a sledge-hammer had swung into the side of my chest.

I felt like I was going to pass out. I couldn't get any air. I reached up and loosened my tie. "Fuck," I breathed.

"Don't try to talk. Let's get you inside." He half carried me through the doors to the station and into my office.

I sank down to my tiny couch and leaned back against the cushion.

"Put your arms up," Cade ordered. "Open your airway."

I crossed my arms and rested them on my head. It helped, but not much. Cade took off my tie and unbuttoned my shirt, spreading it apart. We both looked down at my chest, thankfully covered by my body armor. He leaned forward, then plucked out a bullet. He held it between two fingers. "Shit, Trevor."

I removed the shirt and the vest and examined myself. I had a massive bruise already forming, along with an ugly dark red abrasion right in the middle. I was slowly regaining my breath and was ready to go back out. I opened my tiny storage closet and put on a new vest and shirt. "Let's go," I said to Cade. "We need to catch that fucker."

He knew there was no way to make me stay here. "Yeah. We will. But you're going to the hospital as soon as we're done," he said as he checked his phone. "They're all fine. Fire house is on lockdown. Dad's outside looking for the shooter with the others."

We took off, leaving through one of the side doors. There was no sense in going out through the front and making our presence known. I let Cade take the lead. I was still a bit shaken up, and I hadn't yet regained all my strength.

Was there a weirder sight than a clown with a gun? We had stopped at the side of the building to peer around the corner. Our clown was waving a gun around and maniacally pointing it throughout the crowd. Why he hadn't opened fire yet, I did not know. The crowd was rapidly losing its composure and making it hard for the patrol guys to make their way close to the clown. They were stuck on the outer perimeter of the courtyard trying to work their way into the teeming crowd. I spotted Ben coming from the side of the firehouse, doing the same thing we were. Waiting for an opening to break through the crowd and attempt to disarm him. Officers now herded people out of the courtyard, directing the way into the city buildings and, little by little, the crowd dispersed. Cade and I, along with Ben, made our move and, along with the other officers, we began closing in.

"Freeze," Ben shouted. "You're surrounded." The clown held his weapon straight up, removed the magazine and dropped both to the ground. I was itching to take a shot, but I wanted answers more—plus, I knew better.

"One of you can come and arrest me. I won't move. I'd cross my heart, but you'd probably start shooting," the clown said with a laugh. Ben and Cade approached while I stayed back. I was in a lot of pain and I didn't want to get in the way. That, and I recognized his voice. He was the one who had been calling me. He was probably the man who'd been in Rose's backyard as well. I stood still and kept my weapon trained on him.

Cade picked up the gun and Ben cuffed him. He didn't fight them at all. Ben began reading his rights and he laughed.

"I am an attorney," he said. "And I want to talk to Trevor Hale, and only him." He spotted me and smiled. It was a twisted grin, distorted by all the clown make-up. "How's our little girl, Trevor?" He laughed as they guided him through what remained of the crowd and into the police station.

"They've got him for now. Hospital." Cade demanded.

There was no use in trying to talk to him right now. I turned toward the firehouse.

"Where are you going? We're going to the hospital," Cade insisted.

"What? I'm going to check on my kids and Rose first."

"After. You're still wheezing." He was right. I was wheezing and it was getting worse, not better.

"You're right. The kids probably shouldn't see me like this." I pulled out my phone and texted Rose. "They are all going to head over to Lily's house and stay there tonight. We can head over there after we talk to that freak." I let out a huge sigh of relief. Lily had a huge house and an extensive security system. Her husband Luke would be home at any minute along with her brother Asher. Levi and Jude were going to stay as well. Between all of them, I knew my kids would be safe and secure for the night. "No ambulance," I said to Cade.

"I'll drive," he agreed. And for once, I let him.

I watched the trees fly by as we sped to the hospital. Cade drove with lights and sirens on. My breathing had not improved much, and it was starting to worry me. It was not a quick trip. I had a chest x-ray and a CAT scan. They gave me oxygen, a breathing treatment, and pain medication. Since my ribs weren't fractured, my lungs were clear, and my breathing had finally gone back to normal, I was able to leave the hospital. I had extensive deep tissue bruising and swelling, along with a minor pulmonary contusion—a lung bruise—right where the bullet struck. It corresponded with the circular abrasion on my torso, from which the bruising radiated out. I was lucky my ribs did not break and that none of my injuries would cause permanent damage. The doctor tossed around phrases like, "restricted duty" and, "take it easy." I had never been shot before, but I knew the protocol. I already expected to ride my desk for a week or two. I was fortunate that we didn't exchange fire, or it would be much longer, regardless of the severity of my injuries.

After my discharge we left for the station so I could question that son-of-a-bitch and determine what was going on. Cade had kept in contact with Ben while we waited through all the tests and treatments. He'd gone through booking and was currently sitting in a holding cell refusing to speak to anyone but me.

My breathing fully returned to normal on the way back to the station. I was okay, except for the soreness, and ready to put an end to all of it—all the worry and fear, the doubt and sleepless nights. He would answer for all of it.

Ben waited for us in the front reception area. "His name is Neil O'Donnell, thirty-eight years old, and he really is an attorney. He's in interrogation. Ready, Trevor?"

I started down the hall. I knew that the room had cameras, the mirror was a window, and Ben would be on the other side. As I walked, I tried to calm my temper. This asshole had stalked and terrorized me for months, threatened my daughter, my woman, *my family*—and he fucking shot me. I took a deep breath before entering the room.

"Hi, Trevor," he said with a smile.

I glared at him. His clown makeup was gone, and I recognized him. He was the process server who'd given me the papers demanding the DNA test. I'd already figured out there wasn't an actual lawsuit filed, but it still pissed me off.

"I guess you have some questions for me," he said amiably. "Just so you know, I am an attorney. I've already signed papers waiving my right to one. So, go ahead, sit down and ask away." His hands were cuffed to the table, but he still tried to gesture to the chair across from him.

I sat down. "Why?" I said simply. I had the feeling he wanted to tell me everything, and I was going to let him.

"Tara was a bad girl. She needed a firm hand. You didn't appreciate her. You didn't ever really love her, did you? Not like she needed to be loved. That's why I had to punish you. That's why I called you and demanded money. You owed me my money back."

"What money?"

"The money you got from blackmailing her," he explained, growing frustrated with me. "I gave her everything. I gave her money when you were making her pay to see the kids. Shame on you." My jaw dropped. My late wife was something else. It was quite possible that she was never being blackmailed by anyone at all.

"Did you believe everything she said?" I asked, incredulous. Tara had her brother giving her money, this guy giving her money, and like a fool, I gave her money to spend on the kids when she had them.

"She wanted to be with me. But you wouldn't let her have a divorce. You punished her for loving me, and you couldn't stand it that she had to cheat on you to be with me." He was smug. He wasn't a bad-looking guy. He could have done a lot better than a lying troublemaker like Tara.

"Why did you shoot me?"

"I didn't mean to." My eyebrows shot up. This was too easy. "Back to Tara. Why wouldn't you divorce her?" he asked.

"You have that backward. I had papers drawn up and she wouldn't sign them. I could show them to you if you like." His face twisted. It was time to enlighten him. "You do know she left after Maddie was born, right? Was she with you during the time she was gone?"

"She had to go. Her mother needed her after the heart attack."

"Tara's mother died when she was twelve. I could get the death certificate, or bring her father and brother in to talk to you." I could tell the wheels were spinning in his head as he took my words in.

He shook his head side to side. "No. She loved me. She did. She did. She did. She told me so."

"It seems like Tara told a lot of people a lot of lies," I stated.

It was starting to sink in with him. The fact that he had ruined his life over a faithless witch like Tara.

He had turned pale as he shook with anger. "I did things for her, gave her money. I bought her a car and paid her rent. She was using me? This whole time? She ruined me and now she is gone. She's gone. I know Maddie is not my child. I saw you through your front window. I heard the doctor tell you the news. I have nothing. No more hope, and nothing left. I'm going to be alone." He stared off into the distance as his sad truth spilled from his mouth.

I tried, but I couldn't find any sympathy for him. "Don't worry. It's hard to be lonely in prison," I said and left the room.

He'd confessed to shooting me, admitted to calling and threatening me, I could ID him as the fake process server, and Rose could also ID him as the man in her backyard. He was screwed, and I was done. Time to get back to my family. I signaled to Ben that I was ready to leave.

Cade and I headed off to Lily's house. I was ready to hug my kids and go to bed with Rose, determined to never spend a night away from her again.

Chapter 27
Rose

It took me a minute to remember I was at Lily's house. I turned the bedside lamp on and rolled over. I sighed with relief when I saw Trevor lying next to me. That relief vanished when I saw the state of his chest, and his side, and—oh my god, it went around to his back too. It was a huge bullseye bruise with a bandage in the middle. I gently tugged the sheet further down his body, relieved when I didn't see any further damage.

I got up and walked down the hall to check on the kids. They were all still asleep. I about jumped a foot when I saw Cade sitting in the window seat at the top of the stairs. He sat still as a statue as he stared out the window at the dark outside.

"Have you slept yet?" I asked.

"No, I haven't been to bed. Is Trevor asleep?"

"What happened to him? He was shot, right?"

"Yes, but his vest saved him. The doctor said he's going to be fine. No worries."

I sighed. "Good. How was it? Did you catch him?"

"Yeah, we got him. You're going to have to do a line-up

and ID him as the guy in your yard. And Rose, he's crazy. Totally wacked."

"I got a bad feeling from him when he was on my porch. I just turned and ran away. Maybe if I'd hit him or something, Trevor wouldn't have been shot."

"Or, he could have hurt you instead. No point in debating what could have happened. It's done. Everyone got lucky," he insisted.

"Are you okay, Cade?" He worried me, sitting alone in the dark. "You need to sleep."

"I'll be fine. I'm just sorting through the day. Sometimes, when I can't sleep, I just sit and think it all away." Sitting and sorting through problems seemed much healthier than shoving them aside and going into denial. I admired Cade for his coping skills. Maybe I would take a page from his book.

"That's good. If you feel like talking, I'm always here. You know that, right?" I offered.

"I know. I'm going to go to bed." He stood up. Then sat right back down. I turned back to him. I knew something was on his mind.

"Rose, do you remember when Dad got shot?" We were kids. Mom tried so hard not to scare us by freaking out, but we knew. We knew it was bad.

"I remember. Stupid old drunk Mr. Patterson." He'd shot my dad in the side and said if he were sober, he would have hit him in the stomach like he'd meant to. Mr. Patterson left town soon after he got out of jail. No one would talk to him, unless it was to tell him to sell his house and move away. This town loved my dad.

"Yeah. I've been thinking about that. About Mom and us kids, how scared we all were. I don't ever want to scare anyone like that. Then I thought about you, and Mikey and

Maddie, and how it would be for you guys if Trevor's injury had been serious. All Trevor could think about was putting that guy out of commission, so he couldn't go after you and the kids. Then getting back to you all."

"What are you saying?"

"I'm not saying it affected his job, if that's what you think. If anything, it made him more focused. I'm saying I don't want to ever get married again. It's too much. There would be too much to lose. And not just for me."

I was not expecting that at all. "Oh, Cade. Life is full of risks. Look at my job, for example. You'd think being a kindergarten teacher would be low risk, right? We're having an active shooter lesson on Monday. I have to teach my kids—my tiny little five-year-old sweethearts—about 'Run, Hide, Fight.' That fucking sucks. But this is the world we live in now, and you can't let it stop you from living your life. You just be the best you can be and stay vigilant. Go and be the good in the world. Be a good cop, like you already are. Then be a good husband and father and set positive examples. That's what you can do." Wow, I reminded myself of Dad just then. I grinned at Cade.

"You're right, I guess. I just—I saw him after he had been shot. It could have been so much worse. It was terrible, even though he had a vest on, and it shook me a bit. Didn't shake Trevor though." He laughed. "I had to practically force him to go to the hospital. You might want to talk to him about that. That bullet knocked the air out of him, but he was still raring to go. Huffing and puffing and staggering all the way." Indeed, I would talk to him about that.

"I will, for sure. Cade, don't keep yourself from falling in love again because you're scared. You will make a great husband and father someday."

"Thanks, Rose. And what about you? Plan on having any rugrats soon?"

I shrugged. Hints at having *more* with Trevor had definitely been dropped. But this girl could not live on hints alone. This girl needed tangible evidence that we were on the same page. Things like rings and wedding certificates and co-habitation. "I don't know, I'd like to—someday," I answered.

"Well, you'll make a great mother Rose. I'm really going to hit the sack now. I'm wiped. Goodnight."

"'Night, Cade." I took his place on the window seat. He walked down the hall, then entered one of Lily and Luke's guest rooms. This house was huge. The kids were sharing rooms, but all the adults had their own. No way I would ever want a house this big. I couldn't imagine how long it took to clean it. Of course, Luke had money. They probably had a housekeeper.

I thought about what it would be like to be married to Trevor. Would it have felt any different tonight? Would I have worried more? My father was the Chief of Police, and I grew up the same way as Mikey and Maddie. I knew the different stresses that came with having a family member in a dangerous profession because I'd watched my mom experience them all at some point. I had felt it too, but not like she did since she'd protected us from the worst of it. I hadn't even thought of Trevor's job and how it could come between us, until now. I sank back into the cushioned side of the bay window and stared out the window, just like Cade had done before. We'd switched places. I'd helped him calm down, and in the process, I'd worked myself up.

I turned when I heard footsteps padding slowly down the hall. "Baby, what's wrong?" Trevor said when he reached me.

"Nothing. I just can't sleep," I whispered.

"Bullshit." His reply was simple. And correct.

"You're right. I'm just freaking out a bit." I smiled sadly. "I didn't want to worry you, but we should talk about it. I don't want to make the same mistakes anymore." No running, no hiding—never again.

He held his hand out to me. "Let's go back to bed. I'm sore, and sitting feels better."

"Did they give you anything for the pain?"

"In the hospital. I could probably take some ibuprofen now though."

"I have some in my purse."

He kept hold of my hand as we walked back to the bedroom. I was so busy tonight with Mikey and Maddie and making sure they didn't get a sense of what was going on that I didn't think about how I'd felt. It hit me now, and he must have sensed it because he wrapped his arm around my shoulder and pulled me into his side. He held the door for me, and I broke free to rush to my purse, then I headed into the bathroom for water. I found him slowly inching back into the pillows to recline against the headboard. He winced and took a deep breath while he reached for the pills offered in my outstretched hand.

"Sit by me. Let me hold you," he said after he finished swallowing the medicine.

"I'll hurt you," I murmured. I wanted nothing more than to curl up at his side and hide from this wretched night, but I didn't want to cause him any more pain. I didn't want to burden him with my fears, even though we'd promised to be honest with each other. I put a knee to the bed and stayed still with indecision.

"You'll be gentle with me. I trust you." He smiled softly through his clenched jaw.

Carefully, I scooted over to him and sat next to him, up against his good side. His arm wrapped around my shoulders and he pulled my head to his chest. I did not relax. I hovered against him, caught between relaxation and fear. Caught between the need to sink into him and let him absorb my anxieties, and the warring desire to protect him from further harm. I wanted him to quit being a cop and do something else, like knit sweaters for puppies or become an accountant. But then he could get bit by a puppy or stuck with a knitting needle or suffer from a calculator mishap or piss off a stockbroker. Hell, I was a kindergarten teacher, working with tiny little children, and that wasn't even without risk.

Nothing is safe anymore.

Since nothing was safe, we needed people like Trev. He was doing what he was meant to do, what he loved to do. And I loved him for it.

"Did you get lost in your brain, Rose?" He chuckled softly.

"What? No. I'm here."

His eyes were gentle on me. "Then come here, baby," he whispered.

"Okay," I whispered back, then gave him my weight. He didn't even flinch. I was beginning to think he was strong enough to handle anything. I wrapped my arm low around his waist, avoiding the worst of the bruises.

"You're scared," he said simply. I nodded against his chest. "I'm always careful, Rose. That is all I can promise."

"I know you are. I mean, I grew up with it. I should already be used to what it's like. But I'm not, and this is different. If I lost you, I don't know what I'd do. I don't want to think about this anymore. But that doesn't mean I want to keep it from you . . ." Tears were forming again. I was tired of crying. Heck, I was just *tired*.

He kissed the top of my head. "Let's sleep. Some things don't need to be said out loud for me to understand. If we're together, everything will be okay." He said softly, his breath ruffling my hair.

I turned my face up to his. He smiled down at me and kissed my lips. "Goodnight." I said.

"Night, princess." His head dropped back against the pillows propped against the headboard. He fell asleep almost immediately. A wave of tenderness washed over me, and I reached down and pulled the covers over us and let myself drift off again. Then I drifted off to sleep as well.

"Daddy, your boob is purple and green." I opened one eye and saw Maddie and Mikey standing at the side of the bed. Then I shut it real quick. I wanted to hear what they had to say. I had no doubt it would be entertaining.

"It's not a boob," Mikey hissed. "Boobs are soft and round, like what Rose and Aunt Lily have. You've hugged them both Maddie, think about it. Daddy has muscles. Those are hard and square, duh."

Mikey was right; Trevor did not have boobs. Trevor had a magnificent chest, glorious abs, and all kinds of other beautiful things to see, if one decided to peruse him up and down extensively.

"It looks like a boob to me. And Rose is laying on it. Why would Rose sleep on something hard when she could have her own pillow?"

"Don't be a dummy, Maddie. And don't tell Daddy he has boobs. It's mean. You'll hurt his feelings."

"I'm not a dummy. *You're* mean, Mikey." I opened my eyes before they could start fighting.

"Good morning, guys," I said.

"You're sleeping on Daddy's boob. Are you married now?" Maddie asked.

Mikey sighed with frustration, "Maddie! It's not a boob." He studied my face. "So, are you going to live with us?" He stared at me with wide, hopeful eyes. God, Trevor's kids were awesome.

I blinked at him. "No. Not yet, anyway."

"So, it's just a sleepover at Auntie Lily's house then," Maddie said.

"Something like that. Your dad needs to talk to you about what happened last night." I gently nudged Trevor's shoulder. He was still out like a light, the poor thing.

"Hey." He smiled at the kids when he opened his eyes, "Good morning, baby." He turned to me, and his sweet smile turned into that half grin I never could resist. It wasn't fair that he could still be that hot after being shot and losing almost a whole night of sleep. I was sure I looked frightening. I could feel how big my hair was, and I couldn't remember if I'd taken my makeup off before I went to bed. Oh well. It didn't seem to bother him. Who am I kidding? If it bothered him, I wouldn't be with him.

"Hi, Daddy. Rose was sleeping on you, but you don't have boobs." Maddie smiled huge at him and patted his arm.

"No. I don't have boobs." Trevor said with a bemused smile. Mikey just sighed and rolled his eyes. He shook his head dramatically and flopped down at the foot of the bed.

I sat up to take a mental picture of this morning. I wanted to remember it always. No matter that it had a scary, injury-filled, insomnia-inducing prelude—this morning was precious. This was the first morning with Trevor and the kids, all of us together, and I never wanted to forget it.

"Why are you purple and green? It looks like a humongous owie is all over you." Maddie asked and gently touched part of the bruise with her pointer finger.

"I do have a big owie. I got hurt last night, but I'm okay. I'm going to be fine, Maddie." He gestured for Mikey to come up and sit by him, I scooted over, and Mikey took my place. "Mikey, I'll be fine. I promise," he said. I stood up and helped Maddie settle in on Trevor's other side.

He smiled and mouthed "thank you" to me.

"I'm going to go shower, then check on the breakfast situation around here. I heard Saturday morning doughnuts are real popular in these parts." I winked, then headed into the bathroom so he could have some time alone with his kids. I wasn't sure how involved he wanted me to be in the discussion about his injuries. And I didn't want to be here if they asked him about if we were married or moving in. Awkward.

I hurried through my shower. There were five kids and one pregnant Lily in this house, doughnuts wouldn't last long, and I really needed a doughnut. Or three.

I loved how Trevor was with his kids. So hands-on, always thinking of them and making sure they were okay. Would I really be able to fit into their circle of three? Sure, both kids liked me, and it seemed like they wanted me around more. But would they eventually think I was intruding? God, I hoped not. I could love them both. I could love them just as much as I would love a child of my own. I wanted that chance. I wanted it so bad that it might just drive me crazy.

I opened the bathroom door and peeked out. Trevor had moved to the center of the bed. Mikey and Maddie were cuddled up to him on either side, and they were giggling about something. My heart lurched; I wanted in that bed with them in the worst way. But I didn't want to interrupt them. I didn't want to be a third wheel. No, fourth wheel? I did not want to be a wheel, damn it. Being a wheel sucked. I was tired of feeling like a loser-wheel. *I just want to belong somewhere.*

"Rose! Yay, you're finally done in the shower. Come on." Maddie said and patted the bed next to her.

I'm not going to lie—I felt my eyes start to sting like I was going to cry. My heart got all Grinchy again and felt like it grew.

Trevor stretched the arm he had wrapped around Maddie out further and I sat down, staying at the edge of the bed. "Come on, Rose." He chuckled. "Get in here."

"I don't want to hurt you. This is your bad side," I whispered.

"Sit here," Maddie said and moved from his side. I took her spot and Maddie sat on my lap. Trevor hugged me to his side, and I wrapped my arms around Maddie. She turned around and looked back at me. "That's better," she said with a sigh and cuddled into me. My eyes stung again, and my heart started to pound. Sitting here like this reminded me of when I was a kid—when my brothers and sisters and I would pile in my parent's bed with them and watch movies. This felt like *family*. This felt like everything I'd ever wanted.

"You look funny, Rose. Your face is all scrunchy," Mikey said. "Are you going to sneeze? I hope you don't get snot on Maddie's head."

"Be quiet, Mikey!" Maddie yelled, lunging forward and pointing in his face. Trevor let out a huff because she'd landed an elbow in his stomach when she did it. Luckily, she somehow missed all the bruising.

"Alright. Quit it." Trevor said with a huge sigh, "I just

wanted one moment—just one—to relax with you guys. Can't I have that?"

Maddie flopped back down in my lap and I was the one to let out a grunt. Then I laughed, because while it had felt like a family before, it had been a little too perfect. Now it felt like a *real* family, fighting and all.

I could get used to this.

Chapter 28
Rose

Saturday afternoon for me usually meant sleeping in, procrastinating on household chores, loafing around in my pajamas, and getting lost in a good book. But that wasn't happening today. After coming home from Lily's house, I was full of energy. I'd already scrubbed my house top to bottom, finished my lesson plans, and done all my laundry. I wanted everything to be perfect for Trevor and the kids. I wanted them to feel at home here.

I was ecstatic about dinner at my parents' house tomorrow. Trevor had been to one of my mother's Sunday dinners —the one my dad brought him to when he first moved to town and I had made a dramatic exit in an attempt to avoid him. The kids had been to a few, with Lily. This would be the first time we would all go together. My whole family would be there. It would be like telling them all, "Here is my boyfriend, commence forming your opinions and offering them." My family was nosy, especially my mother. Luckily, Trevor was not new. He had met most of them already. Just not all at the same time. And not as an official couple.

After dinner tonight, we were going to talk to the kids about me being around more often. It felt like we were getting close to living together and I was happy about being with him more. But I wanted to get married. I wanted babies. I wanted a bigger house and maybe a dog, and possibly a minivan. I had needs—lots of them. He had never brought up marriage, and it worried me a tiny bit. What if he was afraid to get married again? I decided not to say anything until after the whole clown-weirdo situation was completely resolved, and he was rotting in prison. Once that was over completely, then I would bring it up. Or not—I couldn't picture myself proposing. Could I be that bold?

I also had to find a good dinner-at-my-parent's-house outfit. But nothing too fancy. I wanted something that said, "Marry this girl," to Trevor, and, "Don't tease Rose," to everyone else. It was a fine line, but I was determined. I wasn't too worried about him spending time with my family. For the most part, they were all friendly and welcoming. I just wanted this day to be perfect, because it felt like an official beginning. Trev said he had bought flowers for my mother. I still remembered the beautiful flowers he gave me, and was curious to see what he'd picked out. I didn't have to worry about my dad or Cade since they both already loved him—so much so that they would probably choose to keep him, instead of me, if we ever broke up. My grandma could be a handful, but if I kept her away from the tequila, she probably wouldn't flirt too much. Grandma acted like a Blanche, but she was so old she looked more like a Sophia. My oldest brother Asher was a wildcard; he would either be quiet and friendly, which was his usual personality, or he would glare at Trevor with a big-brothery hostile stare all night. Violet was awesome and her sons were wonderful, but if she brought her husband—*yeesh.*

Holly would be cool, if she came. Jude and Levi were younger than me and therefore feared my wrath. And Lily knew Trevor before any of us and was like a brother to her. I probably didn't need to worry at all, but I couldn't help myself.

I finished packing up my tote for work on Monday and headed to the bathtub. Dad had grumbled and complained the whole time we were installing it and all my brothers had needed to help because it was massive. I could sink down all the way to my chin in the water. I twisted the handle and dropped a pink and blue bath bomb under the stream. I sighed as I finally sank into the warmth, enjoying the steamy, scented water, cucumber slices on my eyes, and my favorite relaxation playlist. I was lost in blissed-out bath mode when I heard my mother's voice *yoo-hooing* me from the living room. What the heck? I'd locked my door. Then I heard my grandma's voice. I guess the nosiness was starting early today.

"Hey, sweetie," Mom said as she poked her head through the bathroom door. I was home alone, so I had left it open. I looked down the length of my body in the tub. I was pretty much covered by the pastel swirls in the water, courtesy of my bath bomb. I uncovered my eyes and set the cucumbers on the edge of the tub.

"Dahlia, come out here and wait for her. She could be entertaining herself in there. Don't just barge in," Gram shouted from the living room. *Holy crap.* I did a simultaneous head shake, cringe, and "Ew, yuck" face at the thought of my mother and grandmother catching me "entertaining myself."

"I'm not entertaining myself, jeez!" I shouted. "I was trying to relax in my own bathtub in my own dang house!"

"I can see that you have a bath bomb. Which one is

that? Is it from Lush? It smells so good. Ooh, and cucumber slices. Nice touch," Mom complimented.

"Oh my god, can I finish in here? I feel like I'm a teenager again," I grumbled.

"Okay. Sorry, sorry. We're here to pick you up. We're going to get manicures and pedicures. My treat!" Mom announced, before turning around to head in the direction of my bedroom. I loved her, but, *what the hell?*

"I'll pick an outfit for you to wear tomorrow night. I'm so excited! It's official now. My Rosalie has a handsome boyfriend. And he's such a good catch. He's a good man, and he'll treat you right. Your father just loves him, and his children are so wonderful. I want at least two grandchildren from you. Try to make them little red-heads—red-headed babies are just the cutest . . ." she babbled from inside my bedroom. I heard my closet door open. God. Did I wake up this morning and time-travel back to age sixteen?

"Mom, you are seriously in my personal space. I am in the freaking bathtub!" I called out.

"Rosalie, you came out of *my* personal space. I'm just here because I love you, sweetheart. I'm going to help you land him for good," she informed me, popping her head back through the doorway.

"Dahlia, leave her alone. Rose is shy. She doesn't talk about her boyfriends." Gram shouted from the living room. I rolled my eyes and pulled the plug. So much for relaxing. So much for privacy. So much for being an adult. A pedicure sounded nice though. I sighed and glanced at my fingernails—I needed a manicure too. *Why not?* I decided to let her have her way. For now, anyway.

"Hi, Gram!" I shouted.

"Hi, sugar pie!" she hollered back. "You don't have to wear what she picks out. She's in a pushy mood today!"

I laughed. "Thanks, Gram."

"You two hush," Mom shouted from my bedroom. "I'm just happy for you, Rosalie. It's about time someone realized how perfect you are." Aww, that was nice. "Anyway, Violet and Holly are going to meet us at the salon, so we need to get a move on. Lily might show up, if she feels better. Morning sickness has kicked back in, the poor thing." Lily had been miserable at work lately—so much peeing and throwing up. It was constant, and it made me go back down to being only ten percent jealous.

I wrapped myself up in my robe and peeked out to wave at Gram before I went into my bedroom. She waved back and blew me a kiss. Gram was the one who'd chosen my name, after her mother and herself; we were all roses. She'd wanted me to have something special. Luke and Lily were soulmates. It was obvious even as infants—those two came out of the womb and cried for each other. At least, that's what we'd always been told. Gram said I was going to be the girl in the middle. The middle child of the family, and in the middle of Luke and Lily. But Gram never made me feel like I was in the middle. Maybe she'd played favorites a tiny bit with me when I was growing up, but I'd needed it.

"How about this?" Mom asked. She held out my fluffy grey cardigan. It was soft and cozy, kind of sexy too, and it was one of my favorites. "I'm looking for those jeans you have that make your bottom look so nice. You and Lily have the cutest, round little tushies," she said.

"You're welcome!" Gram shouted from the living room. Lily and I took after Gram: short like her, red hair like hers used to be, hazel eyes like hers. And apparently a rockin' ass like hers, too.

"Uh, thanks. You mean these?" I held out a pair of

skinny Levi's. She nodded and snatched them out of my hand.

"Yes. And I brought you this to wear with the sweater." She handed me a cute little white tank top with eyelet lace straps and trim. It was cut low under the arms and up the sides, and was kind of skimpy. I gave her a quizzical side-eye. But I took it because it would look cute with the sweater over it. She smiled conspiratorially at me. "During dinner, let the sweater sleeve fall off your shoulder. Then after the kids go to sleep, just take the sweater off." My jaw dropped. I decided not to respond. "Oh, and I have a present for you in the living room!" She patted my cheek, then headed out of my room.

I shut my bedroom door and dressed quickly. I put on some mascara and pinched my cheeks. I loved presents, and my mother always gave good ones. Gram had settled on the chaise part of my sectional, texting on her phone. She smiled when she saw me. My mother handed me a pair of boots. Black leather, stiletto-heeled booties with a red sole. They were beautiful.

"Are these the expensive kind? You know I can't accept them. I don't want that kind of responsibility in my life." The thought of wearing expensive shoes freaked me out. If a shoe cost more than my house payment, I wanted nothing to do with it. I mean, what if I stepped in dog poo or something?

"Oh, pish, they aren't that expensive, and they will look nice with those jeans. Try them on," Mom insisted. Gram laughed, and Mom sent her a "shut up" look. "Come on, you know you like them. Put them on." I put them on. I held out my foot. I turned it side to side. I admired, then I went into denial. I was keeping them. These were too pretty to make her take them back.

"Thanks, Mom," I said. I hugged her, she squeezed me back. She looked surprised. I usually didn't accept super-expensive gifts from her because it made me feel self-conscious. I couldn't shake the feeling she was planning something and that I was walking right into it. It was her smile; she had that sneaky smile that told me she was up to no good. Maybe I'd laugh about it in a few years, or maybe I would end up scarred for life. Who knows?

"You look so beautiful. And you are the sweetest girl in the world. I'd marry you if I were Trevor. Put on some lip gloss and let's go."

We met Violet and Holly at the salon. They were all seated in the comfy chairs with their feet soaking in the little tubs and drinking coffees when we got there. Violet kept smiling at me. I was glad she was in a better mood. I smiled back, and she laughed. *Weirdo.* Something was up. I looked at Holly, who just waved and sipped her coffee.

Gram and Mom were at the nail polish display, fighting over colors. "No, that one won't photograph well. It has to look perfect." I thought I heard Mom whisper.

"Shush, Dahlia. I'm telling you—red is classic," Gram insisted. What were they on about?

Chapter 29
Trevor

We were finally home from Lily's house. The kids were upstairs with my mother and I sat on the couch to stare at the wall. I needed a brain-break. I thought back to the morning with Rose and the kids. It had been perfect. Even the kid's fighting hadn't ruined it—it had just kept it real. Rose fit in better than I could have ever hoped for.

Yesterday at work, before I'd gotten shot, I'd asked Ben permission to propose to Rose. He said yes. Well, what he actually said was, "Hell yes!" and then he'd hugged me, complete with a few slaps on the back for good measure. It was old-fashioned and outdated, but I did it anyway. I wanted everything to be right when I finally made Rose mine. In about an hour I was supposed to pick Lily up to go ring shopping. I had no clue about what to choose other than it should be big and shiny and take up most of the available credit on my card.

I should probably make some sort of plan for the proposal. Or maybe I should take her on a fucking date first. I sighed. Damn, why was my life so complicated? I wanted

Rose, every day, every night. No more sneaking out before the kids woke up. I wanted to marry her, get a big house with a big yard, and make some babies. I would even drive a minivan if she was going to be in it with me. I wanted it all with her. But I couldn't shake the feeling that I should wait until everything settled back down. I couldn't stop thinking that I was being selfish.

I pulled out my phone and sent Lily a text. I looked up from the screen when I heard a knock at the door. The kids were upstairs with my mother. My mother was thrilled I was going to propose. She'd met Rose a handful of times at the school when she was picking up the kids, she liked Rose, and she approved. Not that it would matter if she didn't. Nothing would change my mind. I crossed to the door and opened it cautiously. I was sick of front door surprises. It was just Lily. A surprise, yes, but a pleasant one. I was supposed to pick her up.

"No changing your mind." She pointed a finger into my face, before I could even say hello.

"Do you read minds?" I laughed.

"Just yours. You and your guilty doubts. Having second thoughts? Planning to postpone your proposal?"

"I want to marry Rose. But I want it to be the right time."

She sighed. "No. Just, no. There is no such thing as the right time. It doesn't exist. You love each other. You've been putting off too much, for way too long. You both deserve to be happy. We're going. Today. To Portland. We're going to Tiffany's. And you're also taking me to lunch." She held up her hand. "But let me in first. I have to pee before we leave." I stepped aside and let her pass. She rushed to the bathroom and shut the door. She was right. I didn't want to put it off. Plus, I did not want to argue with Lily. She could be scary when she got mad. And aside from the scary temper, she was pregnant. Pissing off scary-tempered pregnant women was always at the bottom of my list of things to do.

I heard a noise from the top of the staircase. I looked up to see a smiling Mikey.

"Were you listening?" I hadn't told the kids about my plans yet.

"You're going to marry Rose?" he asked when he finished walking down the stairs.

"I want to. I was going to buy a ring today. I was going to talk to you and Maddie about it when I got home, before I ask her—" Telling them right before it happened would ensure the surprise. They tried, but keeping secrets was not a strong suit for either one of them.

"It's okay. I want you to marry Rose. She's nice, and not just to you. Rose likes me, and Maddie too. She might even love us." He stopped, lost in thought for a second. "Can I give her a ring too?" I smiled. I kind of already knew they would be okay with this.

"That's a great idea, Mikey. Should I pick one out for you today?"

"Yes. Then we should make her dinner, and we can all give her a ring. Get one for Maddie to give to her too. And I won't tell. Maddie can't keep secrets like I can." I held out my fist and he bumped it. Then I picked him up and hugged him.

"I love you, bud. I'm glad you love Rose too."

"I love you too, Daddy. We're all going to be just like a real family together," he whispered. *Just like a real family.* Just like what I'd always wanted. Just like what my kids needed.

Lily came out of the restroom, discretely wiping her

eyes. "Did you catch that?" I asked as I grinned at her. She nodded and hugged Mikey.

"I'm so happy for you guys," she said.

"Aunt Lily, it's so weird that Rose looks exactly like you. But you aren't alike at all." Mikey said.

"It's almost like we're two different people, isn't it?" she answered him with a laugh. Mikey didn't catch the gentle sarcasm though.

"Yeah, like two different people," he mused, then ran off up the stairs. "Don't forget my ring," he shouted. I should probably plan the proposal on the way to the jewelry store. Mikey could keep a secret, but he couldn't keep his voice down.

After lunch and about ten trips to the bathroom for Lily, we were finally in Tiffany's to shop for the ring. It didn't take long to find the perfect one for Rose. A diamond heart surrounded by tiny little diamonds. Lily said it was a halo. I liked the idea of giving Rose a ring with a halo. She deserved a halo—she was an angel in my life. I had asked Lily about Rose's love bucket list. She'd refused to give me the actual list, but she did say that receiving a heart-shaped engagement ring was one of the things on it. The rest of the day passed by in a blur. All I could focus on was dinner tomorrow night with Rose's family and my plans to make her my wife.

Sunday evening had finally arrived. I was a little bit nervous. Rose had warned me that we would be the center of attention. Clearly, her warning came with no knowledge of the fact that I was going to ask her to marry me today. I'd say that being the center of attention was inevitable. Her family was so huge, it triggered my public speaking phobia.

I took a deep breath for courage—they would be my family too, if I had my way.

"Daddy, let's go. Let's go, go, go." Maddie was doing her excited dance in my doorway. She had her school backpack slung over her shoulder. Mikey was standing behind her, not quite jumping up and down, but still excited. He smiled at me and pointed to his hand. I nodded; I had the rings and today was the day. He grinned at me and I grinned back.

"Why do you have your backpack?" I asked.

"Rose is going to help me with my heart word flash cards. I want to pass the pink, so I can get the purple ones," she told me. *Hmm.*

We loaded up my Jeep and headed out. It felt like more than a drive to a family barbecue; it felt like we were driving into a different life.

Chapter 30
Rose

I had planned on wearing the new booties my mother gave me yesterday, along with the jeans and skimpy tank top/ fluffy sweater combo. But it was just too hot. We were having one of those weird, late-fall, hot-weather days. The sun was out, and it was warm enough for shorts. My brothers decided to barbecue out by the pool instead of letting Mom make one of her fancy dinners that she would have undoubtedly cooked up to impress Trevor. Nature deciding to give me a day perfect for casual outdoor dining was an unexpected bonus. I had been bracing for an around-the-dinner-table judgement-fest. This was shaping up to be a fun pool party with lots to distract from the newfound couple-hood of me and Trevor. I was not in the mood for a momquisition. Oh, and I *was* wearing the skimpy tank—over my bikini top. Instead of jeans and the booties, I was in denim cutoffs and flip-flops.

I pulled into my parent's long, brick driveway. Luke's dog, Rocky, shot toward my car like a brown and white blur and jumped up, putting his front paws on the edge of my open window. His doggy grin was irresistible. I let him kiss me, even though it was a little drooly. "Hello boy. How's my pretty puppy?" He panted and licked my face, then darted back to the sprinklers spraying in arcs over the sprawling front lawn.

"Hey, Aunt Rose! Come on!" Dylan shouted from within the midst of the misty spray.

"Auntie Rose!" Mara shrieked, then ran up and hugged me. She was dripping wet. And since I now was too, I darted into the spray with the kids. In addition to Dylan and Mara, I spotted Mark and Bella.

"Hi, Bella. Is your mom working?" Bella nodded. Poor Harper—she missed all the fun.

"Rose," I turned. Lily sat in a folding chair at the edge of the lawn, near the front porch. Showing off her tiny bump in a maternity bathing suit and sipping a delicious-looking frosty glass of lemonade. I reached for one of the empty glasses near the pitcher, but she shook her head and pointed to the cooler next to the porch. I grabbed a Diet Coke and sat on the grass next to her. Pregnant Lily usually went through lemon cravings at some point, and she did not share —I learned that lesson the hard way when she was pregnant with Calla.

I had only been sitting for a minute before my feet were pulled out from underneath me, my legs were stretched out and I was involuntarily moving across the grass on my back and into the sprinklers with the rugrats. *Yes!* Dylan and Mark each had one foot and Mara and Bella were both aiming squirt guns my way. It was so on.

I turned my head back toward Lily. "You armed?" She smirked and without a word, tossed me a squirt gun. I caught it—it was full, but really?

"Come on," I grumbled. She rolled her eyes and slid a

Super Soaker my way. Truthfully, I didn't see her roll her eyes, but I know she did it.

"Thank you, Miss Grumpypants." Dylan let go of my foot and cracked up when I said that, giving me the opportunity to roll away and squirt both of the little foot-snatching boogers in the face while I was at it.

"*Boo-ya!*" I yelled at Mark and Dylan while they laughed and shot me back. Suddenly, Mara and Bella started little girl squealing. I whirled around in time to see Maddie running their way, Mikey running toward the boys, and Trevor standing by his Jeep with his sexy self. He was sporting an irresistible grin on his gorgeous face. This was the second time he'd caught me acting like a nut. I worried for a second, then let it go. I *am* a nut—he should be used to it by now.

I kicked off my flip-flops and jogged toward him. I stopped short of jumping on him. I didn't want to hurt his sore ribs any more than they already were. I had a lot of plans—heck yeah, the naughty kind—and he needed to be in tip-top shape. I finally had a man, and it looked like he would be the kind to stick around, so I had started up a new list.

"Baby, come here," he invited, arms wide.

I stepped into them like I belonged there—because I did. "Hi," I whispered.

"Hi." He laid a hot one on me. I knew it was hot based on two things: 1. The "ew gross!" shouts from the kids and the cat-call from Lily. 2. I was soaking wet with cold water but he sure as heck warmed me up. Oh, and 3. He slipped me the tongue.

"Hello!" We turned to my shouting mother standing on the porch, smiling and waving. Her happy smile fell away when her eyes found me. "You're a mess, Rose!" she cried.

"Let's go fix your makeup." I rolled my eyes, but I still wiped underneath them with a fingertip, seeing mascara on my finger. *Yikes*.

"You're beautiful." Trevor murmured and kissed my forehead. I smiled up at him.

"Oh, Dahlia. Take a chill pill." Gram griped as she sat on the porch swing.

"Mom, you know why I—" she hissed at Gram, then her voice trailed off. "Uh, never mind—who wants to swim?" she shouted to the kids as she switched off the sprinklers. Naturally, they all wanted to swim, so they ran around her through the front door, dripping wet and covered with grass. "Don't slip on the tile!" she shouted at their backs. "Everyone is in the backyard. Hello, Trevor, I'm glad you're here." She greeted him with a huge smile. That smile made me suspicious. She had plans; I could tell. Lily gave me big eyes before following behind the kids.

Violet pulled up next to Trevor and me in her Range Rover. I turned away from her car when I saw Tom sitting in the passenger seat. I took the squirt gun from my waist band and handed it to Trevor. "You'd better take this, or I'll end up squirting that fucker in the face," I whispered. He choked back a laugh and took it from me.

Finn and Nick exited from the back seat with frowns on their faces, and all but ran into the house. Uh-oh.

"Hey guys—" I said to Violet and Tom.

Tom looked me up and down with derision. "Soaking wet in your clothes. Are you ever going to grow up, Rose?" he sneered.

I inhaled sharply and bit the inside of my mouth.

Violet whirled on him with an outraged gasp.

Trevor shot him in the face with the squirt gun. "Rose is

perfect as she is. And you'd better watch yourself," he bit out through his clenched jaw. *Oh. My. God. Hot.*

I grabbed his hand, and he clenched mine back. I couldn't help it. The smile that split my face was massive. It surpassed my wonkified happy smile by a mile. I needed new adjectives to describe this feeling. He stuck up for me. He wasn't afraid to offend or upset anyone, and I wanted to jump him immediately.

"Don't listen to that asshole," he said angrily. "Don't listen to your mother either. You don't need makeup, you're stunning. You could be soaking wet or dressed for a night out—it doesn't matter, you will always be beautiful." *Gumph.*

Violet tossed her keys at Tom. "Go home." He scowled at us and drove off in a huff. "I'm so sorry," she said to me.

"You didn't do anything," I answered through the stars in my eyes and the mush in my brain caused by Trevor's epic, amazing *epicness.*

She nodded back with tears in her eyes that she quickly blinked away. "So, everyone is out back?" Fake smile firmly back in place. My heart broke for my big sister. She deserved so much more. So did Finn and Nick, for that matter.

"Yeah, don't try for the lemonade though. Lily has the lemon craving again." I informed her.

She laughed. "I always craved milk when I was pregnant with the boys. I swear I'd drink a half gallon a day. Tom used to say—" Her eyes drifted away from me, lost in a memory. A terrible, wistful expression crossed her face. I knew they'd loved each other once, even though her pregnancy is what made them get married. "It doesn't matter. I'm going to try and wrestle Calla from Luke. I need a baby fix." She breezed past us towards the porch.

"Well, that was sad," Trevor said.

"Yeah. Thank you for defending my honor." I smiled up at him.

"Always." He pocketed the squirt gun then brought his lips to mine. It was forceful, it was aggressive, and I couldn't help but worry about his ribs. That worry melted away as he backed me into his Jeep with his body. I felt the cold metal of his belt buckle firm against my stomach as his hips pressed against me. He wrapped an arm around my back and tugged me against him. I tried to give as good as I was getting but I just couldn't. I could only cling to him and let him take what he wanted. He overwhelmed me in the best way. "I've missed you—" he whispered against my lips before he went back in, thrusting his tongue into my mouth and grinding his hard thigh up between my legs.

All I could think was *more and yes and don't stop*. But we were in my parent's driveway. Who knew who would drive up next? Was everybody already here? His hands gripped my bottom and pulled me higher up his body. "God, Trev." I gasped against his lips. "Your ribs, the bruises, the driveway—we have to stop."

He pulled back then leaned forward for one more wet kiss. "We'll finish later," he promised with a growl.

"Tonight," I agreed. He smirked and pressed my lower lip with his thumb, I kissed it then touched it with my tongue. His eyes grew hot on me before he took a step back. I held out my hand, he took it, and we headed for the back yard.

We exited the patio doors to a chorus of whoops and whistles and a small round of applause. "What's going on?" I looked around, confused.

"You two didn't even see me drive up, park my car, get out, beep the locks, walk past you, then go into the house.

Go Rose!" Holly laughed and tossed me a beer. My face grew hot. Even though their teasing would be gentle and not mean, I still hated being the center of attention. It wasn't a role I was comfortable with. I was the one who blended into the middle of my family and disappeared. Being front and center was a new experience for me. I passed the beer to Trevor.

"Thanks, baby." He pulled me over to a patio chaise near the pool, then into his lap as he sat down. I curled up between his legs and leaned back into him. He pulled me close and kept his arms around my waist.

The kids were swimming, along with Finn and Nick, Cade, and my father. Levi and Jude were at the grill with Asher and Liam, Luke's friend and business partner, and pretty much the newest member of the family. Violet was sitting on a quilt on the grass holding a napping Calla. Lily was next to them, sprawled out against Luke, who was sitting behind her and massaging her neck. Mom and Gram were at the patio table sipping iced tea and nibbling on the snacks that covered the table. Holly sat next to me and Trevor on her own chair. "I've missed these dinners," she said.

"I'm glad you're here. We always miss you." I smiled at her.

Out of the corner of my eye, I saw Lily nod her head and Luke help her up. "Come on!" she shouted. Maddie and Mikey got out of the pool, followed by everyone else.

I turned to watch Levi piling burgers onto a plate from the grill, and Jude carrying another platter of hot dogs to the table. Okay—she was just calling them to dinner. I let out a soft laugh. I kept getting an odd sensation that everyone was watching me. *Quit being so paranoid . . .*

I smiled as Maddie headed over to us carrying her backpack from school. "Will you help me with my heart word flashcards Rose? Please."

I patted the chaise in front of me and sat up. She handed me the little pink cards and I held the first one out.

"Will," she read the word on the card. I smiled at her and held out the next card.

"You," she read with a small smile. Next.

"Marry." I turned the card around; that wasn't one of my heart words...

I showed Maddie the next card in the stack. "My."

What? And the next...

"Dad," she read as her small smile turned huge. *Oh god. Oh my god...*

Trevor's arm left my waist. I tried to keep breathing and functioning even though my stomach was swirling, and I felt a bit light-headed. *Am I dreaming?*

My mouth dropped open. The patio took on a light-filled, hazy focus. I blinked in confusion—and hope. Was this a proposal?

I turned back to him with a questioning look. He held a small box in his hand. Tears filled my eyes as they quickly drifted around the patio. Everyone watched us with smiles on their faces. Violet was crying through hers, as were Lily and Holly. My mother smiled from ear to ear, with tears shining on her eyelashes. My father was next to her aiming a video camera my way—no wonder she had wanted me to fix my make-up and get a manicure with her yesterday. She blew me a kiss and I choked back a sob. My eyes slid back over my shoulder to Trevor. I turned halfway in my seat, so I could see his face.

"I love you, Rose. I will spend the rest of my life loving you, if you'll let me. Will you marry me?" He asked with a gentle smile.

I nodded. I tried to say yes, but I couldn't get the word out. Tears fell from my eyes and I just kept nodding.

He chuckled and took my hand. "So cute," he murmured as he slipped a beautiful heart-shaped diamond on my finger. A heart-shaped diamond, just like on my list. My eyes snapped to Lily, who shrugged and laughed through her tears.

"Say yes!" Mikey held out a box of his own. He opened it and showed me a dainty blue sapphire eternity ring. "Marry us!" he yelled with a huge smile. I kept on nodding, and I kept right on crying.

I cried harder when little Maddie opened a box of her own and held it out to me. It was an eternity ring, like Mikey's but with pink and white alternating sapphires. "Say yes, Rose," she whisper-spit in my ear.

"Yes. Yes, yes, I will marry you Trevor. And you Mikey, and you too, Maddie." I managed to choke out through the giant lump that had taken up residence in my throat. Mikey and Maddie each slipped their rings on my finger, right on top of Trevor's heart.

"See, Dahlia? She didn't need to redo her make-up. Look at all those tears—it would have been ruined anyway," Gram said to my mom. She winked at me.

I winked back and collapsed in a smiling, sobbing heap onto Trevor's chest. Mikey and Maddie crawled into my lap and wrapped their little arms around my neck. I hugged them back as Trevor wrapped us all up. I wanted to live in this perfect moment for eternity, surrounded by everyone I loved most in the world, sitting in the arms of the man who now owned my heart, and holding the two children that had snuck in and stolen two of the pieces for their own. We were a family now, and I was going to kick so much step-mother ass.

Chapter 31
Trevor

She said yes.

Yes.

And now she was here. In my bed, with the bright morning sun shining on her beautiful face. We would wake up together, make breakfast together, and start our day together. It would always be like this. No more separation, ever. I brushed her hair back and kissed her forehead, but she didn't stir.

"Daddy," I heard whispered from the crack in the doorway. I had unlocked the door after Rose and I had finished. We'd celebrated our engagement with large amounts of naked enthusiasm.

"Come in, Mikey." He was up early. I usually had to wake him, and it always involved a lot of whining, complaining, and hiding under the covers.

Already, our life was better with her in it. But I knew better than to expect Mikey's voluntary morning wake-up to be a permanent thing. "Rose is here. Is she going to live with us now?" He looked hopeful.

"Yes. We're going to get married. We'll have to find a bigger house." I sighed, because real estate in this area was expensive and scarce. But, we were together, and that's all that mattered.

"Daddy." Another early riser. This was going to be a great day. Maddie didn't wait to come in like Mikey did. She crossed the room and climbed into bed and cuddled on my lap. Mikey followed suit and sat next to us on the edge of the bed.

Rose stirred and rolled toward us. She opened her eyes with raised eyebrows, then a gorgeous grin lit up her face. "Good morning," she murmured. She opened her arm out.

Mikey crawled over and curled up next to her. "Good morning, Rose," he said and hugged her back.

"Best morning ever. Even better than Christmas," Rose said.

I smiled down at her. She was right; having her say yes was absolutely better than Christmas.

"So, what do we do? Get dressed for school, then breakfast? Or breakfast, then get dressed?" she asked.

I stared down at her. My heart started to pound hard. I was going to have help. She couldn't know how much that meant to me. "We usually . . ." *Run around like chickens with no heads, whining and nagging until we were all ready to go.* Mornings were not our forte. We were much better in the afternoon. "Um . . ." I didn't know what to say.

She laughed. "Dylan usually whines about getting up and complains about getting dressed. Most of the time he can't find his shoes, then he grumbles that there are no doughnuts for breakfast. I mean, you can't have doughnuts every day. I'm going to guess that we're all happy this morning because we had a great Sunday night, and the excitement isn't gone yet. Maybe we need a new routine together?" She finished. *My God, I fucking love her . . .*

"That sounds perfect," I finally answered.

With a nod, she gave Mikey a squeeze, kissed Maddie's cheek, kissed my lips, and got up. "I showered last night. I just need clothes. Trev? Go shower. Maddie and Mikey, you picked clothes last night, so go get dressed, brush your teeth, and comb your hair. I'll make breakfast. And just so you all know, I don't cook. So, when I say 'make breakfast' that means Pop-Tarts or cereal. Sound good?" The kids nodded at her. "Trevor, I get my coffee from Violet—okay with you?"

I nodded. The kids got up and headed to their rooms. I seriously almost started crying. All I had to do was shower. No one was crying about how tired they were, how cold it was in the morning, their pants being too bunchy at the bottom (Maddie), or that they couldn't find their favorite shirt (Mikey), or that there were no more Strawberry Pop-Tarts (that would be all of us—strawberry was our collective favorite). To be fair, there would most likely be complaints about the lack of Strawberry Pop-Tarts this morning because we were out. But that's okay, nothing could be perfect. But to me, this imperfection was perfect.

Rose and I met in the kitchen before the kids made it downstairs. She looked beautiful. I tugged on her scarf, which was silky and printed with Dr. Seuss characters. God, she was cute. I lifted her onto the counter and stepped into her body, tugging her against me. "Good morning fiancée," I whispered before I kissed her.

She melted against me. "It's the best morning, future husband." She sighed and wrapped her legs around my waist.

I kissed her once more, then pulled back. I looked at her

and marveled at the drop-dead gorgeous, sexy girl with the twinkling eyes and shy smile sitting in my kitchen like she belonged here. Because she did. She belonged with me—wherever I am, and wherever I will be. I ran my hands over her hips, past the curve of her waist and up to cup her cheeks with my palms. "I love you, Rosalie. I'm going make you so happy. I promise."

"I love you too. And I'm already happy. So happy, you wouldn't believe—"

"Ew, gross! Kissing again." I tore myself away. Mikey was smirking in the archway entrance to the kitchen. "Pop-Tart, please. Is Grandma still driving us to school? Or can we ride with Rose?" he asked, just as the doorbell rang.

I helped Rose get down. She crossed to the pantry to find breakfast. And I left the kitchen to answer the door.

"Hey, Ma." I greeted my mother with a hug.

"Did you do it?" My smile must have been answer enough because she burst through the door and rushed inside. "Yay! Congratulations! Is she here?"

"Hi, Mrs. Hale." Rose laughed when my mother accosted her in the kitchen with a hug.

"Call me Deb, or Mom! Oh my gosh, I am so happy for you two—no, you four. Hi Mikey, sweetheart. Are you ready?"

He nodded, then yelled in the direction of the stairs. "Maddie, Grandma is here."

Maddie came bounding down the stairs, "I'm ready." Her lips were pink—just like Rose's.

"Did you get into Rose's make-up?" I turned to Rose. "I'm sorry," I mouthed.

She just laughed. "Oh, Maddie. You look pretty. But you're too young to wear my make-up. I can get you some fun lip-balm after school, if it's okay with your dad."

I nodded. I had no problem with lip-balm. I hugged the kids good-bye, Rose gave them each a Pop-Tart and a hug, and they were off with my mother.

"I have to go too. I could probably take them to school with me in the mornings, if your mom wants to let that go," she offered. "But I usually have meetings after school, so I wouldn't be able to bring them home. I should probably trade in my car and get something bigger . . ." she mused.

And just like that, my life had changed. I smiled at her and swept her up in my arms and kissed the hell out of her —kissed the hell out of my future wife.

"I'll see you later this morning." I whispered against her delicious mouth, then kissed her again. I just couldn't seem to stop.

She smiled against my lips. "For the 'Run, Hide, Fight' lessons?"

"Yep. It will be me, Cade, and a few of the patrol officers dropping into the classrooms this morning. I am on restricted duty for two weeks, but I think I can probably handle a few elementary school kids, right?"

She laughed. "Oh, I don't know about that. Some of my kindergartners from last year are currently busy terrorizing the first-grade teachers. Better keep your eyes open."

"I'll keep my guard up."

"Are you going to Violet's?" she asked.

"No, I usually make coffee here or grab some at the station. I only went to Violet's when I was missing you," I admitted.

Her smile softened. "Trev," she breathed. I loved how I could see what she was feeling. I loved how she let me know when I touched her heart with something I said or did, or if I just made her happy. After my experience with Tara, Rose was like sunshine on a spring day. I had come to count on her and her guileless reactions to me.

She kissed me goodbye before heading to her car parked in the driveway. "See you later," she called on the way.

"Bye, princess." I called back, just to see if I could make her blush. I was not disappointed. I found myself smiling as I watched her walk away.

Chapter 32
Rose

I always dread this lesson. Teaching about active shooters and potential bad guys—it was nearly impossible to teach kids "what if" without scaring the ever-loving crap out of some of them. Every year, without fail, a few of my kids would cry and shake in their shoes no matter how gently I framed the instruction. Kindergarten should be the safest place in the world for my kids, aside from the arms of their parents. I was resentful that the violence of the world had infiltrated the haven of my classroom. Violet and Harper would be my volunteers this afternoon. I needed friendly faces, sweet smiles, and soft arms to hug my scared littles when we finished. I also needed help with clean up, because I always threw a cupcake party on the big-kid playground when I finished this lesson. I was a believer in combining negative and positive experiences. It usually helped to mitigate the trauma.

I had taught the portion on when to "run", including where we go and what we do when we get there. We sallied forth through the "fight" section, talking about what to throw and how to get away. We were now in the "hide" portion of this big, fat treat of a lesson. The kids huddled en masse in my little alcove library corner, squished together and doing their best to be silent. Violet and Harper were in the hallway to test their quietude. I ready-set-go-ed them, and unbelievably, they got even quieter. It was both heartening and sad to see them so earnestly following my instruction. Heartening, because they were cooperating and taking care of each other in their huddle. And sad because they shouldn't have to do this in the first place. Later this morning Trevor or Cade or one of the other officers would be dropping by each class to check in and congratulate the kids on their jobs well done.

"Shh," I reminded, then walked around the shelf that bordered my library alcove and opened my door. "Violet, Harper, did you hear anything when you were in the hallway?" I asked.

"We didn't hear a peep. You were each as quiet as a tiny little mouse. Great job kids," Violet announced.

I looked over the top of the shelf. They were still silent. Some were just ambivalently quiet—for them, this was just part of their day. But a few had big eyes full of unshed tears, and it broke my heart. If there was ever a time that I wished for superpowers, this was it.

"Let's go to the carpet and sit in our circle. Find your spots," I instructed.

We settled into our spots on the carpet with Violet and Harper joining us in the circle. "I know that was kind of scary." I saw nods and a few trembling chins. "You are all brave, and I am so very proud of you. Let's hold hands and share our courage with each other." We joined hands. "Some of our friends were more scared than others. But when I looked around, I saw some of you being great helpers and encouragers, and that made me so happy. I love how we take care of each other. I want us to always do that. Looking out for one another is important. Kindness is a gift, and we should give it to everybody."

Cade poked his head in the doorway. "How are we doing?" he asked as he stepped inside.

"They did great," I answered. "I have some brave kindergartners this year."

"I'm so happy to hear that. I'm just stopping by to remind you kids that the Sweetbriar Police are always here to help. But an important part of that is knowing when to ask us to help. So, if you see something out of the ordinary, something that gives you a bad or dangerous feeling, tell someone. Tell Miss Barrett, or another teacher, or your parents. Tell one of the Sweetbriar officers or your principal. Don't keep it to yourself. It could be important, and it could save a life. Now, I heard that you're going to have a cupcake party on the big-kid playground." There was a collective gasp from our circle at that. "I wish I could join you, but I have to go back to work. Have fun, and be safe." He smiled and headed out with a wave.

I looked around the circle to see that the tears had disappeared, replaced with tremulous smiles on some and big grins on others. The trembling chins were all gone, and our collective mood had improved. "Are you ready? Clap one time if you are."

They all clapped.

I smiled huge and stood up. Violet also stood and headed for the doorway "If you are sitting in a red square, line up by Miss Violet." I went on through the colors until they were all in line. I gestured for Violet to go ahead and lead. "Remember, quiet in the hall until we get to the playground."

Harper followed along the side of the line. I grabbed the

cupcakes, napkins, and a package of baby wipes, and took my position as the caboose.

Recesses at my school were on a schedule and had educational assistants to monitor them. But each teacher could use a bonus recess as a reward for good behavior if they chose. The kindergarten had its own playground. We usually walked down the hall and passed the library to exit through the double doors that led right to it. A short fence bordered it, and it had a bin with jump ropes and balls as well as play structures designed for tiny humans to enjoy. The fence came in handy because it prevented said tiny humans from running away and going nuts as some (most) were prone to do.

The big kid playground was a rare treat that I only allowed when I had volunteers available. I mean, I couldn't watch all the kids and chase down a potential escapee at the same time. It sat in the rear of the huge outdoor area and the only fencing was what lined the perimeter of the school. The school was shaped like a two-story letter L. The grounds were within the L shape and fenced in to make a large rectangular lot. Sweetbriar was on a mountain. The fence at the rear of the property led down the mountain; jump over that and bye-bye to you. The side fence bordered the next-door junior high grounds, and the front fence led to the street with a driveway for garbage and delivery trucks. The cafeteria sat at the front of the school with dumpsters and recycling bins lining the side of the building near the fence.

I led the kids to the edge of the bark chip-filled big-kid playground. I sat the cupcake box on one of the buddy benches and opened it. "Find a seat on a bench and we'll pass the cupcakes out," I instructed with a smile.

Once cupcakes had been consumed and faces were

wiped, I asked for a volunteer to run the box to the trash. Maddie volunteered, so I passed her the box and watched as she started across the playground toward the garbage cans near the cafeteria doors. Violet and Harper circled the playground and kept an eye on the kids while I watched Maddie. She was such a sweet, responsible little girl. I felt more than pride as a teacher; I felt maternal pride. I loved that little girl, and I couldn't wait to become part of her life permanently.

"Miss Barrett!" I turned at the scream. It was Bella, and she was pointing toward the fence near the dumpsters.

I squinted my eyes and spotted a man cutting the lock on the gate. He pushed it open and ran toward Maddie.

"Maddie!" I yelled, but it was too late—he had already grabbed her. The box of cupcake trash fell to the ground and she screamed.

This wasn't happening. *I would not let this happen.*

"Kids! Library! Go!" I screamed at Violet. I spared a glance in her direction to see her gathering the kids and lining them up. Harper was at the other side of the playground helping.

I ran as fast as I could toward Maddie and the man, who I recognized as I got closer as the man from my yard the other night. She kicked back into his body with her feet and thrashed against his hold. I couldn't let him get out of the gate with her. *Keep fighting baby girl! I'm coming.*

I gathered speed when I reached the slight slope down toward the row of dumpsters near the cafeteria section of the building and the gate that led to the street. I took a few running leaps—like a hurdler—to gain distance. It worked, and I was able to take one more jump and grab hold of his neck. I wrapped myself around his body like a stuffed Velcro monkey. I stuck my fingers in his nose and mouth and pulled and poked and pounded my fists one at a time against his face and upper chest. He stumbled but did not fall. I could hear him grunt every time I struck him.

"Maddie, go limp! Like your Mooshka doll!" I yelled.

She went limp, and was dead weight in his arms. She sagged down in his grip and he lunged backward to counter-balance. I tightened my legs at his waist and tried to climb higher on his body. I wanted to topple him over, to make him fall.

Maddie squirmed. Luckily, his grip on her was around her arms, not underneath them and it made it easier for her to wiggle her way closer to slipping free. I had managed to get a good lock on his neck with my left arm, squeezing hard. I could feel his hot breath puff out over my arm.

Maddie got free and stumbled to the side of our scuffle. "Run to the library," I gasped.

He stopped in his tracks and shook his body side to side trying to get me off.

"Rose!" Maddie cried.

"Run, Maddie, run. Now!" I shouted. Her footsteps pounded on the asphalt. Then they stopped.

"Maddie! Sweetie come here!" Violet shouted. A small sigh of relief escaped me. Her footsteps pounded the ground once more, and I redoubled my efforts to knock this fucker to the ground. *No one messes with my kids, especially this one.* Maddie was not just my student; she was going to be *my* kid—*my daughter.*

I let go of his neck, stumbling back a few steps until I regained my balance.

My dad always said for someone small, like me, surprise would be the best offense. So, I took my shot with no hesitation. I was glad I had worn my Doc Marten combat boots with my leggings and tunic because he doubled over with a horrific gurgle, then vomited after I gave him my best purple belt worthy *kin geri*, a.k.a. a front kick to the balls. *Good. I hope he chokes on them.*

I rushed toward him and shoved him. Then I balled up my fist and punched him in the nose. I turned and started running away as he staggered backward. I glanced over my shoulder as he regained his balance and came running and swinging for me. I was able to turn and duck the first hit, but the second one struck the side of my face. I only saw one star cross my vision—I took that as a good sign. I lurched to the side and spun around. Running again was my only option. He was way bigger than me, and he was no longer surprised. Plus, I could tell I had completely pissed him off. I had righteous fury, but he had psycho fury, and I feared I couldn't match that.

I managed to run out of the dumpster area and back into the main area of the deserted playground. The school would be on lockdown by now.

I didn't dare look behind me, I could hear his footsteps running just as fast as I was. It seemed he wasn't only just bigger than me, but faster as well. I went stumbling backward when his hand pulled my hair. Of course, this was the one day I'd decided to leave my hair down and not bun it.

"Stupid bitch," he grunted before spinning me around to slap me.

I flew to the side, but kept on my feet and clenched my jaw. *That fucking hurt.* He swung at me again, but I sidestepped it. Using his forward momentum against him, I shoved him on his side before taking off back in the direction of the dumpsters. Hopefully I could find something to hit him with back there, because there was no way I could take him down on my own. He outmatched me with just his size, nevermind his strength and wacked-out rage. He was a big guy who apparently resided in Crazytown, and all that crazy energy was fueling him.

Yet again, he caught up to me. How could someone that huge be so fast? I braced myself to take another hit and was not disappointed. He let my arms go and slapped me again before I could raise them to protect myself. At least he didn't punch me; it would have knocked me out for sure. But it hurt, and I had no choice other than to try and fight back. I punched him in the nose again, flinching when I felt it break beneath my fist. Blood ran freely from his nose, but it didn't stop him. He came at me again, fists flying. I ran backward; I didn't dare turn my back to him. He smiled at me, sick and crazy. His chest heaved with grunting breaths. *I am going to die back here, right next to the fucking dumpsters.*

"She's mine!" he screamed. "Tara belongs with me."

I heard sirens in the distance and footsteps running in my direction.

Violet came flying around the corner of the cafeteria section of the building, near the rows of dumpsters and recycling bins and landed on his back. *Maybe I wouldn't die today.*

He shook her side to side, but she managed to hold on. I gathered my wits, doubled my fists and punched him in the gut. He grunted. Violet was losing her grip, and I was running out of energy. *We were both probably going to die back here—right next to the fucking dumpsters.*

He lunged forward, then quickly back. Violet landed on her ass with a thud. He turned to kick her, so *I* jumped on his back. We seriously needed some new moves.

Violet scrambled backward like a crab. I held on for a few more seconds before he threw me off again and turned to face me with murder in his eyes. He had gone beyond rage, and the energy radiating from him was horrifying.

He reared back an arm to hit me. Violet lunged up and grabbed it before he could make contact. He quickly turned to the side, swinging into her and shaking his arm loose from her grip. He shoved her with both hands, and she went stumbling back into the recycling totes, knocking them over. Paper flew behind her and littered the ground underneath her supine body.

I shoved his back and he fell forward a step before turning around. This was it. My arms were up. But I already knew he hit hard, so it was more a gesture of hope than an actual defense.

I gasped when Trevor came charging out through the cafeteria door next to the row of dumpsters. Cade was close behind him, and Violet had gotten up. Police cars pulled up next to the gate, with sirens blaring.

With a leap off the steps, Trevor landed his fist in Mr. Crazy's face. One hit was all it took to send him reeling back with a crash into the nearest dumpster. But Trevor was not finished. He took hold of the man's shirt and held him still as he pummeled his face with more hits.

"Trev! Stop, man! Let me cuff him," Cade shouted.

Trevor shoved the man away and he landed with a crash on the ground. Abruptly, he turned and stalked toward me, face suffused with concern and rage. He didn't stop until I was in his arms with my cheek pressed against his heaving chest. "Are you okay?" he asked against the top of my head before his lips pressed a kiss there.

I could only stand there. I was no longer processing what was happening around me. The relief was almost too much to bear. My adrenaline levels dropped, and it felt like I was floating instead of standing on my own. Floating, but heavy at the same time. Violet grabbed my hand as Trevor's arms tightened around me.

"The kids?" I asked her. My voice sounded strange, echoing in my ears like it belonged to a stranger.

"All of them are fine, I took attendance. They are in the library with Lily, Harper and Mrs. Lawrence. Lily has Maddie—she's scared but okay. The school is on lock-down." More relief swamped me, like a weight around my shoulders.

Trevor addressed Violet, "Are you okay?"

"I want to kick him," she snapped.

Trevor let out a startled laugh. "What? Why? Cade just cuffed him. He's under arrest."

"We just taught, 'Run, Hide, Fight.' We scared the absolute shit out of those kids with that lesson. We made them feel a little bit better about it with cupcakes, but then this motherfucker shows up and takes them straight back into the trauma zone. They will be scarred for life because of this asshole, especially Maddie. Let me kick him. Just one time."

"Sorry, Violet. No kicking," Cade answered.

I stood there in a daze and listened to Violet rant. I felt like I had been in a battle, like I had been at it for hours. But in reality, this whole thing probably hadn't even lasted for ten minutes. My head spun as I tried to concentrate on Violet's words.

"She's going down," Violet said. It sounded like it was coming from under water. Her voice echoed in my ears as Trev's arms tightened around my waist.

I was not going to pass out. I had just accomplished some serious feats of bad-assery and bad-asses did not pass out.

I opened my eyes. *Did I just take one really long blink?*

I looked up into Trevor's face as he smiled softly at me. I was in his arms, like a bride. Except we were next to a bunch of dumpsters and nowhere near a threshold or a church.

I sighed with relief and looked around. The gate to the street was open, and blue and red lights flashed, signaling the end of our ordeal. Officers were loading Mr. Crazy into a squad car and Violet stood next to Trevor, grinning at me with a bruise already forming on her cheekbone. I was sure I was going to have at least one bruise to match hers, because my cheek throbbed and felt hot. I wiggled my jaw side to side.

"Be still, baby," Trevor said. "We need to get an ice pack for your cheek. You too, Violet."

"And you need one for your hand Trevor. Fists of fury—woo hoo," she teased. "And you wouldn't even let me kick him one time." Violet always made jokes when she was upset.

"I can stand now." Trevor put me down and I melted into Violet's arms.

She held me and inhaled a deep shuddering breath. "Rosy Posy," she whispered.

"Violet, if you hadn't come out, he would have—"

"Shh, don't say it. Lily and I were throwing fits over the phone for them to let me out of the school. She wanted to come out too, but I said no way. I mean she's pregnant, plus Maddie was in hysterics. Lily snuck me her key card. No way I was going to leave you out here alone." Violet looked over my shoulder at Trevor. "Don't worry, Trevor. Maddie is okay. Lily was calming her down when I snuck out."

"I should have never left the school today after the assembly. Or we should have all just stayed in the house. Who would have thought that fucker would make bail? He shot me, for fuck's sake. Someone is going to answer for this."

"My dad is going to lose his mind," I said.

"Oh, he's already lost it," Cade interjected. "The judge that set bail is an old college friend of this jackass. He's in for a world of hurt."

"Unbelievable," Trevor grumbled. He reached out to pull me away from Violet and back into his arms. Tipping my head back with a gentle finger beneath my chin, he grimaced. "Baby, does it hurt?"

I shook my head. "No. It's not too bad, at least, not yet."

"I'll take care of you when it does. Don't worry. God, you're so damn brave. Rose, you saved Maddie. I owe you everything."

"I—you don't owe me anything. I love her. I would have done anything—"

"Thank you," he cut me off with a whisper and a kiss.

I tuned out of the conversation and relaxed into his arms as Violet and Cade discussed what had happened and the other officers drove away.

Chapter 33
Trevor

I was almost certain that I'd had a heart attack when the call came over the radio sending all available officers to the kid's school this morning. Then it felt like I'd briefly died only moments later when Ben called me and informed me that O'Donnell was out on bail. But it was all over now. Everyone was safe and O'Donnell was back in jail, and Mikey declared we should all celebrate at Joe's Pizza with video games and extra cheese. Maddie still looked shaken up, but I thought doing something normal and ordinary might help. Tomorrow I would call our family therapist for an emergency appointment.

Rose still had me worried. She sat in the passenger seat in a daze, staring out the window, not saying a word. Every so often she would twirl the rings we gave her around on her finger and well up with tears. None of the tears spilled over, and I got the feeling that she didn't want me to notice, so I didn't say anything—yet.

I pulled into Joe's next to Lily's Expedition. She, Luke, and the kids were waiting inside of it, along with Violet and her twin sons. Wow—that was three adults, two teenage boys, a kid in a booster seat and a toddler in a car seat, all in one vehicle, and they didn't look squished. I added a large SUV to my list of future car possibilities along with mini-vans and station wagons. I glanced at Rose again. "What do you think of an SUV? Should we get one?"

She slowly turned her head to look at me. "Huh?"

"You okay, baby? You seem a little out of it," I asked gently.

"I'm fine. Or I will be. I just need to think it out. Cade does that. He thinks about stuff instead of ignoring it . . ." She stared out into the distance again.

"You tell me when you need me. Promise?"

"Yeah, I will." She smiled slightly, then went back to her daze.

I sighed and shut off the car. "Come on, kids. Are you ready for some pizza and games? I'm going to get a whole roll of quarters for each of you."

"All right!" Mikey shouted. He unbuckled himself then scooted over to unbuckle Maddie. He held her hand and said. "Maddie, we can play the car racing game together. I'll let you sit in the red one."

I turned to peek through the front seats. Maddie grinned at Mikey and the weight on my heart eased a little bit. She was grinning at Mikey, and that felt like a great sign.

"Really, Mikey? I can be red?"

"Heck yes. You didn't get hurt today, and I am so happy that I still have a sister. Do you want to win? Because I'll let you, if you want."

I choked up like I always did when my kids were being nice to each other. It made me feel like I wasn't a failure as a father. Mikey had a huge heart underneath the mischievous exterior.

"I want to win," Maddie said with a huge smile. Every time I brought them here, they always fought over the red car, Mikey always won the game, and Maddie always threw some foot-stomping attitude when she lost.

Rose chuckled in her seat as she listened to the kids. "I'm glad you're okay too, Maddie." She turned to peer through the seats. "Let's go play some games. I kick booty at ski-ball. Who wants to challenge me?"

"I do! I do!" Mikey answered. "Can we get brownies too?"

"Are we at Joe's?" I asked and I reached back for a high five.

I got out of my car, and Lily immediately grabbed me into a hug. Her tiny baby bump was hard between us and it reminded me of all I could have lost today. I could have lost my daughter, could have lost Rose, and could have lost all the possibilities that came with her. I swallowed down the sudden burst of emotion. Now was not the time to give into it. I could work that out later, with Rose.

"Oh my god," Lily cried against my chest. I hugged her and patted her back.

Luke stood behind her, holding their daughter and grinning at me. "I'm glad this is all finally over."

"Me too, man." I smiled back.

"I sent the boys in to get a big table," Violet said. "Let's go sit down. I want a glass of red wine the size of my head. Rose, do you want one too?"

"Sure, but only a normal sized one." Violet laughed at her and held her hand out for a high five.

We traipsed through the parking lot and spotted Violet's sons at the big wooden table near the arcade platform at the rear of the restaurant. They waved us over and we headed to join them.

"All right kids. Who wants a Shirley Temple?" Violet offered.

"I do, Miss Violet," Maddie said. "What's a Shirley Temple?"

"Oh, honey bunny, I'm your Auntie Violet now. My sister is going to marry your daddy," Violet informed Maddie.

Maddie gasped. "Mikey, we have an Auntie Violet now!"

"And an Uncle Luke." Luke added. He smiled at her and patted her head. He finished strapping Calla into a highchair, then sat down. Maddie beamed up at him.

"And an Uncle Levi, Uncle Jude, Uncle Asher, and Uncle Cade. And an Auntie Holly. You've already had Aunt Lily, but now it will be official. Plus, you're going to get a new Grandma and Grandpa. Watch out for my mom, Trev. She'll spoil the crap out of them," Rose warned with a smile.

"I love getting the crap spoiled out of me!" Mikey shouted. "This is so awesome."

"Hey, Mikey! We're going to be cousins for real," Dylan said. Mikey beamed at him.

"Maddie, I'm glad you're still here to be my cousin." Dylan leaned over in his chair to side hug her.

"Thanks, Dylan." Maddie hugged him back. "You know what?" Her tiny voice cracked as tears filled her eyes. I put my arm around her and patted her shoulder.

"What?" Dylan and Mikey whispered back.

She took a huge breath. "Rose kicked that man and she hit him and then I got away and ran to Auntie Violet," she informed us all with a tremulous smile. Tears sparkled on her eyelashes.

I pulled Maddie onto my lap. She snuggled her head into my chest and wrapped her arms around me.

"You beat up that guy?" Mikey asked Rose. Clearly, he was impressed. "*You* saved my sister, Rose."

Rose cleared her throat. "Um, yeah I did. I kicked him, and I hit him too."

Maddie turned her face to Rose. "You saved me, Rose," she sobbed. "You didn't let him take me away and he hit your face. Your cheek is all red and purple. Auntie Violet's face is hurt, too."

Rose scooted her chair closer to mine and cradled Maddie's face. "Of course I saved you. I love you, Maddie, just like you were my own little girl." Rose scooped Maddie out of my lap and held her close as she cried, rocking and holding her close she settled down. It didn't take long. Maddie usually burned her feelings out fast with a lot of drama, but they seldom lingered past the flame-out.

"If we have all kinds of new aunts and uncles, then we need a mom too." Mikey declared. "Can we call you Mom?"

Rose's eyes filled with tears. "Yes, baby. I would love that. More than anything in the whole world." Mikey got up to put his arms around Rose and Maddie, and it was all I could do to keep it together.

"Oh my gosh!" Violet cried. "This is gorgeous. This is like watching a whole family being born right in front of my face. Hug me, Nicky." She turned to her nearest son, who put his cell phone down, smiled, and hugged her.

Maddie pulled her face out of Rose's neck. "I can call you Mommy?"

Rose choked back a sob. "Yes, you can, honey."

I reached over and swiped away Maddie's tears with my thumb. "It's amazing that such a horrible day could turn out like this, isn't it?" I asked her.

"Yeah, Daddy." Rose leaned into my side and I wrapped my arm around her.

The moment ended when pizzas started arriving, along with pitchers of soda. Which was weird, because I didn't remember anyone ordering anything.

"Who ordered?" Lily said as she wiped under her eyes with a tissue.

"I did. With Daddy's phone. I went on their website." Mikey said and held up my phone. "I got extra cheese pizza, pepperoni pizza, sausage pizza, and pineapple pizza." He wrinkled his nose at Maddie—pineapple pizza was her favorite. "And I got—"

"Yes! Mikey got the brownies," Dylan yelled when he saw the tray. Joe's was famous for their triple chocolate brownies, and I often used them as a bribe.

Mikey fist-bumped Dylan. "I would not forget the brownies."

Violet laughed when a huge glass of red wine was placed in front of her on the table. "Aw, Mikey you remembered." She winked at him.

He winked back at her. "It doesn't look like it's as big as your head. Sorry." He shrugged, and I shook my head while reminding myself that I needed to watch him every single second.

"It's okay, sweetheart. This is perfect." Violet said and raised her glass. "To the best horrible day ever."

Chapter 34
Rose

I remembered the first time I saw him: standing in Lily's front doorway, smiling at me with a look in his eyes, a certain smile on his face—an expression that had always been just for me. As I held my father's arm, I could see that same smile shining back at me from the end of the flower-strewn aisle. We weren't in a church; we were in the old barn on Luke and Lily's property. It was New Year's Eve, midnight was moments away, and I was about to become Trevor's wife. I knew fairytales were not real, but I was getting my happy ending all the same. This Cinderella was sure as heck *not* running away at midnight. I was here to get my midnight kiss, my prince, and a little prince and princess too. Trevor and I weren't just getting married, we were creating a family.

"Are you ready, sweetheart?" Dad asked.

"Yes. I'm ready." I squeezed his arm and beamed up at him. My dad was as handsome as ever in his black tuxedo and bow tie.

"I'm happy for you, Rosalie. He's a good man. The best." He leaned down and kissed my cheek. His eyes were shining, and his grin faltered for a second. "I know you're grown. I know you've been taking care of yourself for a long time now, but this still isn't easy."

I took a huge breath. "Oh, don't make me cry, Dad." I tucked my bouquet under my arm, so I could fan my face with my other hand as I blinked furiously to combat the tears I felt prickling behind my eyes. "Violet will kill me. She spent forever on my makeup."

He laughed. "We can't have that. Let's go."

As we walked, I caught my reflection in the window. I was in full princess mode. Maddie was with me when I went dress shopping with the rest of the female side of my family. Unsurprisingly, Maddie fell in love with everything that had sparkles and beads, and the fuller the skirt the better. My dress was strapless satin gown adorned with glittering crystal beads, a full skirt, and a small train trailing behind. Cinderella herself would be jealous of this dress. My hair sat piled on top of my head with a few curls trailing down here and there. At Maddie's insistence, I wore a tiara. Maddie had one too, and of course, it matched mine. She'd had a hard time deciding between a tiara and a flower crown, but in the end, the bling won.

Tiny white lights formed an arch over the entire ceiling of the barn, giving it a magical glow. Pink and white roses were strategically placed at different intervals to "highlight the rustic beauty," according to my mother. It all led to an arch at the rear center of the barn where everyone waited for me.

I saw smiling faces and a few tearful ones as I made my way to the flower-and-light bedecked arch. I had refused to choose one Maid of Honor, and all my sisters shared the honor tonight. Maddie was my flower girl, and she did a great job; I could feel my dress sweeping up the petals as I walked. Trevor had asked Mikey to be his best man—then had to actively prevent him from using Google to figure out how to throw a bachelor party. Cade and Trevor's brothers were groomsmen. Maddie was grinning hugely and jumping up and down. Violet was smiling through her sobs, and Lily's and Holly's eyes were shiny with tears. And Trevor . . .

He gasped and covered his mouth with a hand as tears filled his eyes and flowed freely down his cheeks. One of his brothers put a hand on his shoulder and grinned at him.

The thing I loved the most about Trevor was that I always knew how he felt. I could read it on his face, in his demeanor, in everything he said and did. He loved me, and he showed it to me every day. But this moment would be burned on my soul forever. He stood unembarrassed as his tears fell freely down his cheeks. He removed his hand from his mouth, smiled and mouthed "Beautiful. I love you". My return smile was so huge it cramped my cheeks. I had never been happier in my life.

Everyone could see how much he loved me. And I guess they could see how much I loved him too, since I had stopped simply walking faster and had stepped it up to a jog. My dad laughed as he kept pace with me and there was a round of applause when I finally reached the altar. Dad gave me a nudge toward Trevor as he held his arms out and swept me up the steps to stand by his side. He held my hands in his and everything else disappeared. It was just him and me underneath the glowing lights, waiting to finally start on our future.

The vows and the ceremony went by in a blur and then there I was, dancing in his arms.

"Rose," he whispered. I leaned back to look expectantly at his face. "I can't believe that I was able to convince you to marry me without ever taking you on one single date." He grinned down at me with a twinkle in his teasing eyes.

It was true, we had not gone out together on a real date —ever. I giggled. "This is kind of a date right now." He raised an eyebrow in response. "I mean, we planned it in advance. We're dressed up. There will be dinner and champagne, and we're already dancing."

"So, then this is our first date." He chuckled.

"Yep. Married on the first date. You're good, Detective Trevor Andrew Hale."

"You're even better Mrs. Rosalie Victoria Barrett-Hale."

"I love the sound of that."

"Me too, princess. I love you."

"I love you too. Always, Trev." He had time to kiss me one time before Mikey cut in.

"I want to dance with her too," he demanded.

"Me too, me too!" Maddie chimed in.

They were both too adorable; Mikey in his mini-tuxedo, and Maddie in her rose-gold sparkles with her hair up high on her head to match mine.

"Come on," I said, and opened an arm. Trevor did the same, so that we made a circle. The four of us danced and twirled together, spinning away into our happily ever after.

Scan the code for an exclusive bonus scene!

More Sweetbriar

From the Heart

I was his one who got away, or so he said.

Falling for Jake was not part of my plan. I should have stuck to rebuilding my life as a divorcee.

My ex-husband's irresistible best friend was the last kind of complication I needed at this point in my life even though he was the one I saw first all those years ago.

Being with Jake was a risk I was afraid to take but I couldn't resist him and he knew it.

And after spending years with the wrong man, I finally feel wanted, beautiful, adored.

But now things are even more tangled because our one accidental night together has me unexpectedly expecting.

Will he be the one to stay?
Or become my one who got away?

In My Heart

Luke was my first love, my first kiss, my first everything.
He always swore I was his reason to live but he lost himself
in the army then I lost him.

I never thought I could be with anyone after him, but I was.

I never thought I'd go back to the small town where we grew
up, but I did.

Running back to my family as a thirty-year-old widow was
never in my life plan. But for the sake of my children I
returned home to the memories I had fought so hard to
leave behind.

What I didn't know was that Luke was back too. With only
one thing on his mind. Me.

But there is something he doesn't know and our son can't
wait to tell him what he's missed.

Our past brought us back together but if we can't trust each
other it will tear us apart.

Change of Heart

He's Sweetbriar's most devoted cop, my ex-husband, and
the man I've avoided for the last ten years.
He might also be my only hope.

More Sweetbriar

Cade Barrett was my first crush, my first kiss, my first
everything.
I thought we'd last forever.
But we wanted different things.
He was a hometown boy through and through while my
ambitions reached far beyond our small town.
So we let each other go and I left to chase my dreams.
Now I'm back with a secret—the dangerous kind.

He vowed to keep me safe.
While I promised myself to guard my heart.
Until one accidental kiss reignited the fire between us.
And it was hotter than ever before.

Will one final night together extinguish the flames?
Or should I stay and take the one and only chance I have to
get him back?

Heart to Heart

Just friends.
That's all Liam Carter and I can ever be.

Sure, we've shared a kiss or two and our chemistry is off the
charts.
And yeah, pretending I don't want to date him when he's
the sweetest, kindest, hottest man I've ever met is almost
impossible.
He's too charming to be real and looks at me like I'm the
only woman in the world.

But I can't have him.

After what he went through, he deserves a fairytale.
And I'm bad at love with the reputation to match.
Add those to the list of reasons why I should keep my
distance.

But here's the big one.
Did I mention we work together now?
I'm the hot mess trying to start up a new business and he's
the got-it-all-together contractor in charge of the renovation.

There are boundaries I shouldn't cross, right?

But I can't keep my eyes off him.
And he can't seem to keep his hands off me.
The more time we spend together the more I want—until I
want it all.

How am I supposed to resist him now?

About the Author

Nora Everly is a lifelong bookworm. She started reading the good stuff once she grew tall enough to sneak the romance novels off the top of her mother's bookshelf and it has been non-stop ever since.

Once upon a time she was a substitute teacher and an educational assistant. Now she's a writer and stay at home mom to two small humans and one fat cat.

Nora lives in the Pacific Northwest with her family and her overactive imagination.

Website: noraeverly.com

Newsletter: https://www.noraeverly.com/newsletter

Also by Nora Everly

The Sweetbriar Mountain Series:

In My Heart

Heart Words

From the Heart

Heart to Heart

Change of Heart

Honeybrook Hollow:

Next to You

Make You Mine

By Your Side

Sweetbriar Short Stories:

Holiday Hearts

Conversation Hearts

Let It Snow

The Cozy Creek Collection:

Fall at Once

From Smartypants Romance:

Oh Brother!

Crime and Periodicals

Carpentry and Cocktails

Hotshot and Hospitality

Architecture and Artistry

Teachers' Lounge

Passing Notes

Star Crossed Lovers:

(*As Piper Everly, co-written with Piper Sheldon*):

<u>Midnight Clear</u>

Get exclusive sneak peeks of upcoming releases through Nora's newsletter and Facebook group, The Everly Afters.

www.ingramcontent.com/pod-product-compliance
Lightning Source LLC
Chambersburg PA
CBHW010558310726
48969CB00009B/2475